beyond *the* carousel

THE WYATTSVILLE SERIES BOOK 5

BETTE LEE CROSBY

BEYOND THE CAROUSEL
Wyattsville Series, Book Five

Copyright © 2017 by Bette Lee Crosby
Cover design: damonza.com
Formatting by Author E.M.S.
Editor: Ekta Garg

ISBN-978-0-9969214-8-0

BENT PINE PUBLISHING
Port Saint Lucie, FL

Published in the United States of America

To
My Husband Richard

Thank you for making the ups and downs
of this crazy carousel life
more wonderful.

beyond *the* carousel

EMORY HAWTHORNE

They say that every man has a story to tell, and I believe this to be true. My story is one of a terrible happening, something that will send you scurrying to give your children one last kiss before you sleep. It is a tale of murder and heartbreak. Only now, after it has come full circle, can I find the strength to give it voice.

Although this is the story of my life, I am not the central character. I am a bystander, a man who could do nothing to spare those I love. I walked beside them and shared their grief but was helpless to lift it from their shoulders.

I suppose you could say the story began with my father, a man so foreign to me that if we were standing face to face I wouldn't know him. As a boy I was told we possessed the same features—a squared-off jawline and wide-set eyes—but I had only my mother's word on this. Once he was gone, she relied on a few faded memories for comparison. My father is only a bit player in this tale, yet he is the reason we came to live in the house on Chester Street.

The day we moved into that house I was a man bursting with pride, confident that nothing but good fortune would come to us. Nothing bad could ever befall us again. Now that I have grown old with hair as white and fluffy as a cotton ball, I realize how foolish such a thought is.

Life is made up of good times and bad; sometimes in equal measures, sometimes unjustly weighted on one side of the scale or the other. When bad times come, as they most certainly will, you can only trust that sooner or later Justice will lift the blindfold from her eyes and the scale will again be balanced.

This has finally come to pass, and after so many years my story is ready to be shared.

THE EARLY YEARS

In 1918 Lester Hawthorne died a wealthy man. Wealthy but far from honorable. Decades earlier he'd left Virginia promising to send for Wilma and their boy once he'd established himself. Barely a year old when Lester left, Emory remembered his daddy kissing him goodbye but little else.

In those first few years, Lester bounced from city to city. How he finally came to settle in New York, no one can say. The accounts of his years in New York are sparse. They tell only of how he charmed the ladies with his snappy brown eyes, dark curls and courtly manners. There is no mention of how he came by his fortune.

What is known is that at age 30 he married Imogene Delmont, a well-to-do widow fifteen years his senior. Apparently by then his wife and child back in Virginia were all but forgotten. From that day forward there was no need for Lester to work, and he took full advantage of the situation.

When Imogene passed on in 1912, Lester was left with money enough to live comfortably. In the weeks following the funeral, a twinge of guilt began to pick at his conscience so he wrote to Wilma asking for her forgiveness and saying he'd like to see their boy. The letter was forwarded from one place to another, and after nearly a month it came back marked "Deceased." Believing he'd done all he could to make things right, Lester simply went back to living the good life he'd grown accustomed to.

More than five years later, after a particularly rousing night of partying, Lester had a dream in which he saw the gates of hell open wide with the devil calling his name. He woke to the sound of his own screams and sheets soaked with perspiration. There was no sleep for the remainder of that night. He poured himself a glass of bourbon and sat in a plush leather chair thinking things over. By the time the sun crested the horizon, Lester had made his decision.

That same day he visited the law offices of Vance and Parker and had them draw up a new will. Imogene had it set in stone that upon his demise the bulk of her estate would default to the countless heirs of the Delmont clan, but he was free to do as he pleased with his portfolio of stocks. In an effort to atone for past misdeeds, Lester decreed that upon his death, his son, Emory, was to inherit everything in that portfolio.

"To the best of my knowledge, the boy is somewhere in Virginia," he said and left it at that.

Before the year was out Lester was dead, and Archibald Parker began his search for the missing son.

THE LETTER ARRIVED IN AUGUST on a day so hot it threatened to melt the paint on the apartment walls. Weary from a long day of driving the trolley and listening to people complain about it being late, Emory Hawthorne brought the mail in and plopped it on the table without even looking at the envelope. He went to the icebox, poured himself a tall glass of tea then sat at the table and drank it halfway down before he slit the envelope open.

Once he read the letter, Emory sat there rather dumbfounded. Several moments ticked by before he could remember Lester as the daddy who'd kissed him goodbye then disappeared. When he finally did remember he found it almost impossible to believe such an irresponsible man had anything more than a nickel to his name, never mind a portfolio of stocks worth $9,000.

"Please advise if you wish to retain ownership of the stock or would prefer we liquidate these holdings and issue a cashier's check," the last line of the letter stated. It was signed "Archibald H. Parker, Attorney at Law."

For a long while Emory remained in that stiff-backed kitchen chair with his face as white as the paper he was reading. He read and then reread the letter looking for a loophole, a line that would indicate this was a hoax. It wasn't there.

After twelve years of marriage, Rose Hawthorne knew her husband's every expression. When his brows were knitted together as they were now, she knew there was something to fret about. An increase in the rent perhaps or an unexpected repair bill.

"What's wrong?" she asked.

"Read this." Without saying anything more, Emory handed her the letter.

She read it through twice then looked up with a bewildered expression. "I thought your daddy was dead."

"I thought so too," he replied.

"Can this possibly be right?" she asked. "Nine thousand dollars is a lot of money. Where would he get—"

Emory drew in a breath and gave a shrug. "Damned if I know."

THAT NIGHT NEITHER EMORY NOR Rose closed their eyes. While

their daughter, Laura, slept, they sat in bed and whispered about the possibility of such a thing being true and the greater likelihood that it was indeed a hoax. Emory pointed out that while the letter looked authentic enough, his daddy had been a man who'd lie even when the truth was in his favor.

"Who knows if this Archibald Parker actually exists?" he said, but as he spoke the words he was already thinking of what he'd do with such an enormous amount of money.

WHEN MORNING FINALLY CAME, EMORY waited until nine o'clock then went downstairs and asked the landlady if he might use her telephone.

"I've got to call a lawyer in New York," he said. "I'll pay for whatever the charges are."

"Make sure you do," Ida Poole grumbled then begrudgingly motioned him into the apartment.

Thinking it rather odd that a trolley car driver would be calling a New York lawyer, Ida picked up her feather duster and headed for the dining room, which was within easy hearing distance of the telephone. With her ears perked, she began swishing the duster across the credenza.

Emory asked for Archibald Parker then said he was calling in reference to the letter he'd received. He gave his name and address, and for the remainder of the conversation it was mostly yes or no answers. Much to Ida's dismay, there was no mention of what they were talking about.

Five minutes later he hung up the receiver, fished in his pocket and pulled out three one-dollar bills. Emory handed them to Ida and said, "This ought to cover it." With an ear-to-ear grin, he turned toward the door.

Now more anxious than ever to know what was going on, Ida trailed after him saying three dollars was possibly a bit too much.

"That's okay," Emory replied. "Keep whatever is left over."

Taking the stairs two at a time, he bolted into the apartment, lifted Rose into his arms and whirled her around.

"It's true!" he said and kissed her on the mouth, muffling any retort she might have had. With less than twenty minutes before his shift started, he grabbed his lunch pail and hurried out the door.

"I'll give you the details tonight," he called as he started down the stairs.

THAT AFTERNOON AS EMORY DROVE the Broad Street trolley back and forth along the thoroughfare, he slowed at every corner and eyed the houses lining the side streets. Before he returned home at seven-thirty, he knew exactly what he was going to do with the money.

THE FOLLOWING SUNDAY

Sunday was Emory's day off. It was a day when the family went to church then came home and sat down to a leisurely brunch of pancakes with a side of bacon or ham. But this Sunday was different.

Emory insisted on taking Rose and Laura to the Clinton Inn for brunch. As they stood looking at the buffet piled high with meats, eggs, golden pineapple slices, strawberries the size of plums and a dozen different pastries, he said, "Eat up, we have a long day ahead of us."

Not given to such indulgences, Rose found it hard to swallow eggs that came at the price of a family-sized roast. As they sat at the table, she leaned toward Emory and whispered her thoughts.

"Now that you have a few dollars in your pocket, I should think you'd be saving for the future instead of spending," she whispered with disapproval.

Emory reached across the table, gave her hand a loving squeeze and chuckled.

"Don't worry, I've got the future all planned, so relax and enjoy yourself."

"If you say so," Rose replied apprehensively.

That morning Laura, who was eleven at the time, made three trips back to the buffet. Each time she asked the white-gloved server for another stack of blueberry pancakes and a larger helping of honeydew. The third time he added an extra scoop of berries atop the pancakes then laughed and said for such a tiny thing she certainly had a healthy appetite.

Once everyone had eaten their fill, Emory sipped the last of his coffee then brushed a crumb from his mouth and said, "Now we're off to find ourselves a new home."

Although Rose was opposed to extravagances of any sort, she smiled at such a thought. Twelve years of living in a third-floor cold water flat with a shared bathroom was more than enough.

"I hope it's a place with hot water and electricity," she said.

"Oh, it will have that," Emory replied, "and a whole lot more."

CHESTER STREET WAS TEN BLOCKS from the Clinton Inn. It was one of the elegant side streets that ran across Broad Avenue. From end to end the street was lined with large houses, rolling lawns and hedges framing the walkways. Halfway down the block, Emory stopped in front of a two-story gray house with a "For Sale" sign in the yard.

The front porch stretched the full width of the house. At the top of the steps to the right sat a cozy looking wicker settee with plump cushions. On the far side they saw a matching table and chairs. The carved oak door was smack in the center.

Laura looked up at the house wide-eyed. "Daddy, are you going to buy this house?"

"I believe so," Emory answered happily.

Rose whipped her head around and looked at him with disbelief. "We can't possibly afford—"

"Yes, we can," he cut in, "and we'll have a few dollars left over."

Emory wrapped his arm around her waist and tugged her up the walkway. When they stepped onto the front porch, he stomped his heel against the floor.

"Hear that?" he said. "Solid as a rock. A house like this is built to last."

"I've no doubt of that," Rose replied, "but I question the wisdom of spending—"

The door opened, interrupting her, and a middle-aged man stood on the other side.

"Are you here to look at the house?"

Emory nodded and stuck out his hand. "Emory Hawthorne. I called yesterday." He introduced Rose and Laura.

"A pleasure." He lifted Rose's hand into his then gave Laura a smile. "I'm Edward Bernstein, the owner. Please come in." He stepped back and gestured toward the living room.

The moment she stepped inside, Rose noticed the room's beamed ceilings and stone fireplace and fell in love. The practical nature she'd carried with her for as long as she could remember was pushed to the back of her mind. As they walked through room after room, she made no mention of price but took note of things like the tall windows and wide baseboards, floors polished to a gleam and a staircase railing that was sturdier than any she'd ever seen.

When Edward Bernstein led them into the master bedroom upstairs, she saw French doors opening onto a small balcony and imagined the cool night air washing over them as they slept. The bedroom in their apartment, with one small window that at best opened halfway, was unbearably hot in the summertime.

Almost as if he'd read her mind, Edward crossed over and flung the doors open.

"Even on the hottest day of summer this room is comfortable," he said. "Feel that breeze?"

Rose nodded, caught the scent of late-blooming jasmine and

sighed. "Such a beautiful house. Doesn't your family hate to leave it?"

He smiled with a shrug of resignation. "We have no choice; I've been transferred to Cincinnati."

"How sad," Rose replied sympathetically, but a smile curled the corners of her mouth.

Once they'd toured the main rooms, Edward turned to them and said, "If you're still interested, would you like to see the rest of the place?"

Emory and Rose's heads bobbed in unison.

Following along like a line of baby ducks, they went through every inch of the house. Climbing the narrow attic stairs, they peeked into a tiny dormer room that overlooked the street. Even though the room was still unfinished, Rose could easily imagine it with tieback curtains and a window seat for reading.

Room by room, she began to see her family settling into the house. Laura in the back bedroom that overlooked a dogwood tree in full bloom. The small study turned into a sewing room. A spare bedroom for the grandchildren they might one day have.

After she'd mentally placed Laura in the room she already thought of as the dogwood room, Rose asked about schools in the area.

"The elementary school is just two blocks over," Edward replied. "It's a wonderful school; Nora Kelly, the fifth grade teacher, is an absolute gem."

"I'm going into the sixth grade," Laura volunteered.

"Well, then, you'd have Mister Morris," Edward said. "He's everybody's favorite."

Laura looked at Emory and Rose and grinned.

As they headed down for a look at the furnace, Edward snapped on the switch at the top of the staircase and the basement was flooded with light. Trailing behind Emory, Rose poked a finger in his back to catch his attention. When he turned to look at her, she gave an eager nod and mouthed the word "yes." Long before Edward showed them the coal bin and pointed out that the furnace was a steel-riveted Lenox that sent steam heat to every room in the house, Rose had all but moved in.

When they returned to the living room, she smiled sweetly and excused herself.

"Laura and I will explore the backyard," she said, "while you gentlemen go about your business."

IT WAS NEARLY AN HOUR before Emory came out calling for them to leave. Although Rose was bursting with curiosity, she waited until they were nearly to Broad Street. Then she said, "Well?"

"Well what?" Emory teased.

"Did you get the house?"

Emory walked with his back straight and his chest puffed out as he answered, "Yes, I did, and some of the furniture as well."

Ignoring the ladylike behavior she prided herself in having, Rose let out a squeal of delight that could be heard halfway down Broad Street.

Rose Hawthorne

Years ago I spotted a blue silk change purse dropped on the street, and I picked it up. Inside there were two one-dollar bills, a quarter and three dimes. No name or identification, just the money.

I liked the feel of that soft silk in my hand, so I slid it into my pocket and walked off. Sure, I glanced around and didn't see anyone looking like they'd lost a purse, but I didn't go out of my way to find the owner either. We were struggling to make ends meet back then, and I couldn't help thinking of how that money would buy enough groceries for a week. That day I bought a nice fat roasting chicken to cook for dinner, a piece of chocolate for me and a candy stick for Laura. I never mentioned finding the purse to anyone, not even Emory.

All that week I kept telling myself there was no crime in keeping the change purse because I had no way of knowing who to return it to, but no matter how hard I tried to convince myself I still felt guilty about keeping something I wasn't deserving of.

That's kind of how I feel about the house. I want it a thousand times more than I wanted that piece of chocolate, but I still feel guilty having it.

I keep asking myself why. Why would a daddy Emory never even *knew give us all that money? I feel frightened that a day or a week or a month from now someone will show up to tell us it was all a mistake, and we have to give the money back.*

When the sensible side of my brain thinks about that possibility, I focus on the twelve years of washing my face in icy cold water and hauling groceries up three long flights of stairs. Then it's like having that blue silk purse all over again.

FRIVOLOUS THINGS

On the first day of September, the Hawthorne family moved out of the cold water flat and into a house grander than anything they'd ever imagined owning. As luck would have it, Henry Bernstein was moving into an apartment with a spectacular view of the Ohio River but considerably less room. He had no need of the large dining room set, the wicker porch furniture and several other items, so he'd sold them to Emory for next to nothing. The telephone table in the center hall he'd thrown in for free.

Although the apartment in Ida Poole's house had seemed painfully cramped, their meager possessions appeared lost in such a large house. This was particularly true of Laura's room. Back in the apartment she'd slept on a divan small enough to fit in the alcove that served as her room.

Emory eyed the near empty expanse. "Seems to me you need some more furniture in here."

"I don't have anything else," Laura answered.

"Well, then, I guess we'll have to go shopping and find some proper furniture."

Nothing more was said about it until late that night when

Emory and Rose were lying side by side in the old bed they'd brought from the apartment. The mattress sagged from years of wear, but with the smell of jasmine in the air and a soft breeze cooling them it seemed a bit more comfortable.

Although they were both weary from the day of moving and unpacking, she slid closer and eased her head onto his shoulder. For a few moments there was only the sound of their hearts beating in a matched rhythm. Then she spoke.

"You did a good thing buying this house, Emory."

She raised herself up on her elbow then bent and kissed his mouth.

"I know if it were left up to me I would have said let's get a smaller, less expensive place, but now that we're here I can feel how special this house is."

"I've still got almost two thousand dollars in the bank," he reminded her.

"Thank goodness." She dropped down and snuggled into the crook of his arm. "We need to save every penny just in case…"

"In case of what?"

Rose grew up with a mama who never once squandered a cent. From the time she was old enough to ask for candy, Rose was taught that such requests were frivolous and pennies were to be saved for tomorrow, "just in case" her mama had said. But she'd never explained what the "case" might be.

Rose thought back on this and gave a weighted sigh.

"For a rainy day," she finally said. "A time when we have less than we have now."

"That time has come and gone," Emory replied. "We've seen our share of hard times and somehow pulled through. Now we've moved on to good times, so let's just relax and enjoy them."

For several long moments there was only silence as they lay together feeling the rise and fall of each other's breath.

"It's hard to change," she finally said.

Emory gave her shoulder an affectionate squeeze. "I know."

Another few moments of silence passed. It was during those moments of silence Emory could gather his thoughts.

"Please try to trust my judgment," he said earnestly. "I swear I will never do anything to put you or Laura in harm's way."

"I know that," she replied. "But what if something unforeseen happens? Something you have no control over."

"What if no such thing ever happens?" he answered in a voice that was not mocking but gentle and tender. "This house is bought and paid for. It's ours for the rest of our lives. We can pinch pennies and worry about something that may never happen, or we can spend our time and money enjoying each day."

A labored sigh came up from the depths of her chest.

"I realize what you say makes a lot of sense, but I can't help thinking if something—"

"No matter what happens, I'll take care of my girls," he cut in before she could finish the thought. "And if we do happen upon bad times, we'll still have these good times to look back on."

"I suppose," she answered reluctantly.

Emory turned his face to hers and kissed her. It was a soft and tender kiss that asked for nothing in return.

"The thing I want most in life is to make you happy," he said. "My happiness comes from doing these things for you and Laura. Please don't take that joy from me."

With her cheek pressed to his, Rose blinked back the tears that threatened to spill over.

"I won't," she whispered.

It was a promise she made to both Emory and herself. No matter how frivolous a thing might seem, she vowed to stay true to that promise of not taking his joy away.

CHANGE DIDN'T COME EASILY, BUT Rose tried. The following

Saturday Emory suggested they go to J.C. Penney and buy a bedroom set for Laura.

"She's growing up," he said, "and after eleven years of sleeping in an alcove, she deserves to have a nice room of her own."

A wrinkle crossed Rose's brow. Her inclination was to look for a chest of drawers and maybe a chair at the Good Shepherd Thrift Shop. Not a bedroom set per se but a few used pieces still in good condition. She might have suggested this, but she'd caught sight of the pride he took in making such a suggestion.

Please don't take that joy from me.

"That's a fine idea," she replied.

WHEN EMORY PLUNKED DOWN $249 for a bedroom set that included two nightstands, a full-size bed, dresser, mirror and chest of drawers, Rose had to walk away.

"I'll be in the fabric shop," she said.

She didn't mention it, but her thought was before he came around to suggesting they buy curtains and a coverlet for the new bedroom she could stitch them herself and save the money.

That day she bought twenty-two yards of pale pink muslin, and for the next two weeks she sat at the sewing machine pumping her foot back and forth on the pedal as she stitched dainty little ruffles along the edge of tieback curtains and a coverlet. When they were finished, she eyed them and scrunched her nose. On a Tuesday afternoon, with no one pushing her to do so, Rose returned to J.C. Penney and bought nine yards of grosgrain ribbon trim. It was the first frivolous purchase she could ever remember herself making.

On Wednesday afternoon when Laura came from school and saw her room she squealed with delight. Dropping her school bag on the floor, she darted down the stairs to the kitchen and hugged her mama so tight Rose could barely breathe.

"Thank you, thank you, thank you!" she said. "It's the most beautiful room I've ever seen!" Seconds later she was on the telephone with her new best friend, Rebecca, gushing about her wonderful surprise.

Rose was in the middle of chopping onions for their dinner stew, but as she listened to Laura tell of the ruffles and fancy ribbon trim her eyes filled with tears. Not from the onions but because she'd discovered the joy of giving Emory had spoken of.

TODAY IS TOMORROW

You might think with Laura being as close to her mama as she was, she'd pick up the thread of Rose's frugality but she didn't. She had her mama's hazel-colored eyes and loose curls, but she had her daddy's personality. Every day was a day to be lived, and this new environment was a world waiting to be explored.

Laura turned twelve that first year, and up until then she'd been a somewhat reserved child. In their tiny apartment she'd seemed content to sit at the kitchen table watching her mama cook or snuggle into the alcove with a book carried home from the library. For hours on end she would read, jumping from one story into the next.

Now all of a sudden she'd become a giggly girl with a bevy of friends who drifted in and out of the house. Overnight, it seemed, Rose began finding books with the bookmark tucked into the very first chapter.

"Aren't you going to finish this?" she'd ask.

Laura inevitably answered that she would as soon as she had time; then she'd dart out the door because Peggy, Sue Ellen or Rebecca was waiting for her.

In addition to hot water and electricity the Hawthorne family had a telephone sitting on the hall table. Every time it jingled, Laura shouted, "I'll get it!" and came running. It was almost always one of her friends calling. At times Rose would catch snippets of a conversation about movie stars or secret friendships and wonder if she had ever been that young and giddy. If so, she could no longer remember. What she did remember were the endless days of helping her mother with the sewing, snipping the ends of string beans and holding her tongue unless she'd been spoken to.

AFTER THAT FIRST YEAR IN the house, the days fairly flew by. One year turned into two, and in a flash it became three. Twice Emory was given an increase in pay, and the third year he was promoted to the first shift supervisor. Laura grew nearly seven inches in those years. In what seemed the blink of an eye, she went from a stick thin girl to a shapely teen with friends attached to both arms.

The only one who remained relatively the same was Rose, but that was as she wanted it. Old habits were hard to shake loose, and in those early years just the thought of spending a nickel frivolously was like a burr under her skin. Although she didn't approve of wasting money for a standing rib roast simply because it was Sunday, seeing her family happy somehow justified such purchases. The problem was once she came to accept spending money on those things, Emory moved on to bigger things.

The day they went to the J.C. Penney store to pick out a new living room set, she broke out in hives.

She'd not said a word of protest when he suggested the new living room furniture, but as they stood there listening to the salesman tell of hand-tied springs and fabric durability Emory noticed Rose picking at the back of her neck. He moved closer and saw the rash blossoming at the edge of her collar.

Affectionately looping his arm through hers, he told the salesman, "We'll think it over and come back if we decide to place an order."

He steered Rose toward the door. "It's such a lovely day, let's walk through the park."

There was no further mention of the living room set. They walked for nearly an hour then stopped at the Garden Inn for coffee. As they sat across from one another, Emory spoke of possibly putting a small patch of tomato plants in the backyard.

"Last year Herb Korselman set out six plants and got tomatoes enough for the whole summer," he said. "I'm thinking eight plants…"

Rose was only half listening. Her thoughts were stuck on the velour living room set. The truth was the set they'd brought to the house was worn threadbare. The arm of the sofa wobbled if you sat close to it, and the chair had a hole in the spot where there once was a button. She and Emory had gotten that set the year they were married, and it was a hand-me-down back then.

Times were different now. Emory was making a good salary, and they had money in the bank. They could afford a new living room set, and she wanted Laura to feel comfortable about bringing friends to the house. Rose thought back to a few days earlier when Laura hustled Rebecca and Josephine past the living room and up to her bedroom. She hadn't said anything, but it was obvious that the dreary looking sofa was an embarrassment.

She folded her napkin and slid it under the cup. It was a thing she'd done by force of habit for as long as she could remember. She was always protecting things, skimping on today so there would be a safe tomorrow. Now today was yesterday's tomorrow, and she was still skimping. Next year was this year's tomorrow, and before long Laura would be married and gone. Then they'd have no need of a big house or a new sofa.

Emory was in the middle of telling how the tomato plants would do best on the south side of the house, when she cut in saying, "I'm sorry."

"Sorry?"

"About the living room set."

"There's no need to be sorry. We can wait a while until you feel—"

Rose shook her head. "You were right. We need one now. Let's go back to the store and order that furniture."

Emory stretched his arm across the table and took her hand in his. "Are you sure about this?"

She ducked her head and gave a sheepish grin. "I'm sure."

"What about the end tables and lamps? Would you like to wait on those?"

"No. We can go ahead and order those too."

Emory chuckled. "What brought about this change of heart?"

"I realized today is the tomorrow I worried about yesterday."

WHEN THEY LEFT THE COFFEE shop, Rose and Emory walked back across the park and turned toward the J.C. Penney store. This time it was different. Rose's step was a bit jauntier, and her smile stretched across her face.

Much to Emory's surprise, after they'd placed the order for a sofa, matching chair, a coffee table and two end tables with lamps to set atop them, Rose suggested they stop and look at draperies.

They browsed the department for nearly an hour. Rose went along the entire display rack, fingering the fabric of each panel and eyeing the stitches that at times were less than uniform. In the end she told Emory the stitching wasn't quite up to par, but the truth was she'd decided she could make the same draperies for less than half the cost.

ROSE

You might think it's an easy thing to settle into having something more than what you've expected of life, but it's not. When you've spent years believing you're poor, your mind keeps thinking it even after it's no longer true.

This past week when we left Penney's without ordering the furniture we intended to buy, I started wondering how it was I'd come to be saddled with such a fear. Emory grew up poor just as I did, but he's not at all this way. He takes whatever good fortune comes his way, says, Thank you, Lord, and goes about the business of enjoying it.

I thought about this for a long while and realized the only reason I'm this way is because Mama was. She never lived a carefree day in her life. She'd start out the day worrying about what was gonna happen tomorrow; then when tomorrow came and nothing bad happened, she'd start worrying about the next day.

Looking back, I understand Mama was that way because of Daddy. He liked whiskey better than he did his family and made no bones about it. A thousand or more times I heard him tell Mama he should never have gotten married because he wasn't cut out to be a family man. How is hearing such a thing supposed to make a woman feel?

I think somewhere in her heart Mama wasn't just worried about *money. She was worried Daddy would one day up and leave us. Sure enough, he did.*

Understanding this made me realize that being well off and comfortable isn't just about having money in the bank. It's knowing that come what may, the person you love will be there for you. I know I won't ever be poor as long as I've got Emory to love me.

The Parlor

omething about the new furniture changed the dynamics of the Hawthorne household. It was as if the plush velour sofa had an extra layer of sociability built in. What was once called the living room was now called the parlor, a name that seemed more befitting of the luxurious surroundings. The week after the furniture was delivered, Rose walked next door and invited Marion Eastman and her husband, Albert, to dinner without giving a second thought to the cost of a larger roast.

"Nothing fancy," she said, "but I thought it would be nice to get together."

Up until that day Rose and Marion had done nothing more than chat with one another across the backyard. For three years they'd spoken only of laundry soaps, recipes and such, but after that evening they became the best of friends.

Marion invited Rose to join the ladies Wednesday afternoon bridge game, and within a few months Rose had grown friendly with every woman who lived along Chester Street. Tuesdays had always been her day for dusting, but now instead of fussing over furniture that didn't have a speck of dust to be seen she strolled down the block and sat for a cup of tea with Bess Pearson or Emma Applewhite. And they in turn came to visit her.

There was something very special about the parlor. It was a place to invite friends, a place to be proud of and a place where she could wile away the evening sitting across from Emory as he read the paper. When there was an article of interest he read it aloud, and Rose openly offered opinions on everything from President Harding's new import tax to the latest movie featuring Rudolph Valentino. Time, it seemed, flew by in the flutter of an eyelash as she sat on the velour sofa darning a sock or rolling a skein of wool into a ball.

"This is such a pleasant place to be," she told Emory. "Why was it we didn't realize we needed a parlor like this sooner?"

Thinking back on the day they'd ordered the furniture, he smiled fondly.

"Maybe sooner would have been too soon," he said, then moved on to talking about the possibility of the New York Yankees winning the World Series.

THE PARLOR WAS ONLY THE start of the changes that came to the Hawthorne household that year.

For Christmas Emory bought a brand new RCA radio for the family to enjoy together, and on New Year's Day he settled in to listen to the Rose Bowl game. The first kickoff had yet to occur when the doorbell started ringing.

"Marion said you've got a radio," Albert Eastman said. Then he walked in and plopped himself down on the sofa. Right behind him was Charlie Morton and Walter Wetzel. By time the first quarter ended the room was filled with neighbors, and Rose was setting out a platter of sandwiches.

The next day Laura started inviting her friends to radio parties, which made her the most popular sophomore in

Wyattsville High. In the afternoon the girls would gather in the Hawthornes' living room on the pretext of studying, and before long the still-new coffee table would be pushed against the wall and they'd be dancing the Charleston to tunes like *Black Bottom* and *Shimmy Like My Sister Kate*.

On the days when Emory came from work and found the parlor cluttered with teenage girls, there was little he could do. He would on occasion fold his expression into a scowl, deepen his voice and say it was time to start studying, but beneath the stern expression there was generally the hint of a smile. The truth was the energy and vivaciousness of the girls made the house seem more alive. Happier perhaps.

When Laura was in her junior year of high school, everything changed. It began two weeks before Labor Day. Rose was in the kitchen fixing egg salad for lunch when she heard a peal of laughter come from the parlor. The sound was different than the raucous giggling that usually came from Laura and her friends.

Rose tiptoed down the hallway and peeked around the corner. Sitting next to Laura was the Jennings boy who lived at the far end of the street. After seeing the look on Laura's face, Rose stepped into the room and asked if the lad would care to stay for lunch.

"It's only egg salad sandwiches," she said, "but we've more than enough."

The boy looked up with a wide grin. "I love egg salad."

That was the first time Rose actually met Henry Jennings, but before long he became a fixture around the house.

For the remaining days of summer, the lad was practically camped out on their front porch. He showed up early in the morning and didn't leave until the sky turned dark. When dinnertime came and Henry was still sitting beside Laura on the front porch swing, Rose always asked if he'd like to join them for dinner. The first few times it seemed harmless enough, but before long it was just assumed there'd be an extra place setting at the table.

Thinking maybe she could drop a subtle hint, Rose asked, "Do you want me to call your mama to make sure she's not expecting you home?"

Henry shook his head. "I already told her I'd be staying."

Rose knew Edna Jennings, Henry's mother, from the ladies bridge club, so there was nothing more said. When Emory came in complaining that he'd nearly tripped over the boy's bicycle in the walkway, Rose put her finger to her lips and made a hushing sound.

"Lower your voice, or he'll hear you," she said. "His mama is a friend of mine."

"Well, then, it would seem you could—"

Rose again shushed him, this time a bit more emphatically.

The problem seemed to be that Laura liked Henry as much as he liked her, although why Emory couldn't say. The boy was a lanky string bean with knobby knees and oversized feet.

"Laura will be terribly upset if you start fussing at Henry, so try to be patient," Rose urged. "She'll be going back to school in a few more days, and then she's sure to move on to some other interest."

Laura did go back to school but didn't move on to another interest. Every morning when she left the house he'd be standing on the sidewalk, waiting for her so they could walk together. After school he'd swing by his own house, drop his books off then come back to spend time with Laura. When the weather turned cold they simply moved from the front porch to the parlor, and more often than not the boy sat in Emory's favorite chair with his gangly legs stretched out. On the rare occasion when Henry wasn't at the house he'd call on the telephone, and Laura would stand in the hallway for an hour or more talking about absolutely nothing.

As fall turned to winter and then spring, it began to appear as if they were in love. Twice Rose asked her daughter if they had spoken of anything as serious as marriage.

Laura laughed. "Of course not. We just enjoy being together. Henry knows I've still got another year before I finish high school."

"What about him?" Rose asked. "He graduates this year. Has he mentioned what he plans to do then?"

"He's already got a job lined up. The gas station where he's been working part time is going to put him on full time, and they're going to let him buy the 1921 Hatfield they've got sitting out back. It needs work, but Henry's very knowledgeable about fixing cars."

It was not the answer Rose wanted to hear. She knew Emory was hoping the boy would go away to college, but obviously Henry had other plans.

"Before you two become serious, I wish you would try dating other young men," she said.

"Why?"

It was an uncomfortable moment. Rose stumbled over several thoughts then gave what she believed to be the best answer.

"Henry is a nice enough young man, but he doesn't have much ambition. I question whether he'd be—"

"Mama!" Laura cut in sharply. "Why would you say such a thing?"

"Tinkering with cars is fine for a boy, but as a man—"

"Daddy was a street car conductor when you married him!"

"Yes, but your daddy had ambition. He knew he'd have to support a family and—"

"Henry has ambition too," Laura snapped. She whirled on her heel and trotted up the stairs.

From that point on, any discussion about Henry was prickly as a briar patch. When Emory suggested that perhaps he should have a talk with the lad, Laura flew into a fit of tears.

"I'm only saying I think you're too young..." Emory stammered, but by then she'd stormed out of the room.

Emory turned to Rose with a mystified expression. "I simply do not understand teenage girls."

"No one does, dear," Rose replied.

A CHANGE OF HEART

Laura and Henry continued to date all summer. He went to work at the gas station and did indeed buy the Hatfield she'd spoken of. It was a two-seat coupe that rattled as if it would fall apart any moment.

Rose feared once he had the car they would be off riding around to God-knows-where, but such was not the case. If anything the boy seemed to develop a greater sense of responsibility. Any number of times he volunteered to drive Rose to the Safeway store and wait while she shopped. When they arrived back at the house, he'd carry in the groceries.

Such courtesies impressed Rose, and in time she convinced Emory to accept the likelihood that Henry would one day be their son-in-law. Once the thought settled in, even Emory began to see the lad's good qualities. He was polite, came from a nice family, went to church on Sunday, had a job and was apparently willing to wait until Laura graduated high school before even mentioning anything as serious as marriage.

For well over a year all appearances would lead anyone to believe Laura was crazy in love with the boy, but that winter the courtship began to wane. On afternoons when Rose expected to see him at the house, she'd find the living room filled with Laura's girlfriends.

"Isn't Henry coming over?" she'd ask.

More often than not Laura would say he was busy working at the gas station or polishing his car.

Then in February the entire month passed by without Henry at the dinner table even once. It seemed as though once Emory and Rose accepted the lad as a suitable son-in-law, Laura changed her mind.

On the day of her graduation they had no doubt Henry would be sitting beside them as they watched Laura walk across the stage to receive her diploma, but the seat remained empty. Afterward when asked about Henry, she simply said he had to work that day.

"Couldn't he ask for the afternoon off?" Emory asked.

"I told him not to bother," Laura replied. "I'm going to Louise Latham's party anyway, so he'd just be bored."

Later that evening Emory sat in the overstuffed velour chair flipping through the pages of *The Wyattsville Tribune*, but his thoughts kept drifting from the articles back to his discussion with Laura. After months of staunchly defending Henry, she apparently was ready to move on.

Bewildered by such a change of heart, he asked, "Are all young girls this fickle?"

"I can't say," Rose replied. "I know I wasn't. I fell in love with you that day at the church picnic, and I've never once changed my mind."

Emory folded the paper, set it aside and came to sit beside Rose on the sofa. He draped his arm around her shoulder and tugged her close.

"I'm a lucky man," he said then leaned over and kissed her cheek.

After several minutes passed by, he added, "I hope when

Laura gets ready to settle down she'll pick a sensible young man, someone who will love her as much as I love you."

Rose snuggled closer. "I hope so too."

ALTHOUGH AT TIMES IT SEEMED Laura did little or no studying, she was actually at the top of her class. Her typing and stenographic skills were second to none. That summer the Ridge Valley Savings Bank advertised a secretarial opening and seven high school graduates applied for the job, but Laura was the one who got it. She came home glowing.

"I'll be working for Mister Burnham," she said. "He's the senior vice president."

The following Monday she pulled on her crepe middy, dusted powder on her nose, painted her mouth and trotted off to work. Catherine Goodman, the office manager, spent the morning introducing her around and explaining her responsibilities, but once Laura sat down at the desk in front of Montgomery Burnham's oak-walled office there was actually very little to do. That day she answered three telephone calls, took fifteen minutes of dictation and typed two letters plus one interoffice memo reminding employees that all cash drawers had to be rectified before they were closed out for the day.

It was much the same throughout the week. Then on Friday afternoon Franklin Wilkes walked in. He apparently knew exactly where he was going because he crossed the lobby and went directly to Laura's desk.

"Is Monty around?" he asked.

She looked up into what was quite possibly the handsomest face she'd ever seen. "Are you referring to Mister Burnham?"

"Yes, Montgomery Burnham. Tell him Franklin is here."

"Do you have an appointment?"

Franklin chuckled. "I don't think I need one."

Laura motioned to the visitor's chair across from her desk. "Please have a seat, I'll check if he's available."

She stood, smoothed her skirt then walked back and tapped softly at the oak door. After hearing him call out for her to come in, she cracked a narrow opening and stepped inside Montgomery Burnham's office.

"A Mister Franklin is asking to see you, but he doesn't have an appoint—"

Burnham gave a quizzical look. "Mister Franklin?"

"Tall, dark hair, rather handsome—"

"Oh, you mean Franklin Wilkes." Burnham gave a warm chuckle then rose from his seat and followed her out to greet Franklin.

It was obvious they knew one another well in addition to being business associates. They shook hands as old friends do, and Franklin asked about Burnham's family. As they started toward the office, in that last second before he disappeared through the door, Franklin looked back at Laura and smiled.

She returned the smile.

When the day ended at five o'clock, Laura didn't hurry out as she'd done earlier in the week. She stayed an extra twenty minutes shuffling papers from one side of her desk to the other, leafing through the pages of her steno pad as if she might have missed something and even straightening the magazines on the table in the reception area. When there was absolutely nothing more to busy herself with, she reluctantly pulled her purse from the desk drawer and headed for home.

EVERY MONDAY MONTGOMERY BURNHAM HAD lunch at his club

with a group of bankers. It was a thing he'd done for years, and, if nothing else, he was a creature of habit. He left the office at precisely twelve noon and returned at one forty-five.

At twelve-fifteen Franklin Wilkes walked in.

"Is Monty around?" he asked.

After seeing how friendly they'd been with each other, Laura suspected he already knew her boss's routine and that thought settled pleasantly in her head.

"He's out to lunch right now," she said. "Would you care to wait?" *Say yes. Please say yes.*

He gave her the smile she'd been thinking of all weekend.

"If it's no bother," he replied.

Instead of moving off toward the visitors' chairs, he perched himself on the corner of her desk and began chatting.

It was precisely what she'd hoped for. Although she would be hard pressed to say whether it was the way his smile made her cheeks feel flushed or the way he made her think of things that had nothing to do with the bank, Mister Burnham or her job for that matter, something about Franklin drew her to him. His eyes were as dark and rich as chocolate, and the lines that crinkled at the corners made him look as though he was born smiling.

He asked if she was new with the bank and without taking her eyes from his face, she nodded. Trying to recapture the balance of her senses, she told him, "This is only my second week."

"Well, then," he said. "A week of working with Monty is something to celebrate. If you're available perhaps we could have lunch later this week."

Laura hadn't stopped smiling since the moment she saw him walk in.

"I'm available," she said, and just like that they made a date for lunch on Thursday.

He stayed for over an hour, leaning in with whispered tidbits of conversation and tales of how he and Monty had been doing business for the past three years. He told her he was a stockbroker with the Sampson Investment Company and worked in the Morgenstern building in downtown Wyattsville. He said he'd been with the firm for three years, and Burnham was one of his first clients.

All the while he stood there talking, she was imagining what it would be like to have him kiss her, to feel his lips pressed to hers and his arm snug around her waist.

Five minutes before Mister Burnham was due back, Franklin said he'd waited long enough.

"It wasn't anything important," he claimed. "I can stop by again later in the week."

Considering that she was, after all, a secretary, Laura asked if Franklin wanted her to pencil in an appointment or have Mister Burnham call.

"Not necessary," he said and turned to go. Halfway across the lobby he looked back, smiled and gave a wink.

That's when she knew for certain the visit was just to see her.

After Lunch...

On Thursday morning Laura was awake a full hour earlier than usual. She rifled through her closet three times before she finally decided on a pink georgette dress that was nearly three inches shorter than the skirts she'd worn earlier in the week. When she arrived at the breakfast table, Emory raised an eyebrow.

"Aren't you a bit overdressed for work?" he asked.

"There's a special luncheon today," she said, giving the impression it was a group event. To avoid any further questions, she gulped down a few sips of coffee, pulled on the straw cloche with a matching pink flower and hurried out the door.

With more time than usual, she walked instead of taking the trolley. As it happened the Morgenstern building was on the way. Well, sort of on the way. It was a block past where she usually turned off for the bank. It was one of those office buildings she ordinarily hurried past without a second thought, but on this morning she slowed her step as she passed by. The sun was already bright, and the glimmer of something caught her eye. She looked up and saw rays of light flickering off the glass windows like a million tiny fireflies.

He's up there in one of those offices. Which one?

Years later Laura would remember this day. She'd remember passing by the Morgenstern building, looking up at the windows and wondering which one might be Franklin's office.

By then she could no longer bear to walk along Broad Street.

FRANKLIN ARRIVED AT THE BANK a few minutes before twelve.

"I'd like a word with Monty before we go," he said.

As was their routine, she tapped on Burnham's door then opened it and said, "Mister Wilkes would like a moment of your time, sir."

"Franklin, come on in," Burnham bellowed.

He was in and out of the office in less than two minutes. He closed the oak door behind him then offered Laura his arm and flashed the smile she would come to love.

"We're good to go," he said, and off they went.

Laura assumed they'd go somewhere local; the coffee shop down the street perhaps or the Italian restaurant two blocks over. Instead he hailed a taxicab and after she'd climbed into the back seat gave an address on the far side of town. A look of apprehension settled on Laura's face.

"I have to be back at work by one o'clock, so I don't think—"

"No, you don't. Monty said if we made it back by two-thirty, that would be just fine."

"Really?"

Again he gave her that smile. "Really."

THAT DAY THEY DINED AT the Belmont Club, a place that during the day served excellent French cuisine and after dark, when it was supposedly closed, became a speakeasy. As they nibbled on petit fours and sipped a second cup of coffee, Franklin told her the secret of the club. Delighting in such forbidden information, she gave a smug grin.

"I'll bet you've been to the speakeasy, haven't you?" she teased.

"Once," he said, then laughed and told her the thing he remembered most was how the music was very, very loud.

It was impossible not to like Franklin Wilkes. He was the best of all things: handsome, charming and worldly. He had money in his pocket and a touch of mischief in his soul. He made her feel more alive than she had ever felt. Sitting across the table with her eyes fixed on his face, she could feel the warmth of his heart. It was as if she'd been waiting all her life for him, and now he was there.

As they left the restaurant his hand circled the curve of her waist, and she felt the heat of it rising to her cheeks. They stepped to the curb, and he again hailed a cab. It was there in the back seat of the taxicab that he first kissed her.

After the kiss he asked if he could see her again on Saturday. Laura nodded, too breathless to answer. By the time she returned to her desk, she knew she was in love. Not the "boy-down-the-block" kind of love she'd felt with Henry. This time it was an "I'll-love-you-until-the-day-I-die" kind of love.

It was only a day until she would see him again, yet she could scarcely contain the excitement of such a thought. On Friday she ate lunch at her desk, hoping he might possibly stop by or drop in to speak with Mister Burnham. Twice she glanced up quickly and thought she saw the swagger of a figure such as his crossing the lobby. Both times she was disappointed. Other men stood as tall and had thick strands of dark hair falling across their forehead, but no one else had Franklin's smile.

ON SATURDAY MORNING WHEN THE Hawthorne family sat down

to breakfast, Laura was at loose ends when it came to explaining exactly who her date for that evening was.

"A fellow I met at the bank," she said casually.

"Does he work there?" Emory asked.

"He doesn't exactly work there. It's more like he does business with them."

Rose nodded. "Oh, a customer?"

Laura stuffed a chunk of pancake into her mouth and shook her head. Emory looked her square in the face and waited.

"Exactly how did you meet this fellow?" he finally asked.

Chewing on that piece of pancake as she tried to sort through the possible answers, Laura eventually swallowed and said, "Franklin does business with Mister Burnham."

Still not satisfied, Emory asked, "What kind of business?"

"He sells investments. He's a stock broker."

"Stock broker?" Emory's tone indicated his annoyance. "How old is he?"

Laura shrugged and went back to carving another chunk off of the stack of pancakes.

"It's only a date, Daddy. I didn't ask him his life's history."

"You say Mister Burnham knows this fellow?" Rose asked.

Laura could see the wheels turning in her mama's head, and she gasped.

"Don't you dare call Mister Burnham! You'll embarrass the life out of me!"

After answering several more questions and confessing that Franklin Wilkes had been the one who took her to lunch on Thursday, the conversation came to an end. By then Emory was determined to be on hand and check the fellow out before Laura left for her date.

AT TEN MINUTES BEFORE SIX, Franklin parked his car alongside the curb in front of the house. The car was a snazzy Chrysler roadster with a convertible top, chrome-rimmed headlights and fat whitewall tires. He stepped onto the front porch and rang the doorbell. Rose opened the door.

"Good evening, Missus Hawthorne," Franklin said and handed her a bouquet of flowers. "These are for you."

"Good gracious," Rose said with a pleased smile. "What a thoughtful gesture." She pulled the door back and led him into the parlor.

Laura came up behind her mama and greeted Franklin. He put his hand to her arm, and she felt the same tingle she'd felt that first time. Were it not for the mandate her daddy had laid down earlier she would have darted out the door immediately, but Emory insisted on meeting her date.

"Emory, dear," Rose said, "this is Franklin Wilkes. He and Laura are going out this evening."

Emory stood and stuck out his hand.

"A pleasure," he said in a less than cordial manner. He motioned for the two of them to have a seat then asked where they were going.

"I was thinking dinner at the Wyndower Grill on Broad Street." Franklin looked at Laura and smiled. "And perhaps the Rialto Theatre afterward. They're showing the new Ben Hur movie, and supposedly it's quite a spectacle."

Emory gave a thoughtful nod. He could find nothing wrong with that plan. As a matter of fact, he had spoken with Rose about possibly going to see the same movie on Sunday.

He asked, "How exactly did you and Laura meet?"

"At the bank. I represent the Sampson Investment Company, and Montgomery Burnham was one of my first customers."

"Sampson Investments, huh? How long have you been with them?"

Franklin said he'd been there three years, and Emory could

find no problem with that answer either. He asked several more questions, and when he ran out of things to ask about he said, "Did my daughter mention that she is only eighteen years old?"

Rose popped out of her chair and gave him an angry glare then smiled awkwardly at the young man.

"It's been lovely meeting you, Franklin," she said. "Now you and Laura shoo on out of here and have yourselves a lovely evening."

Emory stood and gave another nod. Not changing his tone, he said, "Yes, do have a nice evening. Just don't be too late getting home."

Rose glared at him again, then turned and walked them to the door. Once Franklin's car had disappeared around the corner, she returned to the parlor.

"Why in heaven's name were you so rude to that young man?" she asked.

Emory sat there for a full minute before saying anything. "Did you see the way he was looking at Laura?"

"Yes, I did," Rose replied, "and I thought it was rather loving and sweet."

"He was looking at her the same way I looked at you the night we met."

"And what's so terrible about that?"

Emory leaned back in the chair and gave a labored sigh. "Laura's only eighteen. She's too young to be thinking of marriage."

Rose laughed. "Don't make a mountain of a molehill. It's only a date. Let's not fret about this fellow the way we did the Jennings boy. Laura went with him for over a year, and nothing came of it. The same thing will probably happen again."

Emory gave a doubtful shake of his head.

"Not this time," he said.

A SEASON OF LOVE

Emory was right. That fall before the leaves began to change color, Franklin came to him and asked for Laura's hand in marriage.

"I love your daughter, and I promise to be a good provider," he said. "I've got a steady job, and I've saved a bit of money…"

As Franklin continued Emory sat there with a deadpan expression, giving no indication of whether he would answer yes or no. The truth is he would have said no in a heartbeat, but then he'd have Rose and Laura to contend with. How could he explain how he felt? That he couldn't fathom that some stranger would swoop in and carry off the beautiful daughter he loved so much? Emory had hoped Laura would wait until she was twenty or twenty-one before even thinking of marriage, but that hope had flown out the window when he saw how she fluttered into Franklin's arms the minute he showed up on the doorstep.

"I can believe you'll take good care of my girl," he finally said, "but the problem is I'm not really ready to lose her."

"You wouldn't be losing your daughter," Franklin replied. "You'd simply be adding me and whatever children we have to your family. We'd live nearby, right here in Wyattsville. My job is here; Laura's job is here. We have no reason to go elsewhere. We could come for dinner once or twice a week and have you and Mother Hawthorne on Sundays..."

Emory noticed how he already called Rose "Mother Hawthorne." It was a losing battle. Truthfully, he had never expected to win, but still he couldn't go down without a fight.

"Laura is awfully young to be married. It's a lot of responsibility to be fostered on the shoulders of a girl so young."

"Wasn't Mother Hawthorne seventeen when you married her?"

"Well, yes, but..."

Emory turned and looked Franklin square in the face. He was going to say times were different then, that the world was less complicated, less challenging perhaps, but before he got the words out he saw the beads of perspiration blossoming on Franklin's forehead.

"You really do love my daughter, don't you?"

"Yes," Franklin answered. "With all my heart."

Knowing he had no real choice in the matter, Emory gave an almost imperceptible nod.

"Okay then," he said. "You have my blessing."

Franklin took hold of his hand and shook it vigorously.

"Thank you!" he said. "I swear I won't let you down. I'll—"

He was going to repeat the litany of promises he'd already made, but Emory cut him off.

"I'm not agreeing to this marriage because of what you've promised to do or not do," Emory said. "I'm agreeing to it because I've seen the way Laura looks at you." He drew in a breath then gave a long and wistful sigh. "It's apparent my daughter loves you as much as you do her."

THE FOLLOWING SATURDAY FRANKLIN AND Laura went for an early dinner at Renaldo's. It was a restaurant with a strolling violinist and candlelit tables. He had the ring in his pocket but had yet to decide exactly when he would pop the question. Although reasonably certain she felt about him as he did about her and her answer would be yes, still he was nervous.

Earlier in the week he'd visited the restaurant and reserved a side booth where she would sit next to him rather than across the table. It was a table where he could hold her hand in his, wrap his arm around her shoulder and plant a row of kisses along the edge of her cheek as he whispered the question.

He'd walked through the restaurant and carefully selected the perfect table, one in a shadowy corner, away from noisy conversations and the hustle and bustle of waiters carrying trays of food. To make certain everything would go right, he'd slipped the maître d' a five-dollar bill. Marcel had not only promised to save the booth, but he'd added that there would be a rose at the table for the lady.

Everything should have been as he'd arranged it, but when they arrived at the restaurant there was no Marcel. Four people were crowded into the booth he'd chosen, and the only thing available was a table in front of the swinging door that led to the kitchen.

"We can take that table or go somewhere else if you like," Laura said.

Franklin hesitated. Neither was a good option, and now he'd been thrown off his stride.

"Let's go somewhere else," he said.

As they walked back to his car Franklin tried to come up with another restaurant as romantic as Renaldo's, but there was none. He opened the car door and Laura climbed in. Still trying to come up with a place, he circled around and slid behind the wheel.

"Any place special you'd like to go?" he asked.

She nodded and gave a mischievous grin. "Let's go to that speakeasy at the Belmont Club."

"Tonight?"

"Why not? I've never been to a speakeasy. It'll be fun."

Franklin pictured the look on Emory's face if Laura came home tipsy or smelling of whiskey.

"That's not a real good idea," he said. "Maybe after we're married—"

Laura's head jerked back as she turned to him with a look of astonishment.

"Married?!"

"Damn!" He smacked his hand to his forehead. "Now I've ruined it!"

"Ruined what?"

He pulled the ring from his pocket and held it out.

"I wanted tonight to be special because I was going to ask you to marry me."

"Well, then ask me," she said and smiled.

Already seeing the answer in her smile, he slid the ring on her finger and whispered, "Will you marry me?"

"Of course I will," she answered and kissed him as he'd kissed her that first day in the taxicab.

They did end up in the speakeasy that evening and the music was every bit as loud as Franklin had said, but neither of them cared. Laura had her first taste of whiskey, and they danced until they could barely catch their breaths. As they drove home that night, he apologized for the way things had turned out.

"I wanted tonight to be special," he said.

Laura laughed and put her hand to his face. "It was! I'll remember this night for as long as I live."

In the wee hours of the morning as she closed her eyes and

drifted into a dream of the beautiful future awaiting them, Laura couldn't possibly imagine the heartache that was to come.

THE MONTHS THAT FOLLOWED WERE a frenzy of activity in the Hawthorne household. Yards and yards of silk organza were stretched across the dining room table as Rose cut and stitched Laura's wedding gown.

No matter where Emory went, there was yet another reminder of the upcoming wedding. His quiet evenings of sitting in the parlor were all but gone, because the telephone never stopped ringing. When Rose did have a few minutes to sit across from him, she was busy sewing tiny pearls on the bodice of Laura's gown and not the least bit interested in hearing him read the news of the day.

He thought when the first Sunday of December finally arrived he'd be glad to have an end to all the craziness, but that's not what he felt as he walked Laura down the aisle. At the altar when he passed her hand to Franklin and kissed her cheek, he realized the end of the craziness meant the little girl who once depended on him would now belong to someone else.

He looked Franklin in the eye and said, "You'd better take good care of my baby."

"I will," Franklin replied. "So help me God I will."

FRANKLIN WILKES

I didn't just fall in love with Laura; I fell in love with her family also. Emory is a man I'd be proud to call Dad. And I can say the same for Mother Hawthorne. She and Laura are cut from the same cloth. I consider myself lucky to be marrying into such a family.

Neither of my parents came to the wedding. I sent invitations to both of them, but I guess they were afraid people would talk. More than that, they were probably afraid they'd run into each other. When they got divorced they didn't just end the marriage, they chopped it into a million angry little pieces. They fought tooth and nail over who was going to get the house, but neither of them fought for me. I was the leftover baggage they passed back and forth like a hot potato.

I left Cleveland the day after I graduated high school and never went back again. Sad to say, there's no reason to go back. To Mom and Dad I'm a walking reminder of their failures, and that's something they'd rather forget.

I promised I'd take care of Laura, and I meant it from the bottom of my heart. When you come from a broken home, you know what angry words and thoughtless gestures can lead to. I'll never let that happen to our marriage.

Emory Hawthorne needn't worry about me. I said I'd love Laura until the day I die and that's exactly what I intend to do.

HAPPILY MARRIED

After the wedding, Franklin and Laura drove to Richmond and spent four days at the Algonquin Hotel. They stayed in the bridal suite, slept late each morning and stayed up until all hours of the night dancing to the music of an eight-piece orchestra in the grand ballroom. On their last night in Richmond the band played *Sleepy Time Girl*, and Laura lowered her head onto Franklin's shoulder with a sigh.

"This has been so wonderful," she said. "I hate to see it come to an end."

Franklin held her close as they swished across the floor moving with the music.

"It's never going to end," he replied. "Every year we'll come back here and do this all over again."

She gave a soft chuckle. "You say that now, but when we have a family—"

"We'll bring them with us." He bent, kissed her forehead and cupped his hand around the small of her back. "And when the children are old enough to understand, we'll tell them of how we fell in love and spent a magical four days in this very same place."

THE NEXT MORNING AS THEY climbed into the car and headed back to Wyattsville Laura could almost see her whole life stretched out in front of her, more wonderful than anything she'd ever imagined.

HOLDING TRUE TO HIS PLEDGE, Franklin rented a lovely little three-room apartment that was less than five blocks from Chester Street. In the morning he and Laura would leave for work together. They'd walk over to Broad Street holding hands like the young lovers they were, and there on the corner they'd kiss goodbye. She would turn down towards the bank, and he'd walk three blocks over to the Morgenstern building.

Several times a week Laura would arrive home and find a still-warm casserole or a basket of Rose's fresh-baked muffins sitting alongside the door. She'd scoop up whatever was left there and then hurry inside to call her mama.

"However did you know chicken noodle casserole is Franklin's favorite?" she'd ask.

On evenings when the weather was balmy, they'd have dinner then walk over to spend an hour or two with Emory and Rose. Whatever concerns Emory had regarding Franklin were gone in no time. As soon as they returned from their honeymoon, Franklin took to calling Emory "Dad." The first time he said it, Emory swiveled his head and looked around as if he expected to see someone else standing there.

That spring while Laura and her mama fussed about the kitchen or worked at tatting another new doily, Franklin sat across from Emory and listened to the baseball games on the radio.

"Can you believe those Yankees?" Emory would say with a discouraged nod.

Franklin would bobble his head in almost the same manner. "With this lineup, they're sure to take the pennant. The Senators haven't got a prayer."

Although at one time Emory resented the thought of giving up his daughter, it had come to be exactly as Franklin had forecasted. He hadn't lost Laura at all, and he had gained a son-in-law who was happy to sit and talk about things the ladies had no interest in.

SHORTLY AFTER THEIR FIRST ANNIVERSARY, Franklin and Laura invited Rose and Emory over for Thanksgiving. Laura set the table with the china they'd ordered from J.C. Penney and roasted a turkey filled with bread stuffing. Starting early that morning she made a bowl of candied sweet potatoes, a dish of corn pudding and pickled green tomatoes. Rose brought a basket of biscuits and a maple walnut cake.

When they sat down at the table, Franklin said grace then took out the bottle of wine he'd hidden away and poured a glass for everyone.

"Wine?" Rose said. "Isn't that against the law?"

"Drinking it isn't," Franklin replied with a grin. "Just making it and selling it is. But let's forget about prohibition today and have a toast, because we've got something to celebrate."

"Celebrate?" Emory and Rose echoed in unison.

A secretive glance slid back and forth between Laura and Franklin.

"Do you want to be the one to tell them?" he asked.

Her mouth curled into a grin, and she nodded. "I've quit my job because we're expecting a baby."

Rose squealed. "Oh, how wonderful! When?"

"The doctor thinks it will be the first week of June."

"That's not all," Franklin added. "We bought a three-bedroom house on Madison Street." He grinned at Laura. "We wanted enough room for children."

Rose heard the plural and smiled. "So you're planning on more?"

They both nodded.

"At least three," Franklin said.

Laura laughed and added, "Maybe four."

MADISON WAS A QUIET STREET lined with white clapboard houses and fenced-in yards. Although it was five blocks in the opposite direction, it was closer to Chester Street and the Hawthorne house. A week after they moved in, Laura began stitching curtains for the baby's room. Not knowing whether the baby would be a boy or girl, she decided on white with a border of brown bunnies at the bottom.

Once the curtains were done and the walls painted, they began shopping for a crib. Laura's first thought was to order something inexpensive from the Sears and Roebuck catalogue, but Franklin shook his head.

"We'll go downtown, buy a first-rate crib and a chest of drawers to match," he said. "If we buy something sturdy enough, we can use it for this baby and the others that are yet to come." He gave a grin and added, "Luckily we can afford it."

That much was true. In the five years Franklin had been with Sampson Investments his earnings had gone up steadily, and in 1925 his commissions had more than doubled.

"These are good times," he said, "and it's only going to get better."

A month before the baby was due, he bought a shiny new Chrysler sedan. Three weeks later at 3AM on a Sunday morning,

Laura went into labor and he drove her to the hospital. On the way her water broke, and she started to cry.

"I've ruined our beautiful new car," she said through her tears.

Franklin reached across and took hold of her hand.

"You having a healthy baby is the only thing that counts," he said. "This car's just a car."

Laura winced her way through another contraction but managed to smile back at him. At five minutes before seven their baby girl was born.

Years later, after everything happened, Laura would still remember hearing the church bells that morning as she sat propped against the hospital bed pillows with the baby held to her breast. They named the child Christine. It was Laura's choice, inspired by the sound of those bells. When people asked how she came upon the name, she'd proudly answer, "It means follower of Christ."

PROMISE OF PROSPERITY

Just as Franklin had predicted one good year rolled into another, and with the sale of stocks rapidly climbing he earned a year-end bonus that enabled him to pay down over half of the mortgage on the house.

Before Christine turned two he paid off the remaining balance, and they celebrated by spending the weekend at the Algonquin Hotel in Richmond. Together the three of them strolled Gerard Street browsing the shops; then they returned to the hotel for afternoon tea in the grand salon. Before starting for home, Franklin bought Christine a doll nearly as big as she was, and he bought Laura a gold heart-shaped locket.

"This is to remind you of how much I love you," he said and hooked it around her neck.

With sales continuing to spiral upward, weekends at the Algonquin Hotel soon became a regular thing, and on each trip they returned with a small gift for Christine's grandparents. When Emory was handed his customary box of cigars, he smiled, squared his shoulders and stood proudly. Times like this he knew Lady Luck had tapped him on the shoulder when he said yes to Franklin marrying his daughter.

FRANKLIN'S BEST YEAR TO DATE was 1928, and in December when he received his annual bonus check he invested most of it in the same stocks he'd been selling to his clients. Not only did he invest, he also convinced Emory to take the money he'd set aside over the years and do the same.

Emory had no reason to doubt his son-in-law. The proof was in the pudding. There was no arguing with such success.

That Christmas Franklin brought home a tree tall enough to touch the ceiling, and there were more presents than a person could count. The week before Christmas, Laura and Rose took Christine downtown for a visit with Santa at Miller's Department Store. They shopped for a while then had lunch at Anne's Tea Room. Afterward they browsed the festively decorated windows along Broad Street, and when Christine saw the displays of toys her eyes sparkled.

"Are you excited to see Santa?" Laura asked.

Christine nodded and happily hiked her shoulders toward her ears.

Rose laughed. "Laura, this child is you all over again."

It was true enough; although she was still a toddler Christine was the spitting image of her mama.

When they finally got to Miller's and she saw Santa dressed in his red suit and surrounded by elves, Christine could barely contain her excitement. She climbed onto his lap and chatted happily, but when he asked what she wanted for Christmas she couldn't think of a single thing she didn't already have.

IN JANUARY THE YEAR STARTED off with the same robust sales, but near the end of March stock prices began to fall. Like many of the Sampson clients, Franklin had invested most of his money in the market and the slowly declining prices made him sit up and take notice. At first he'd figured it to be nothing more than the natural fluctuations of the buy and sell market, but after a week of closing on the down side every day he started to get apprehensive. He thought about it for most of the weekend, and on Sunday evening as he and Laura were climbing into bed he told her of his concerns.

"We've been lucky," he said, "but maybe it's time we took some of that money out of the market and stuck it in a savings account."

Laura agreed. Remembering her mama's frugal nature, she said, "You should also telephone Daddy tomorrow and have him do the same."

"Okay," Franklin replied; then he snapped off the light and went to sleep.

ON MONDAY MORNING FRANKLIN WENT into the office with that intention, but before he got situated at his desk all hell broke loose. Stock prices plummeted. Late in the afternoon he started calling clients who had bought stocks with a partial down payment to tell them the firm was calling their margin. This meant they now had to pay more than what the stock was worth.

George Feldman, a welder who worked for the Reliable Steel Company, was one of those clients. When he'd heard his friends brag about making money hand over fist in the market, he'd taken a mortgage on his mama's house and invested every last cent. Hearing of the firm calling in their margin, he flew into a rage.

"You saying you sold me no-good stock?" he snapped.

"That's not it at all," Franklin said and again explained how buying on margin worked.

"You bought Broadhurst at seventeen dollars a share," he said.

With a snarl in his voice George said, "Yeah, but now you're telling me it's worth eight dollars and fifty-seven cents! I ain't paying seventeen dollars for something worth eight-fifty-seven!" With that he slammed down the telephone.

It was the same story all afternoon. Some clients blew up and shouted; others, like the elderly Louisa Burns, cried. When Franklin arrived home that night, he told Laura of the day he'd had.

"It's a good thing you transferred our money into a savings account," she said.

Franklin put a hand to his forehead and rubbed his fingers across his brow.

"There was no time," he said. "I didn't get to it."

"But you did call Daddy, didn't you?"

He shook his head. "I didn't do that either."

"Dear God," Laura said with a moan. "Mama is going to have a conniption."

ON TUESDAY THE TRADING ACTIVITY was considerably calmer. Although there was no upswing in prices, the downward spiral had slowed to a crawl. As soon as he got to the office, Franklin telephoned Emory.

"You'll take a hit but better safe than sorry," he said.

"A good point," Emory said. Then he remembered the inheritance he'd gotten because of his daddy's stocks. He changed his mind and told Franklin to hold on to the blue chips.

"I doubt anything can happen to those," he said.

Before noon Franklin had sold the majority of stocks in his account and a percent of what Emory had. He transferred the money into individual savings accounts. They'd taken a hit, but neither of them had gone into debt.

Franklin spent the remainder of the day calling clients. Those with blue chip holdings he told to sit tight; others with more speculative stocks he advised to sell and cut their losses. On Wednesday morning Charles Mitchell, a highly respected banker, held a press conference and told reporters that the downturn was nothing but a hiccup in the market.

"I intend to continue lending money," he said and reassured those listening that the market would rebound before the week was out. The evening newspapers reported the story word for word, and by Friday what Mitchell forecasted had come to pass.

The following Monday George Feldman called Franklin.

"What kind of shit are you giving me saying my stock's no good? The newspaper says Broadhurst is selling for seventeen sixty-three!"

"The market rebounded at the end of the week," Franklin replied. "But since you're in such a speculative position, I'd suggest you sell the stock and break even while you can."

"I ain't gonna sell nothing!" George replied. "My money's good as the next man's. I ain't looking to break even; I'm looking to make money. If you got a nickel's worth of brains, you'll make sure I do."

Four times Franklin explained that there was no guarantee with the market and twice he added that he didn't feel good about what was happening, but George refused to listen.

That evening Franklin waited until Christine was tucked into bed. Then he sat beside Laura and told her that despite the market surge, he was not feeling good about things.

"I think we should leave our money in the bank," he said.

Laura nodded and said she was fine with whatever he decided to do.

FRANKLIN STUCK WITH HIS DECISION even after the market soared in June and July. With his brows pinched together and a worried expression tugging at the corners of his mouth, he advised many of his clients to do likewise.

"Don't you read the newspapers?" Emma Pearl asked. Then she went on to tell him the market was at an all-time high, and indications were it would keep on going.

"Read the article on page seven of the *News Leader*," she said.

Of course Franklin had read the article. But he'd also been keeping an eye on other indicators. The steel mills were cutting back on production, not as many new homes were being built and automobile sales, which had skyrocketed for the past five years, had now slowed dramatically.

After almost three months of advising clients to sell despite the boom market, Franklin was tagged a pessimist. A few of the clients listened to his advice but most did not, and a few even moved their accounts to a different brokerage firm.

HIGHS & LOWS

That summer Laura and Franklin made just one trip to Richmond. It was to celebrate Christine's fourth birthday. Again they stayed at the Algonquin and took tea in the grand salon, but instead of browsing the shops along Broad Street they went to the city park and rode the carousel. It took three tries but Franklin finally caught the brass ring, and Christine was given a free ride on the white horse that moved up and down in time with the music.

Franklin lifted her onto the horse, buckled the strap around her waist and stood beside her as they circled around and around. Laura stood beside the carousel and snapped a picture each time they came around.

After dinner, with Christine tucked safely into bed and the third-floor maid keeping an eye on her, Franklin and Laura went downstairs to the Madison Ballroom and danced. As the evening grew late, a willowy blonde stepped to the microphone and sang *Someone to Watch Over Me*. As they moved with the music, Franklin tightened his arm around her waist.

"I'll always be here to watch over my two beautiful girls," he whispered.

She leaned her head onto his chest and sighed. "I know you will."

IN THE FIRST WEEK OF September, the Dow Jones hit an all-time high. Despite his son-in-law's apprehension, Emory took the money from his savings account and reinvested it. That same week Franklin lost three more clients. They claimed when it came to predicting the market he didn't know his ear from his elbow, and at that point he was beginning to wonder if perhaps they weren't right.

Seeing such a dramatic increase in the stock, George Feldman took the last $200 out of his mama's savings account and bought another ten shares of Broadhurst Steel. When Franklin got the call from George telling him to buy the ten shares of Broadhurst, he started to voice his doubts about the stock.

"I ain't interested in your opinion," George said and hung up.

Not anxious to lose yet another client, Franklin took the transaction and put through a buy order.

The following week Broadhurst took a dip along with a number of other stocks, but it was only a few points so nobody did anything. The days of the month rolled by with investors expecting a rebound, but it didn't happen. By early October a number of Wall Street brokers were scratching their chins.

The *News Leader* jumped back and forth with a diversity of opinions. One day they'd interview a banker who assured readers the market had reached a sustainable high and was certain to stay there. The next day they'd quote an economist who claimed such expectations were unrealistic.

The fourth week of October when Laura's parents came to Sunday dinner, Franklin took Emory aside.

"I know a lot of people disagree, but I think we're in for a rough ride," he said. "Play it smart; take the money you've reinvested back out of the market."

"With the prices down?" Emory replied skeptically.

Franklin nodded. "Last week was a roller coaster ride, but it's going to get worse. I'm certain of it."

Over the past few years, Emory had come to have great respect for Franklin. He was a man who took care of his family, and there was nothing Emory Hawthorne appreciated more than that.

"Okay," he said. "Do it."

ON MONDAY MORNING WHEN FRANKLIN got to the office, the first thing he did was to execute the trade for Emory. By then the value of the account had dropped by nineteen percent. Franklin telephoned Emory and gave him the news.

"I'm sorry I got you into this," he said, "but I'll make it up to you, I swear I will."

The money he'd lost was the equivalent of three months' pay for Emory.

"I'm not happy losing all this money," he said, "but you don't have to make up for anything. Taking care of my little girl as you do is payment enough."

BEFORE NOON THE MARKET WAS in free fall, and there seemed to be no way of stopping it. Franklin remained in the office until eight-thirty that evening, calling clients and advising them of the situation. Some said to sell as soon as the market opened the next morning; others said he'd been wrong before and they had little reason to believe he was right now.

He came home that night bleary-eyed and exhausted.

DESPITE A LACK OF SLEEP, Franklin was awake before dawn and anxious to get to the office. He slipped out of bed quietly, got dressed then kissed Laura's cheek and said he was in a hurry. He took the car and drove to work instead of walking as he usually did. Two hours before the market opened he was at his desk writing up the sell orders he'd taken the previous night.

When the opening bell rang on Tuesday, Franklin's sell orders were a fraction of what poured in. There were no buy orders, just sells—so many that by noon the ticker couldn't keep up with them. By close of business, the ticker tape was more than two hours behind.

That day Franklin skipped lunch and drank nine cups of black coffee. It was after ten when he finally telephoned Laura to say he was at long last starting home. He'd parked the car on a narrow side street in the downtown area, not a place where there would be other people walking around at that time of night. Halfway down the block he heard footsteps behind him.

"Hey, Frankie, wait up!"

Franklin hadn't been called Frankie since he was in kindergarten, and even then he hated the name. He turned and saw the figure staggering toward him. Something was wrong with the man.

"Do you need help?" he asked.

"Yeah, I need my money back!"

Franklin recognized the voice then saw the man's face. George Feldman, drunk as a skunk. After a day such as he'd had, his patience was at an end.

"What do you want?"

George moved closer then stopped. From two feet back, Franklin could smell the whiskey on his breath.

"Gimme my money back!"

"I don't have it," Franklin said. "It's in your account. Tomorrow you can close out the account and—"

"I want my money now!"

George shifted something from one hand to the other, but what it was Franklin couldn't say. A bottle opener or maybe a knife.

"All I've got is three dollars in my pocket," Franklin said. "If you need money you're welcome to it, but I can't get a nickel out of your account until the market opens tomorrow morning."

He nervously reached into his pocket, pulled out the three singles and handed them over. George snatched the bills and clumsily thumbed through them.

"You got balls, Frankie, you know that? You take everything I got and give me three lousy, stinkin' bucks..." He shoved the money into his pocket.

Taking advantage of the momentary diversion, Franklin jumped into his car and drove off.

FRANKLIN DIDN'T DRIVE STRAIGHT HOME. He headed north, turned at the Safeway store and then doubled back along Wilmont. He drove past the house, looking to make sure there was no sign of trouble then continued for three blocks. At Brewster he turned into the side street, parked the car and walked back. George Feldman had seen the car, and a man in such a state of mind could be crazy enough to come in search of it.

As Franklin walked he turned back several times, trying to see into the dark shadows and listening for the sound of footsteps behind him. If George Feldman was waiting to jump him from behind a bush Franklin could handle that, but the one thing he didn't want to do was lead a crazed man to his wife and daughter. Franklin kept walking and circled the block three times until he was absolutely certain he wasn't being followed. By the time he pushed through the front door, his face was ashen and his mouth drawn.

"You look terrible," Laura said. "Are you okay?"

"For now," Franklin answered. He explained his encounter with George Feldman. "This market situation isn't going to settle down anytime soon, and I'm concerned that he won't be the only one acting crazy."

A knotted line of ridges settled on Laura's forehead. "Perhaps you should call the police."

"And tell them what? They can't arrest a person for being angry."

"Maybe they could question him, say they're keeping an eye on him or do something that would scare him enough to leave you alone."

"It's not me, I'm worried about," Franklin said. "It's you and Christine."

"Us? Why?"

It was all but impossible for Franklin to explain the level of hatred he'd seen in George Feldman's eyes.

"I can take care of myself," he said, "but I'm worried about you and Christine being here alone."

She eyed him with a look of concern. "Christine is just a child. Surely you don't think—"

"Of course not," he said. "But if a stranger knocks at the door, don't answer it."

He gripped her shoulders and held her at arm's length with his eyes looking directly into hers. His intent was to warn Laura but not frighten her out of her mind.

"Understand this," he said in a dead serious voice. "George Feldman might or might not be dangerous. I don't know, and I don't want you to take chances. If Christine goes outside, keep her in the backyard and stay with her."

The fear in his voice was something Laura had never heard before.

"Franklin, you're scaring me," she said nervously.

"I don't want you to be frightened," he replied. "But I do want you to be cautious."

He saw the fear in her eyes and drew her to his chest. "I'm probably just being over-protective, but it's only because I love you so much."

Even as he spoke he was remembering the previous year's kidnapping of ten-year-old Rose Budd. It was almost eleven o'clock by then, too late for making telephone calls, but still Franklin dialed the Hawthornes' number. Emory answered in a sleepy voice.

"I hate to bother you at this time of night..." Franklin began. He told Emory of the incident with a disgruntled client.

"I'm not expecting trouble," he said, "but I'd appreciate it if you or Mother Hawthorne could stop by to check on Laura and Christine during the day."

"Do you really think anyone would—"

"I doubt it," Franklin said, but his voice was edgy and filled with concern.

FRANKLIN

*L*ast night when I asked Dad to stop by and check on Laura, I could hear the anxiety in his voice. He's concerned, and he's got every right to be. He loves Laura and Christine as much as I do. He suggested I report it to the police, but I told him the same thing I told her. Right now there's nothing to report.

Hopefully last night was a single confrontation, and Feldman got the anger out of his system. If he steps back and looks at the whole picture, he'll realize the market isn't something I can control. I told him to take his money out while he still could, but the man's a hothead and not one who is likely to listen to reason.

The thing is George Feldman didn't flat out threaten me. I doubt he's even interested in a man-to-man fight. If that's what he was after, he would have come at me last night. The apprehension I felt wasn't because of what he said, it was because of the crazed look in his eyes. He was more than just a belligerent drunk. He was a man who'd lost all reason. With a man like that, I worry he'll follow me home.

Being a stockbroker is like being an amateur psychiatrist. You're supposed to know what's in the client's head and what their expectations are. When I look at Feldman, all I see is a man hell bent on revenge. In his mind I've taken everything from him, and I think he'll be looking to do the same to me.

Even a fool can tell what's most important to me. There are pictures of Laura and Christine all over my office. That's what has me worried.

From here on in you can be sure I'll be looking over my shoulder when I leave the office at night. And on days when I drive, I'll be parking the car at least three blocks from the house. I'm praying I've seen the last of George Feldman, but if he does show up here again I'm going to report it to the police.

DARK DAYS

On Thursday Franklin didn't hear from George Feldman but the selling frenzy continued, and by the end of the day the New York Stock Exchange announced they would remain closed on Friday.

Late that afternoon Franklin called George's telephone number but got no answer. Since George seesawed back and forth on buy and sell orders as he did, Franklin figured it unwise to close out the account without an actual request to do so. Rules were rules. The account had already dropped to a value of less than $100 and wasn't likely to go lower.

On Monday when the market reopened, he called George again. Still no answer. By noon the stock exchange had already announced it would be closing at one. It remained that way all week: sellers frantic to get rid of their stock, shortened market hours and long waits for everything. The market decline continued through most of November, and by the time Thanksgiving rolled around there was little to be thankful for. Rose and Emory came to dinner, and they celebrated with a much smaller turkey and less trimmings.

"We're not as bad off as some are," Laura told her mama.

"Franklin isn't making any commissions, but at least we have some savings."

NOVEMBER TURNED INTO DECEMBER, AND George Feldman held on to his Broadhurst stock still believing it would bounce back as it had before. In January the company declared bankruptcy and closed its doors, and George went on a bender that lasted six days. When he finally sobered up and returned to work, he found he'd been fired.

"I got a mortgage payment due," he said grimly. "How the hell am I gonna make it with no job?"

"That's not my problem," the foreman replied and told George if he wasn't off the lot in thirty seconds they'd call for the police.

That same afternoon Sara Perkins, a loan officer for the bank, called. She said there were two mortgage payments already overdue and the third would be coming up in another week. George told her she could go straight to hell then ripped the telephone from the wall and started stomping on it.

Mama Feldman heard him cussing and hurried in from the kitchen.

"That was the bank calling again, wasn't it?" she said.

"Yeah, Mama, that was the bank," George snapped. "They want their money, and I got nothing to send them."

"What's that mean? They gonna throw me outta my own house 'cause of a dumb ass thing you did?"

"How the hell should I know?" George yelled. He gave the broken telephone one last kick and sent it flying across the room.

"You happy now?" she asked sarcastically.

"Mama, I swear, if you don't leave me alone—"

"You'll what? Move out? There ain't nobody but me who'll have you!"

"Shut up, Mama, just shut up!"

"I'll shut up when you get off your lazy ass and go back t' work so's you can pay the bank and pay me for that broke telephone."

"I can't get t' work," he said. "I got canned."

Earlier in the day George thought he'd simply find himself another job and say nothing about being fired, but in the heat of the argument it came out. When his mama heard that, she about went crazy. She began beating her fists against his chest and calling him every name she could think of. Once he was able to get loose, he ran up the stairs and disappeared into his bedroom.

It was the start of an argument that raged on through the middle of February. Every time George ventured out of the room, his mama came at him screaming like a banshee.

With each day that passed, he became more desperate. He'd thought finding a job would be easy enough, but now it seemed there were no jobs. Nothing. Not even sweeping the streets or emptying out trash cans. After nearly a month of looking he went back to the steel mill thinking he'd beg to have his old job back, but by then they'd already laid off forty-two men and weren't willing to even talk to him.

With the telephone no longer working, the bank began sending a barrage of letters. Each one was more threatening than the previous one. Looking at them when he had no money and no way to get any was depressing, so after a while George stopped opening the envelopes and just tossed them into the trash.

IN LATE FEBRUARY HE WAS lying in bed one morning thinking of what he might do when he heard the hammering at the front of the house. His mama heard it also. She was the one who opened the door and saw the bank's foreclosure notice nailed there. Seeing that, she stormed up the stairs and pounded on George's bedroom door with both fists.

"What now, Mama?" he hollered and stayed where he was.

"Don't you get sassy with me! Open this door right now!"

George was already dead tired of arguing and he knew opening the door would only mean a bigger fight, so he did nothing.

For a good five minutes she stood there banging on the door and yelling cuss words at him. Then she stopped as suddenly as she'd started. He heard a groan and the thump of something hitting the floor.

"Mama?" George called. "You still there?"

When he got no answer he twisted the lock, pulled the door open and saw her lying there. He inhaled sharply and kneeled beside her.

"Mama!"

She was breathing, but her hand was clutched to her heart.

"Get an ambulance," she wheezed.

George was halfway down the stairs before he remembered his bout with the telephone. He ran across the street and pounded at the door. Bertha Paulson was an old woman and slow as molasses. When she finally opened the door he said, "Mama's sick, call for an ambulance."

"I don't have no telephone," she replied.

George went from one house to another, and it was almost five minutes before he found someone to make the call. By the time he got back to the house, his mama was no longer breathing.

"Mama!" he cried. "Don't do this! Please don't do this."

When the ambulance finally arrived, Anna Feldman's skin had already taken on a ghastly pallor. George stood at the window and watched as they lifted the stretcher into the ambulance and pulled away.

"I'm sorry, Mama," he said then dropped down on the sofa and buried his face in his hands.

ANNA FELDMAN WASN'T NECESSARILY A good mother, but she was all he had. Now he had nothing. No job, no home and nobody who gave a damn whether he lived or died. With that thought in mind, he pulled his last bottle of corn whiskey from the cupboard and poured himself half a glass.

For a long while he sat there thinking back on what had gone wrong. He remembered how at first buying the Broadhurst stock had seemed such a good idea. He could still picture the way Franklin Wilkes stood and shook his hand. Back then Wilkes treated him as an equal, but later on, after the stocks had become almost worthless, he'd doled out a measly three dollars. It was a handout, given to him as if he were a vagrant standing on the corner with a tin cup.

Shoved the money at me then drove off in his fancy car.

George poured another drink and gulped down a swallow. He could still picture Franklin Wilkes with a suit and tie.

Wearing a smug grin.

He stood and walked back into the kitchen. On the counter was the dishtowel where his mama had been wiping the dishes.

She's not coming back.

There would be no one to wash the dishes, or cook the supper, or even yell at him for the stupid things he did. She was gone, and in a few days or weeks the house too would be gone. They'd put a padlock on the door and tell him to go find another place to sleep. George drained the last bit of whiskey then refilled the glass.

It's not fair. Mister big shot with money taking advantage of poor folks.

As he thought it through, he came to the conclusion Franklin

Wilkes was responsible for everything. The lost job, the lack of money and now his mama's death.

A man like that don't deserve to live.

YEARS EARLIER HIS MAMA HAD a gun. George remembered it. The first time he'd seen it he wondered why she had a gun, and she told him it was for protection in case his daddy came back. His daddy never did come back, but chances were she still had the gun. George finished his drink and poured another one. He gulped a swig then headed for his mama's bedroom.

If she still had the gun, that's where it would be.

One by one he rummaged through the drawers, tossing aside bloomers, baggy brassieres and flannel nightgowns. Nothing. No gun. No bullets. He searched under the mattress, beneath the bed and in every corner of the small closet, but still nothing. Not even some loose change he could use.

After nearly an hour of searching, he flopped down on the bed and gave the iron footboard a kick. That's when he heard it: metal hitting metal. He bolted up and looked at the bed again. That's when he noticed the blue string tied around the center post of the headboard. Sliding his finger beneath the string, he pulled.

Up came a black drawstring bag; in it he found a Smith and Wesson .38 and a box of bullets. He took six bullets from the box, slid them into the chamber one by one and then headed back to the kitchen to finish his drink.

Leaving the glass on the counter, he headed out the door. The only thing he took with him was the loaded Smith and Wesson.

REVENGE

Franklin Wilkes normally left the office at six o'clock but on Friday, February 21st, he worked late. Reginald Parris, one of his few remaining clients, had passed away two weeks earlier, and his widow requested a recap of what was in the investment portfolio. They'd been loyal clients and stuck with him even through the madness so Franklin couldn't very well refuse, especially since Washington's birthday made this a long three-day weekend.

At four-thirty he called Laura and told her he'd be working late.

"Don't wait supper," he said. "It could be eight or eight-thirty."

He promised to call when he was ready to leave the office.

GEORGE FELDMAN TOOK NO CHANCES. At five o'clock sharp he was standing across the street from the Morgenstern building. The front exit was the only way in or out so sooner or later Franklin

Wilkes would come through the door, and then George would have his revenge. This time he was not going to accept a few paltry dollar bills. He wanted what was coming to him and would take nothing less.

Between five-thirty and six o'clock a rush of employees poured from the building. George stood carefully scanning the crowd. His eyes moved from face to face as he watched for Franklin. At six-thirty a delivery truck pulled up in front of the building and blocked his line of vision. It was only for a few seconds, no longer. George stepped to the right and continued watching, confident it had not been long enough for him to miss the man he was waiting for.

By seven he began to wonder if Wilkes had somehow slipped out in the crowd of people and gone undetected. The longer he stood there the angrier George became. He paced back and forth picking at the loose thread hanging from his pocket and thinking about Franklin with his fancy car, tailored suit and red tie. He pictured the house a man like Franklin would live in; a mansion probably, with columns flanking the front entrance.

For sure Franklin Wilkes doesn't have no foreclosure notice tacked to his door.

Every new thought was like an icepick chipping its way into George's brain.

At seven-thirty the lights in the lobby of the Morgenstern building grew dim, and it became more difficult to see. He waited another fifteen minutes, but only one man came from the building. The fellow was wearing a hat and walking fast with his head ducked down. Before George could catch sight of his face, the man disappeared around the corner.

George hesitated a moment then followed after him. Crossing the boulevard, he hurried along the street and turned where the man had turned. There was no one in sight. Picking up the pace, George moved to the end of the block and looked both ways.

Nothing. No man. No car.

"Sum a' bitch," he grumbled then headed back toward the boulevard.

He was reasonably certain the man he'd seen wasn't Franklin. At least that's what George told himself.

Too short.

Returning to the same spot he resumed his waiting and watching, but before ten minutes had passed George lost his patience. He looked up at the windows of the building. Except for a scattered few, they were all darkened. Once again he'd been played for a fool. It was what he should have expected.

The likelihood was Wilkes had slipped out in the middle of the crowd. While George was standing there with his guts tied up in knots and the wind blowing cold against his neck, Franklin Wilkes was probably at home sitting at the dinner table and joking it up and laughing. No doubt he was bragging to his wife about how he'd given poor stupid Feldman the slip.

George felt the prickle of anger crawling across his skin, and something rose up in his throat. Bile, bitter and sour as week-old milk. He heard the sound of his mama's voice in his ears.

Don't just stand there looking stupid! Do something!

With long deliberate strides he crossed the street, grabbed the handle of the glass door and yanked. The door didn't budge. He tried another door and then another. Locked, all of them. There had to be another way. If Franklin Wilkes had left the office, he was probably at home. Maybe if he knew where Wilkes lived…

As he stood trying to remember if there'd ever been mention of an address, George heard the click of high heels crossing the marble-floored lobby. He stepped back into the shadows and waited. Seconds later a young woman hurried out and turned onto Broad Street. As the door swung back, George grabbed it seconds before it clicked shut.

Once inside the building he knew where he was going. Using

the back staircase, he walked two flights to the third floor. At the end of the hallway was the Sampson Investment office with its shiny brass lettering on the door.

Okay, Sampson, now let's see how strong you are.

The front door was locked. George looked around and, seeing no one, took out his pocketknife, slid the blade in and pushed the latch open. The moment he stepped inside he spotted the light coming from Franklin's office. That door was standing open, and he could hear movement inside the office. Still careful not to make a sound he reached into his jacket pocket, pulled out the gun and started inching his way down the hallway.

Focusing on the account ledger in front of him, Franklin was unaware of anything until Feldman's shadow fell across his desk. He lifted his head and froze when he saw George standing there with a gun pointed at his chest.

"Wait—"

George pulled the trigger. The first shot hit just below Franklin's collarbone, and he dropped back into the chair. Franklin opened his mouth, but nothing came out.

"I ain't nearly as stupid as you thought," George said with a vengeful sneer.

He pumped another five shots into Franklin's chest then slid the empty gun into his pocket and walked out as if nothing had happened.

THE ONLY OTHER PEOPLE IN the building that night were Abraham, a porter who emptied wastebaskets and mopped floors, and Margery Kramer who was working on the fourth floor at Brentwood Accounting. Margery heard the sound but guessed it to be a car backfiring. She listened for a few moments, and when there were no other sounds of disturbance she went back to typing. As was his routine, Abraham had started on the first floor and worked his way up through the building. He was on the seventh floor when it happened and heard nothing.

LAURA EXPECTED FRANKLIN TO CALL. He'd said maybe eight or eight-thirty. By nine-thirty she still hadn't heard from him, so she called his office. The telephone rang and rang, but there was no answer.

Perhaps he's stepped out to use the men's room. She waited ten minutes then called again. Still no answer.

Even during the worst days of the market crash, Franklin had not been this late and not told her. And now with business down to barely a trickle, he'd been coming home earlier than usual. Laura dialed the number again and again. After nearly a dozen calls, she telephoned her parents.

By then it was after ten-thirty, and when Emory answered she could hear the sleepiness in his voice.

"I'm sorry to wake you, Daddy," she said, "but I'm worried about Franklin."

After explaining the situation, she asked if he'd drive down and check the office.

"Could be Franklin's busy and doesn't want to take time for telephone calls," Emory said, "but I'll go make sure."

"Cross over Wilmont and drive down Broad Street just in case he was on his way home and had a flat tire or car trouble," she said. "But if he's still working, tell him to call me right away because I'm worried."

"Okay," Emory replied.

As soon as he hung up, he changed from his pajamas into a pair of slacks then pulled on a jacket and headed off. The

Morgenstern building was a twenty-minute walk, but the drive took less than five minutes and this time of night there was little traffic.

As Laura had suggested, Emory drove along Broad Street. When he saw no sign of Franklin's car, he parked in front of the building. Opening the door with the spare key left with him for safekeeping, he climbed the stairs to the third floor.

It struck him as strange to see the front door of Sampson Investments standing wide open. Emory stepped inside, listened for a moment then called out, "Anyone here?"

When there was no answer, he called out again. Still no answer. He spotted the light coming from Franklin's office and headed toward it. Franklin was slumped in his chair, his chin dropped down on his bloody chest and his arms hanging limp.

Emory jerked back with a gasp. He whirled around looking side to side and behind him. Nothing was disturbed. The office was exactly as it would have been any other day. It seemed apparent that whoever did this was no longer there. With his heart pounding against his chest, he cautiously moved toward Franklin and felt for a pulse. There was none.

"Dear God," Emory said through a moan as his eyes filled with tears.

The thought of Laura still waiting flashed through his mind, and for a moment it felt as though every drop of blood in his body had suddenly turned icy cold. With a heart that was carrying the weight of the world, he lifted the telephone receiver.

"Number, please?" the operator said.

"Get the police," he said sorrowfully. "A man's been murdered."

AS HE WAITED FOR THE police to arrive, Emory stood there in the stark silence remembering Franklin as the young man who'd come to him asking for Laura's hand in marriage. They'd known each other for what, five, maybe six years? Yet they were close as father and son.

A stream of tears rolled down Emory's face, and he brushed them away with the back of his hand. He had more than himself to think about. His grief was nothing compared to what Laura would feel. And Christine; poor little Christine.

Standing guard over the body of a man he not only respected but had come to love, Emory swore a vow.

"I won't rest until I find the person who did this," he said solemnly. "And for as long as I live, I will care for your family just as you would have."

His promise seemed so small in a time of such great grief, but it was all he had to give.

A WIDOW'S TEARS

Two uniformed officers arrived eight minutes after Emory made the call.

"Did you touch or move anything?" the older one asked.

"Only the telephone."

Emory explained that Franklin Wilkes was his son-in-law, and he'd come to check on him because his daughter had been calling the office and became worried when Franklin didn't answer the telephone.

"I keep a set of spare keys in case of an emergency, so I unlocked the downstairs door and came up. When I got here the office door was standing open, and I found Franklin..."

A lump of sadness welled in his throat, and his eyes again filled with tears.

"Laura doesn't know...I have to go tell her."

"Before you leave, we have a few more questions."

The older officer asked the questions while the younger one called for a crime scene investigator.

"You said Mister Wilkes's wife had been calling the office; do you know what time she made the first call?" he asked.

Emory gave a puzzled looking shrug. "I'm not sure. Sometime after eight, I guess. It was ten-thirty when she called me."

"Mister Wilkes and your daughter, were they were having some kind of marital problems? Money, maybe? Infidelity?"

Emory pinched his brows into a sorrowful knot and shook his head.

"Not at all," he said. "It was just the opposite. Franklin was a good provider, and they were very happy." A sigh with the weight of a boulder rolled up from his chest. "I never saw two people more in love with one another."

"What about Mister Wilkes's working routine? Was it customary for him to be here in the office this late in the evening?"

"Last fall maybe, but not recently. He's been coming home earlier than usual."

One question followed another, and Emory assured the officer there was not the chance of a snowball in hell Laura had anything to do with Franklin's death.

"Anyone who's ever seen them together knows…"

His words drifted off; there simply was no way of explaining a relationship that was beyond perfect.

The officer switched his train of questioning.

"What about enemies?" he asked. "Did Mister Wilkes have any enemies?"

"He had problems with a few people who lost money in the market, but I doubt that would be enough."

"You never know what can set a person off. Sometimes one little thing that you'd never give a second thought…" The officer didn't finish the sentence and moved on to other questions.

After nearly a half hour of repeating that he knew nothing, Emory gave the officers Franklin's home address and said he had to go tell Laura.

"Please don't come to the house until I've had time to tell her," he said then started toward the door.

As he stepped out into the night air, Emory felt the tremendous weight of what he had to do. He wanted—no, needed—Rose by his side. On the way to Laura's house he stopped at his own.

"At a time like this, our baby is going to want her mama to be with her," he said.

What he didn't say was breaking Laura's heart was something he couldn't face alone. He would be strong enough to deliver the news, but Rose had to be there to wipe away the tears that followed.

She pulled a coat over her nightgown and climbed into the car.

WHEN THEY ARRIVED AT THE Wilkes house, Emory knocked at the door.

Franklin never knocked; he used his key. Wary of strangers at this time of night, Laura called out, "Who is it?"

"Mama and Daddy," Emory answered.

She recognized his voice and yanked the door open. Seeing her mother standing there in a nightgown, Laura knew something was wrong.

"Franklin," she said in a voice that trembled. "Has something happened to Franklin?"

Emory nodded and pulled her into his arms.

"I'm sorry."

Pushing the tears back, he explained that Franklin had been shot.

The reality of death wears a thousand different disguises. Even when the ugliness of it is staring you in the face, you believe it to be something else: bad luck, misfortune, a serious accident, but not death. Only when it grabs hold of you with its bony hand do you see the truth of what it is and realize it has come to take someone you love.

Despite the grim look on her daddy's face, Laura clung to a tiny grain of hope.

"Is he in the hospital?" she asked fearfully.

Emory shook his head. "There was nothing anyone could do; he was gone when I got there."

Laura felt the bony hand clawing at her heart.

"No," she said, her tears coming fast as she shook her head hard. "No…"

Her knees gave way, and as she started to fall Emory held on to her. He helped her into the living room and sat beside her on the sofa.

"This can't possibly be happening," she said through her sobs. "Not to Franklin. Maybe you were at the wrong office. Franklin's there, he's working late, he'll be home—"

Emory wrapped his arm around her trembling shoulders.

"I wish I were wrong," he said. "But it was Franklin. I saw him."

Laura dropped her head into his lap and cried with huge shuddering sobs.

"Why?" she asked through a moan. "Why?"

Emory had no answer. He and Rose sat there whispering words of sympathy and tenderly rubbing small circles across her back, trying to comfort her as they did when she was a baby.

While little Christine slept, the three of them remained huddled together on the sofa. Laura stayed in the center, and on each side were the pillars who would hold her up and give her enough strength to get through the night and the terrible, terrible days that were to follow. The long night stretched into morning, and when the sun began to streak the horizon Laura knew her life and Christine's life would be forever changed.

AT SEVEN O'CLOCK THE NEXT morning the doorbell rang.

"Sergeant Carroll," the man said and handed her a card that read "John Carroll, Sergeant, Wyattsville Police Department."

He was a tall man with a face that had a look of intensity etched on it. He removed his hat and gave a sympathetic nod.

"I'm sorry for your loss," he said politely. Without a moment's hesitation he added, "I regret having to intrude at a time like this, but we're trying to find the person who shot your husband and hopefully you've got some information that can help us."

Laura stood there with expressionless eyes and cheeks pale as milk. He too was a reality hard to accept. She looked at the card, read it letter by letter then held a shaky finger to her lips and made a whisper-thin shushing sound.

"Our daughter is only four, and I haven't told her yet."

She turned to Rose and said, "Mama, can you keep Christine busy for a while?"

Rose gave a nod; then Sergeant Carroll followed Laura back into the kitchen.

Once they settled at the table he said matter-of-factly, "This wasn't a random break-in. Nothing was taken, and none of the other offices were disturbed. My belief is that the person who killed your husband came there looking for him."

Laura looked at him with a bewildered expression. "Why?"

Sergeant Carroll shrugged.

"Once we know why, we can figure out who," he said then asked if Franklin had any enemies.

"Franklin? No." Laura absently folded and then unfolded a napkin that had been left on the table. "Everybody loved Franklin. He was kind, goodhearted, generous…" Her eyes welled with tears.

"I'm sorry," Sergeant Carroll said, "I know this is tough."

He hesitated a few moments before moving on to the next barrage of questions. He asked about Franklin's friends, business associates and neighbors.

"What about his clients?" he said. "Did he ever talk about his clients? Did he ever mention someone blaming him for the money they'd lost in the market?"

The way he asked the question brought to mind that night four months earlier. Franklin had come in looking like he'd seen a ghost, and for a few weeks afterward he called home several times a day to check on them. But time passed, and the encounter was forgotten. Laura could even remember Franklin saying he'd obviously overreacted because it turned out to be nothing.

"Never heard from the guy again," he'd said.

"There was this one incident last October…" She told the story of that night. "At the time Franklin thought the fellow could be dangerous, but then later on he said it was nothing."

"Did he mention a name? Or what the guy looked like?"

Laura thought for a few minutes and while she could easily picture the look of concern on Franklin's face, she couldn't recall the man's name.

"Do you think you'd know it if you heard it?"

She nodded. "I believe so."

THAT AFTERNOON LAURA TOLD CHRISTINE her daddy had gone to heaven. She didn't share the awful truth of what happened; that was something she alone would live with. She held the child to her chest, and in a brokenhearted whisper created a fantasy claiming Franklin's last words had been to say how much he loved her.

Christine pushed back and looked her mama in the face. "But isn't Daddy coming back?"

Seeing the innocent look of her child's face, Laura prayed for the strength to hold back her tears.

"I'm afraid not," she said softly.

Christine's eyes filled with tears. "I don't want him to go to heaven."

"I don't want him to go either," Laura replied.

"We could tell Daddy how much we love him so he won't go to heaven."

Laura gathered Christine into her arms and held her close.

"Daddy knows how much we love him, but he can't come back," she whispered.

THE NEXT DAY SERGEANT CARROLL returned with a list of Franklin's clients. It was a list that stretched back to the day he'd joined the firm. He handed the list to Laura and waited as she looked through it.

Using her index finger she inched her way down the page, stopping on every name and trying to recall the sound of Franklin saying it. She hesitated for a moment at Gordon Edelman and then moved on. When she came to George Feldman, she could almost hear Franklin's voice speaking the name.

"George Feldman," she said. "That's it."

"Are you pretty certain?"

"I'm very certain," Laura replied.

THAT AFTERNOON SERGEANT CARROLL AND two uniformed police officers knocked on George Feldman's door. They banged on the door for a full ten minutes before Bertha Paulson hobbled across the street and said Missus Feldman had passed away two days earlier.

"What about George?" Sergeant Carroll asked. "Does he live with her?"

Bertha gave a disdainful look. "Sponges off of her is more like it."

She went on to explain George was Anna Feldman's son but hadn't been seen around since his mama's death. Sergeant Carroll eyed the foreclosure notice on the door and then gave the patrolmen an okay to break it down.

Laura Wilkes

I t doesn't matter that your heart is breaking, that your life will never be the same. When someone you love dies there are responsibilities, arrangements to be made, details to be taken care of. You feel dead inside, but still you go through the motions as if you are a puppet with some unseen hand pulling the strings. You do what you're expected to do, even though inside you feel as though the earth has shifted beneath your feet. At the funeral parlor I thought, Surely hell itself is no worse than this.

People mean well, but they have no idea of what is going on inside my heart. They hug me and tell me how much Franklin will be missed. Do they think I don't know that? They kneel, say a quick prayer, then move on. For me there is no moving on.

Were it not for Christine, I would have jumped into that grave right alongside Franklin. I tell people I have to be strong for her, but the truth is she gives me purpose enough to keep on breathing. Without her I don't know if I could go on.

Louise Wilkes, Franklin's mama, came to the funeral. She didn't come to our wedding, but she came to the funeral. The poor woman looks almost as dead as her son. I can't help but wonder if her heart hurts as much as mine. I look at Christine and know how I would feel if something happened to her. Missus Wilkes sat beside me at the services, and we held hands. Her fingers were as cold and bony as my own. I wanted to shake her and say, It's too late for showing Franklin you care; you should have done it years ago instead of worrying about your own hurt feelings, *but I didn't have the heart. Adding that misery to what she already has won't do a thing but cause more heartache, and God know there's been enough of that already.*

She asked if Christine and I needed anything; I said no, we'll be fine. The truth is I don't know what we need or don't need. I can't think about tomorrow because I can't move beyond the minute I'm standing in.

I try to remember things I'm supposed to do, but all I can think about is Franklin. You might think I'd remember the moments of passion and big events like our wedding, but it's the small everyday things that are stuck in my head. I remember how he walked the floor with Christine when she was teething, and how some nights when I didn't hear him come in he'd sneak up behind me and kiss the back of my neck. Yesterday I was standing at the sink washing out the coffee pot and started thinking how he'd never again kiss the back of my neck. I began bawling like a baby. How can I not?

Being left behind is in many ways worse than being dead. Thank God for Christine; she's my reason to go on living.

The Years That Followed

After the funeral Laura and Christine settled into a new
normal. Emory and Rose begged them to come live at
their house, but Laura refused.

"This is our home," she said. "It's the home Franklin made for
us, and if I leave here it would be like leaving him behind. As long
as we're here, I know he'll be watching over us."

In an odd way this was true for despite the hard times that
came to much of the country, Franklin had left them provided for.
Two years earlier he'd paid off the mortgage, so the house was
free and clear. With the money he'd transferred into the bank and
a double indemnity life insurance policy for $5,000, they didn't
have to make a lot of lifestyle changes. It was nearly four months
before Laura could sort out what they had and didn't have, and
when she finally did it was with the help of Emory.

"If you're careful with your money, you'll be okay," he said, "and
if things get too tight your mama and I will be here to help out."

From the time he'd made his vow to Franklin, there was not a
single day when Emory didn't stop by to check on Laura and
Christine. No matter the time, he'd pop in on his way home from
work.

"You need anything fixed?" he'd ask. "Leaky faucet? Loose doorknob? Squeaky hinge?"

Emory was also the one who time and time again called Sergeant Carroll to inquire how the investigation was going.

Within days of the murder, George Feldman was identified as the shooter. The fingerprints he'd left on the doorknob confirmed it, but by then he was long gone. There was no trace of him. Flyers were sent to every state in the union, but George had vanished. He never returned to his mama's house and, as far as they could tell, never again worked as a welder. He was a man who seemed to have no friends and no ties. There was no one to suspect of hiding him and only a handful of people to question about his possible whereabouts.

It was the height of the Depression, and like thousands of others George Feldman simply disappeared into the crowds of unemployed men living in the cardboard houses alongside railroad tracks in one town or another. Men such as that had only a first name or a nickname like Slim, Rusty or Blackie.

That first month when it still seemed possible they'd find George, Emory offered a $100 reward for information leading to his arrest but still there was nothing. On Saturdays he would drive from town to town dropping off copies of the flyers at the police stations and tacking flyers to the walls of the post offices, but in all that time there was never a single sighting of the man.

Every time Sergeant Carroll reported there was still no break in the case, Emory waited until the time was right then told Laura.

"I'm sorry," he'd say then segue into a suggestion about one thing or another that needed to be fixed.

"There's a loose brick in the walkway," he'd claim and ask if it was a good day for fixing it.

On days when he could find absolutely nothing to be done, he'd drop down on the sofa and spend an hour talking about some inconsequential thing that drew Laura's mind away from the heartache she was feeling. Every Saturday morning he mowed the lawn then sat at the kitchen table drinking coffee.

During the day Rose came. She was there most every day, and as the days turned into weeks and the weeks into months she taught Laura the things her mama had once taught her.

She'd show up with a bushel basket of peaches and say, "I was all set to make some peach jam and I got to thinking, 'This is something I ought to teach Laura how to do.'"

They'd spend an entire day cooking and canning then deliver jars of the homemade jam to friends and neighbors.

Laura could get through the days, but the nights were almost unbearable. For hours on end she'd lie awake feeling the emptiness of her bed. At times she tried to imagine the sound of Franklin breathing or the touch of his hand. For over a month she took his bathrobe and placed it beside her in the bed because it still had the smell of his skin. On the worst nights she remembered him ashen and cold, which is how he came to her in her dreams.

When morning finally arrived, she'd wake so weary she could barely hold her eyelids open. On those days it was Christine who gave her reason for living. Although stones of sorrow weighed heavily in her heart, the love of her child enabled her to move through the day.

At times the sorrow was so huge it threatened to suffocate her. During the day she pushed it back and allowed it to surface only at night when she was alone in the room she and Franklin shared. That was the one place where there was no comfort, no hiding from the truth, no distraction to turn her thoughts away. Franklin was gone, and in her half-empty bed there could be no denying it.

A YEAR LATER WHEN CHRISTINE started kindergarten, Laura took out the camera and snapped photos of her in the new pinafore dress Rose had stitched. Click, click, click. After only three shots the roll of film in the camera whirred to the end.

That afternoon Laura dropped the film off at the drugstore to be processed. Five days later she picked up the pictures, and when she pulled them from the envelope there was Franklin smiling back at her. He was standing beside Christine as she rode the white horse on the carousel in Richmond. That afternoon of such great happiness was now a lifetime away.

Laura left the store, crossed the street and sat on the bus stop bench. One by one she went through the photos. Franklin smiling. Christine waving. The two of them laughing together. She could almost hear Franklin's voice in her ear.

I'm still with you, he said.

For over a year she'd remembered only the sadness of losing him but seeing him like that, she began to remember the happiness of having him. That evening she built a fire in the fireplace with rolled newspapers, kindling and then the logs angled just so. It was the way Franklin did it. After the fire was lit, she cuddled beside her daughter on the sofa.

She pulled the pictures from the envelope and showed them to Christine.

"Do you remember this day?"

Christine nodded, and her mouth curled into a grin.

One by one Laura leafed through the photos, lingering over each shot, reminding her daughter of the things they'd done. How they had taken tea in the grand salon of the Algonquin Hotel. How on several occasions they'd strolled Gerard Street and browsed the shops.

"Do you remember when Daddy caught the brass ring for you?"

Christine nodded. "He gave it to me so I could ride the white horse."

Laura smiled. "That's right. He did it because he loves you."

"Can he still love me even if he's in heaven?"

"Absolutely!" Laura answered. "He still loves both of us. And do you know what he told me today?"

Christine gave a puzzled look and shook her head.

"He wants us to always remember how much he loves us."

"Does Daddy have a telephone in heaven?"

"No telephone, but if you close your eyes and remember how good it felt when Daddy hugged you, he'll send a thought to the inside of your head. Then you'll be able to hear him whispering about how much he loves you."

Christine gave a wide smile showing where her front tooth was missing.

THE NEXT DAY LAURA TOOK the film back to the drugstore and ordered five enlargements of her favorite shot: the one where Franklin's face was nuzzled next to Christine's. They were wearing the same broad grins. She bought frames for four of the pictures. One she sent to Franklin's mama; another went to her parents. One was set on Christine's nightstand, and the fourth was placed on the living room mantle.

The fifth unframed picture she placed in the empty spot beside her in the bed. She carefully tucked it under his pillow and kept it there for all the years of her life. On nights when the loneliness threatened to overcome her, she'd pull the picture from beneath the pillow and talk to it.

"I'm missing you terribly tonight," she'd say, then tell him of her day. After a while she'd feel the warmth of him. He was not there, but he was somewhere close by.

Throughout that long winter, Laura lit the fireplace every night. With Christine cuddled close, she told tales of the memories she had stored in her head. She told of their wedding day, trips to

Richmond, the morning of Christine's birth and thousands of other small moments. Although you might think after a while she'd run out of things to tell about, she never did. And so it was that Christine came to know her daddy almost as well as she would have if he'd been alive.

ALTHOUGH LAURA WAS ONLY 23 when she lost Franklin, she never fell in love again. When Rose, Emory or one of her friends suggested this fellow or that one was a gentleman worth meeting, Laura simply shook her head and said she was still in love with Franklin.

"But Franklin has been gone for well over a year," her friend, Elaine, said once.

"He's not gone," Laura replied. "He's still with me."

And it was true. With her memories and stories Laura kept Franklin alive, not only for herself but also for Christine. Not once did she even consider dating.

William Bennett, the good-looking mailman with a friendly smile and easy-going manner, brought letters and packages to the Wilkes house six days a week. At most places he'd simply stuff the letters into the box and move on, but at Laura's house he'd stop and ring the doorbell even on days when there was no mail.

"Nothing today," he'd say and then stand at the door chatting about one thing or another. Laura welcomed the few minutes of distraction, and on days when it was bitter cold or blowing snow she would invite him in for a cup of coffee or just to warm himself for a few minutes. When he asked her out to dinner, though, she offered only an apology.

"I don't date," she said. "I hope I haven't given you the impression that—"

"Not at all," William said. "Not at all."

Two weeks later on a Tuesday morning there was four inches of snow, but when William handed Laura the mail she simply thanked him and closed the door.

PIECE BY PIECE

Five years passed, years that were frequently filled with difficulty and hardship. Despite President Roosevelt's New Deal, there was no end in sight to the Depression. Worried the money Franklin left would not carry them through to better times, Laura, like everyone else, cut back and made do with less. Instead of going out to dinner or taking trips to Richmond, they borrowed books from the library and sat in front of the fireplace reading or talking about the happier times.

On nights when news of the world felt heavy on her heart and loneliness was wrapped around her like a second skin, Laura and Christine walked over to Chester Street. Although coffee was costly, Rose brewed a pot and added an extra spoonful of sweetness to each cup.

"It always makes me feel good to come here," Laura said as she and Rose sat at the table talking.

It seemed that no matter how heavy Laura's heart was when she arrived, it would be a bit lighter when she left.

IN 1937 WHEN CHRISTINE WAS in the fifth grade, Rose passed away. It happened sometime in the middle of the night, but exactly when Emory couldn't say. That morning, believing her still asleep, he climbed out of bed and dressed for work. When he walked back to kiss her goodbye, he found her cheek cold and lifeless.

It was a heart attack that came about with no warning. A number of times she'd complained about indigestion, but after taking a spoonful or two of Phillips Milk of Magnesia she supposedly felt better.

When Emory came and told Laura, she collapsed into his arms.

"How can that be?" she cried. "Mama and I were planning to roast a chicken for Sunday."

The night before it happened, Laura sat across the kitchen table from Rose and talked of how she wished Franklin could have seen Christine growing up as she was.

"He would have been so proud of her," she said wistfully.

"He knows," Rose replied. "You've said so yourself. He watches over you every day. If he watches over you, he sees Christine as well."

Laura smiled at such a thought.

ROSE WAS LAID TO REST on the coldest day Wyattsville had ever seen. The morning broke with icicles hanging from trees, fire hydrants leaking and hoses that had been left out in the yard split open. Before they reached the cemetery, snow flurries started. It was not enough to cover the ground, but, driven by a cold wind, it was enough to sting Emory's face and leave his feet feeling frozen. He stood beside the grave with one arm wrapped around Laura, the other around Christine and a trail of frozen tears stuck to his cheek.

"First Franklin, now Mama," Laura said just before breaking down in sobs.

Although Emory's own heart felt like a chunk of ice splintered into a thousand shards, he tightened his grip on her shoulders.

"We'll get through it," he said. "We've been through hard times before."

"Maybe so," she said, brushing back a tear, "but why is it that the people we love are the ones who die?"

Laura had always been close to Rose, but in the years following Franklin's death they'd grown even closer. Emory knew this and gave her a bittersweet smile.

"Sooner or later everyone dies," he said, "but when it happens to someone we love a piece of our heart dies with them, so we stop and take notice."

He gave a nod to the line of gravestones that stretched as far as the eye could see. "I imagine every one of those buried here was somebody special to someone."

"Maybe so," Laura replied, "but I doubt anyone was as special as Franklin and Mama were to me."

ONCE ROSE WAS GONE, LAURA felt emptier than ever before. It seemed almost impossible to find a bit of brightness in her life other than Christine. When she wasn't thinking about the injustice of losing both Franklin and her mama, she was fretting about Emory being by himself.

Often in the middle of the day, she called to ask if he'd eaten breakfast. If he answered yes, then she'd ask about lunch.

"I worry about you being alone," she'd say. "I have Christine to keep me company, but you have no one."

Unaccustomed to being fussed over in such a way, Emory brushed such questions aside like a flock of pesky mosquitos.

"I have eaten, cleaned my teeth and gone to the toilet," he'd say, "and now if you don't mind I am trying to listen to my radio show."

No matter how many times he gave that answer, Laura continued to pester him. On the evenings when she came with a casserole for his supper, she asked after him. And on mornings when she'd bring fresh-baked muffins, she'd ask again. Each time Emory shook his head claiming it was something he didn't want to discuss.

"You've got your life, and I've got mine," he said.

"Without Mama it's not much of a life," Laura argued, but there was no convincing him.

For over a year he remained in the Chester Street house by himself. He did little more than sleep there, because almost every waking moment he was either at the office or looking for something to do at Laura's house. When he could no longer find something that needed to be painted, repaired or oiled, he built a bookcase for Christine's room. He also taught her how to play pinochle and, when the weather turned warm, how to fish.

That summer he took a group of her giggling girlfriends to his favorite fishing hole, and instead of dropping a line in the water and leaning back to wait for a nibble he spent the afternoon putting fresh worms on hooks and untangling lines. He also escorted Christine to the Girl Scout father-daughter dance.

IN 1939 EMORY TURNED SIXTY-FIVE and was forced into retirement. He was given a pension, considerably less than he'd been making but enough to get by on. At that point Laura told her daddy him not living with them was pure foolishness. Rumors of the United States going to war were already being spoken aloud, and Laura had started working with the Bandages for Britain volunteers rolling balls of gauze and packing boxes to be shipped overseas.

"I don't like the thought of Christine coming home from school to an empty house," she said. "What if something happens when I'm not here? Who knows what trouble a teenage girl can get into?"

The thought of Christine in need of anything stuck in Emory's head, and after weeks of consideration he finally agreed to move in. By then the Depression was nearing an end and although America was starting to feel the bustle of a pre-war economy, a lot of people were still out of work so the market had way more sellers than buyers. After six months of strangers traipsing in and out of the rooms, poking through cupboards and finding fault where there was none, he finally sold the house to a middle-aged couple who offered him half of what he'd originally paid for it.

The closing was on the last Friday of September. When they handed Emory the cashier's check, he took it and deposited it in Laura's bank account. Once that was done he loaded his suitcases into the back of his car, drove to Laura's house and moved into the guest room.

Later that evening he handed her the deposit slip and said, "You're going to need this for Christine."

She took one look at the amount and gasped. "Daddy, you shouldn't have—"

"I've got my pension, and that's more than enough. I won't always be around to see to your needs, so keep the money and use it for whatever you and Christine need."

Laura's eyes filled with water, and a tear rolled down her cheek. She wrapped her arms around Emory and laid her head against his chest.

"You're the best daddy in all the world," she said through her sniffles.

Emory, who was not given to such a show of emotion,

mumbled, "No, I'm not. I'm just doing what your mama would have wanted."

Little of their day-to-day life changed, because he'd been spending most of his time there anyway. The only change anyone might notice was that he became even fonder of Christine. Although he'd been busy working when Laura was growing up, he now had all the time in the world and he spent most of it doting on his granddaughter.

He insisted on driving her everywhere she wanted to go and personally meeting any boy she dated. By then she was a freshman in high school, but the boys she dated were just that: boys. They'd stand with their shoulders rounded and pimply faces expressionless as Emory warned them about trying any "funny business" with his granddaughter.

When he did it, Christine inevitably turned red-faced and exclaimed, "Granddaddy!"

On the evenings when she was out with her friends, he sat in the living room and waited until she was home before going to bed. Once when Christine spent the night at a classmate's slumber party, he paced the floor until almost dawn. Laura told him there was nothing to worry about, but still he worried.

"You're certain this classmate is a reputable girl?" he asked.

"Yes," Laura answered, explaining that she worked with the girl's mama. "There's absolutely nothing to worry about. The girls just like to get together and have fun. They'll stay up most of the night and do silly things like paint their nails or talk about boys."

"Boys?" Emory repeated nervously.

A TIME OF WAR

The Japs bombed Pearl Harbor in December of 1941, and before the week was out America was at war. Fathers, sons and brothers enlisted, and women stepped in to fill the jobs they'd vacated. Laura was one of those women. After only a few weeks of training, she became a stamper in the same steel mill George Feldman had once worked in. The first week she joined the production line, she took to asking fellow employees if they'd ever heard of Feldman. One by one they shook their heads.

"Well, if you hear of him working in another plant, let me know," she'd say.

Although over a decade had passed, Laura never gave up hope that one day her husband's murderer would be found and brought to justice. If she could be the one to make it happen, so much the better.

OVERNIGHT WYATTSVILLE WENT FROM BEING a sleepy little town

to a place where everyone was involved in the war effort. That summer victory gardens began to blossom in almost every yard, and Emory found a new purpose in life. After he'd planted corn, tomatoes, beans and radishes for Laura, he planted five rows of corn and two of summer squash for the Widow Watkins. Then he helped Pastor Ingersoll set up a garden on the back side of the church property.

Emory volunteered to tend the gardens of working women whose husbands had gone off to war. He bought a wheelbarrow, filled it with the things he needed, then went from house to house spreading fertilizer and pulling weeds. After a day of such work, he'd come home whistling a happy tune. Seeing the mud caked under his fingernails only served to make Emory feel he was making his own contribution to the war effort.

Now in her last year of high school, Christine was relieved to be out from under her granddaddy's stringent supervision. That summer while he was off gardening, she signed up as a junior hostess at the USO on Sycamore Street. She went directly from school and stayed as late as seven and sometimes eight. When Emory questioned why she was so late getting home, Christine said she was working for the war effort and gave her mama a sly wink.

THAT SUMMER REMINDERS OF THE war were everywhere. Everyone, including the radio newscasters, spoke of it, and if someone didn't hear news of it the rationing coupons they needed to buy most anything reminded them. There was no escaping the war, and yet these were relatively happy years at the Wilkes house. Emory felt useful and appreciated, Laura was busy working at the factory and without her granddaddy watching her every move Christine was learning what it felt like to be a young woman.

In the spring of 1943 she graduated high school, and to celebrate Laura took her on a four-day vacation to Richmond. It was a trip that breathed life into all the memories they'd shared. They stayed at the Algonquin Hotel, which looked much the same as it did that last time. The chandeliers sparkled, and bellboys bustled to and fro in their red jackets. Only now there was a different feeling in the air, a tenseness that warned of danger. Instead of grand dames in all their finery, the lobby was filled with young servicemen talking and laughing as if there were no threat, as if tomorrow or the day after or a week from then the war would be gone and they would still be at the hotel.

That afternoon when the clock struck three they settled in the grand salon and ordered tea, just as they had all those years ago. Laura looked across the foyer. In the distance she saw a young man who looked very familiar from the side.

"See that gentleman in the dark suit?" she whispered. "He looks like your daddy did when we first got married."

Christine was not yet five when Franklin was killed, and what she remembered of him was only from the pictures she'd seen. But those pictures were enough.

"Oh, Mama," she said with a wistful sigh, "he does; he truly does."

Laura smiled. "Your daddy was the handsomest man I'd ever met. The first time he kissed me, I knew then he was the man I'd love for the rest of my life."

Christine never tired of hearing stories of Franklin. She leaned in and asked Laura again to tell the story of their honeymoon.

"It was the first time I'd ever been away from Wyattsville," Laura said, "and I fell in love with this place. It was as if everything here in Richmond were magical, and your daddy made it all the more so. We stayed up until the wee hours of the morning and danced until the band stopped playing. When we finally headed for our room, your daddy danced me down the hallway singing *When My Sugar Walks Down the Street*, and I laughed so hard I nearly wet my panties."

Christine had heard the stories dozens upon dozens of times, and by now she could tell them herself.

"This place is so special. That's why you brought me here for my fourth birthday, right?"

Laura laughed. "Right. The picture of you and your daddy on the carousel was taken on that trip."

She looked across where the young man who looked like Franklin had been standing. This time she saw an empty spot and sighed.

"There was nothing your daddy wouldn't do for you," she said. "When you wanted the brass ring, he was determined to get it for you."

"Tell me the story again," Christine urged.

"It wasn't as easy as you might think…" Laura's voice was soft and filled with the warmth of remembering. "Daddy held on to the pole and when the carousel circled past where the brass ring was, he leaned out so far it looked as if he were floating on air. 'Get it, Daddy!' you yelled. Then somehow he reached up far enough to grab hold of the ring."

Christine's eyes danced with happiness. "I remember."

The truth was she was too young to remember, but she'd come to know the story through her mama's memories.

"Would you like to go there tomorrow and ride the carousel?" Laura asked.

Christine nodded. "Oh, yes, I would."

FOR FOUR DAYS THEY FOLLOWED the pathway they had walked years earlier, and little by little the stories Christine listened to became her own memories. In years to come she would tell of her mama's honeymoon as if she'd been there. On their last afternoon in Richmond, a young sailor approached Christine and asked if she'd take tea with him.

"I'm scheduled to ship out the end of this week," he said, "and I'd love to have a nice memory to take with me."

Christine looked to her mama.

Laura smiled and gave a nod. "Go ahead, I have some packing to do."

As she walked off toward the elevators, Laura glanced back across her shoulder. She saw Christine's eyes sparkling just as hers once had.

The magic of this place is still here, she thought.

AS THE BATTLE ON THE European front worsened, news of the men lost came to the wives and mothers of Wyattsville. The morning the Western Union man brought news of Private Elliott Browne's death, Laura skipped work and sat with Lillian throughout the remainder of that day and night.

When she wrapped her arms around Lillian's quivering shoulders and said, "I know only too well what you're feeling," the words came from her heart.

The next day she took patches of fabric from her sewing basket, stitched a gold star onto a blue background and made a small flag for Lillian. That night she delivered the flag.

"Here at home we don't get medals for bravery," she said, "but hang this in your front window, and it will show those who pass by that you have sacrificed as much as any man on the battlefront."

Lillian looked at the small flag and shook her head sorrowfully.

"Pitiful exchange, isn't it?" she said. "A single star for the father of my children."

"I know," Laura replied and again hugged the woman to her chest.

BY THE TIME THE WAR ended, twelve husbands and nine sons were lost to Wyattsville. Laura cried for each of them.

During those years of sadness and heartache, Laura and Christine returned to Richmond three times. Each time it gave them a small bit of magic. Not a lot but enough to allow them to believe better days would come.

END OF AN ERA

When the war ended, so did Laura's job. In April of '46 the steel mill went back to manufacturing refrigerator panels and cut back on the work force. Laura had seniority and could have stayed on, but she stepped aside so Mary Beth Monahan could keep her job. Mary Beth had two children and a husband who'd been unaccounted for. Missing in action, they said. Not dead but not coming home either.

That afternoon Mary Beth caught up to her as they were leaving the mill.

"I heard what you did," she said and wrapped her arm around Laura's shoulder. "I can't ever thank you enough. If I lost this job, I—"

"It's okay," Laura replied and squeezed Mary Beth's arm. "I'm looking forward to taking some time off."

There was more than a grain of truth in what she said. Over the past few months Laura had become tired; not the kind of tired that comes from working, but the kind that settles into a person's soul with the weight of years lived. She'd known all but four of the men lost to the war, and she'd cried heartfelt tears for each of them. It seemed as if Franklin's death had started a landslide of

111

heartaches, and the simple, uncomplicated world she once knew had all but disappeared.

TWO MONTHS LATER CHRISTINE QUIT the job she had waiting tables at the Copper Kettle, and together she and Laura headed for Richmond. They checked into the Algonquin Hotel on a Tuesday and stayed for twelve days.

They lived as they had not lived for more than fifteen years, sleeping late and ordering breakfast from room service, sitting lazily by as the bellboy poured steamy coffee from a silver pot and served pastries. Every afternoon they took tea in the grand salon and afterward strolled Gerard Street shopping for souvenirs to bring home. Together they selected a fisherman's knit sweater for Emory, and Laura bought a gold locket for Christine.

"What about you, Mama?" Christine said. "We haven't yet found a gift for you."

"I already have everything I need," Laura replied, but in the end she selected a box of perfumed soaps tied with a lavender ribbon.

On three different afternoons they visited the park and rode the carousel, the same carousel Christine had ridden as a child. The tall wooden stand with an arm that held the coveted brass ring had been taken down, but most everything else was the same. The princely white horse had a chunk of his hoof missing and the painted flowers on his harness had dulled, but the magic was still there. Christine climbed astride and laughed gleefully as the music played and the carousel circled around.

"I can't imagine a vacation more wonderful than this," she said.

Laura answered with a smile. "When your daddy was alive it

was always this way. I'm so sorry you didn't have enough time to really get to know Franklin."

"I do know him," Christine replied. "I know parts of Daddy that most daughters never get to see. You've given me all these wonderful memories; how could I ask for more than that?"

Laura wrapped her arm around her daughter and brushed a kiss across her temple.

"You're right," she said. "How could we ask for more than what we've already got?"

They walked to the edge of the small lake and sat side by side on the bench.

"Did I ever tell you about the time it turned chilly and your daddy…"

Christine smiled. Yes, she knew that story just as she knew all of the other stories, and she treasured each and every one.

It was late when they got back to the hotel and Laura was overtired, so she stretched out across the bed and fell asleep. When she woke long past suppertime, they ordered roast beef sandwiches from room service. Months later Christine would wonder if back then her mama knew what was happening.

LAURA MENTIONED IT FOR THE first time on the drive home.

"On Thursday I've an appointment to see Doctor Moriarty."

She said it in an offhanded way as if it were nothing to worry about.

"Why?" Christine asked.

"I'm just not feeling myself lately." Laura left it at that and said nothing more.

Christine insisted she go with her mama.

"I might as well take advantage of this time," she said, "because next week I'll have to start looking for a real job."

The waitressing job at the Copper Kettle had been a fill-in, something she'd taken the summer she graduated high school. It was a lively environment and the tips were good, so she'd stayed. One month led to two, and before Christine knew it she'd been there for over a year.

"I'd like to get a secretarial spot," she said, "working in a law office or maybe a bank."

"Here in Wyattsville?" Laura asked.

Christine laughed. "Well, of course. Why would I go anywhere else when my family is here?"

"I just thought maybe…"

Laura left the thought unfinished.

DOCTOR MORIARTY HAD HIS SUSPICIONS the moment Laura told him about the two episodes she'd had.

"I threw up something I couldn't remember eating. It was grainy, bitter tasting and black as week-old coffee grinds," she said.

Christine slid a sideways glance at her mama. "You never said anything—"

"I'm sure it's nothing to worry about." Laura looked to Doctor Moriarty and added, "Right?"

He gave a noncommittal shrug. "We'll see. I'll need to examine you, draw blood, take some x-rays and do a few other tests."

He looked down, concentrating on his notes and avoiding eye contact with Laura.

Christine sat in the chair as Laura leaned back onto the examination table. The doctor felt the sides of her neck then moved to the high part of her abdomen. He spent over fifteen minutes prodding and feeling his way across her stomach. As he moved his hands from one spot to another, his eyebrows knit together and his mouth grew taut as if he was holding back something he needed to say.

"What is it?" Christine asked nervously.

There was no real answer, only the same vague sounding, "It's too early to tell. We'll have to wait for results of the tests."

When they left the doctor's office, Laura drove directly to the hospital for the tests he'd ordered. It was after five when they finally left.

"Let's get Granddaddy, and we'll all go out to dinner," Laura said. She tried to sound casual, but her voice was thin and unconvincing.

That evening they all had dinner at the Copper Kettle and Laura tried to act as happy and lighthearted as the environment, but Christine already had a lump of fear settling into her heart.

CHRISTINE PUT OFF LOOKING FOR a job, and two weeks later she went with Laura to find out the results of the tests. This time there was no smile on Doctor Moriarty's face.

"I'm afraid I have bad news," he said. He went on to explain that Laura's pancreas contained a tumorous mass.

Christine's eyes filled with tears. "Now what? Does Mama need an operation or radiation treatments?"

Doctor Moriarty allowed his eyes to meet hers as he shook his head ever so slightly.

"The disease is too far progressed. Radiation would be ineffective at this point. Right now pancreatic cancer is something for which we have no cure. Scientists are working on a drug—"

Christine gasped. "No cure? How can you say there's no cure? Surely there's something…"

He again shook his head. Looking to Laura he said, "What I can do is give you medication to ease the pain. As the need becomes greater, we'll increase the dosage. You won't have to suffer."

Christine brushed back the stream of tears rolling down her cheeks. "Not suffer? How can we not suffer knowing—"

Laura reached across and placed her hand on Christine's arm.

"It's okay," she said.

There was no explanation of what "okay" meant, only the reassurance of those all too imprecise words.

CHRISTINE GAVE UP ALL THOUGHTS of finding a job. She spent every moment at her mama's side. Throughout the summer they sat on the front porch swing, pushing back and forth with easy strokes and talking; not of the cancer but of the good times gone by.

In the fall they took one last trip to Richmond and stayed for just three days. On that trip they didn't visit the carousel but instead strolled through the quiet neighborhoods where brownstones and small apartment buildings lined the streets.

"Wouldn't it be lovely to have an apartment in one of these places?" Laura mused. "Imagine living in Richmond with the magic of this city right here at your fingertips every single day."

"We could move here if you'd like," Christine replied.

Laura gave a saddened smile.

"I'm afraid it's too late for me," she said, "but you could—"

"Mama, you know I'd never leave you and Grandpa," Christine cut in.

"That's what I'm afraid of," Laura said and heaved a great sigh.

They walked on, but as they rounded the corner she turned and took one last look back.

"Living here in Richmond would be a wonderful life for a young woman."

IN NOVEMBER LAURA'S SKIN TOOK on a yellow cast, and Doctor Moriarty said it was jaundice.

"Your liver is starting to shut down," he said and gave her a prescription that hopefully would slow the process.

A few days later she was too weak to get out of bed, so Christine sat by her side. That afternoon she pulled a worn copy of *Little Women* from the bookshelf Emory had made and read aloud. Before she was halfway through the first chapter, Laura was sound asleep.

It was that way for three weeks. Then on a Thursday morning, Laura never woke up. She spent three days in a comatose state and on Sunday evening simply stopped breathing.

The following Wednesday she was laid to rest alongside Franklin.

CHRISTINE WILKES

Yesterday Granddaddy and I buried Mama. He stood next to me with his face set in that same hollow-eyed expression he had when Grandma died. He was trying to hide the pain in his heart, but I saw the tears rolling down his cheeks and disappearing into his beard.

When we left the cemetery and came back to the house, I went to Mama's room and sat on the side of her bed. I thought maybe being there I'd feel closer to her, but when I looked at the pillow still dented with the place where she'd laid her head all I could feel was the pain in my heart. I picked up her pillow and held it to my face just to breathe in the smell of her lavender soap.

Underneath her pillow was the picture of Daddy and me on the carousel. I'm guessing she kept it there all these years. It was crumpled and creased, but I could see how much she'd loved it.

For a long time, I sat there thinking how that picture was all Mama had left of Daddy. One small piece, and yet she hung on to it all these years. I wish I'd known about the picture sooner; I could have slipped it in beside her so she would have it with her when she got to heaven.

I'd like to believe she doesn't need the picture anymore, that she's with Daddy now and he's got his arms wrapped tight around *her. Hopefully he's kissing her face and dancing her across the clouds.*

If that's how it is then I know Mama's happy, and I'll have to be happy for her. I've got to trust that's exactly how heaven is, because if it isn't there's just no sense to life or death.

I'm trying to be as brave as Mama was when she lost Daddy, but right now all I feel is a misery that's like a knife sticking into my chest.

THE LEGACY

In the weeks following the funeral, Christine ambled through the house like a walking ghost. Her cheeks were pale and her eyes reddened from tears. The months of watching her mama slip away piece by fragile piece had taken her spirit and left behind a shattered heart.

Near the end Laura saw this happening, which is why she left the letter. The envelope was addressed to "My Darling Daughter" and placed in the top drawer of her nightstand where she knew Christine would be sure to find it. Her instructions were spelled out clearly.

"I know you are grieving now," she'd written, "but better times will come. When your daddy died the two of us had to make a world of our own, and once I am gone you will have to continue on without me. It will be difficult but not impossible. Look hard enough, and you will find a pathway to happier times. Once that happens, build a place for yourself in that world."

The letter went on to say the box of jewelry Christine should keep, but all of her other personal possessions were to be packed up and taken to Saint Michael's Thrift Shop.

"Please," the note continued with the word underlined, "do

not cling to these things thinking they are what you have left of me. They are only things. I am with you now and forever. When you feel sad or lonely, close your eyes and whisper my name. I'll be there for you just as your daddy was always there for me."

TWENTY-ONE DAYS AFTER THE funeral, Christine and her granddaddy were summoned to the office of Albert Barkley, attorney at law. It was in a small brick building in the center of Wyattsville. When they pushed through the heavy wooden door, Barkley's secretary led them back to his office.

Christine, still red-eyed and weepy, perched on the edge of the chair.

"I didn't know Mama had a will," she said through her sniffles. "It seems as though she would have—"

"Your mama and I have been friends since before your daddy died, Christine," Barkley said. "She was a strong woman and felt there were things you'd be better off not knowing until the time was right."

He pulled two envelopes from his desk, handed one to Christine and the other to Emory.

"Before you open your envelopes, we need to go over the terms and stipulations of Laura's will."

Reading through the document on his desk, Barkley said that the house would go to Emory and Christine would receive all of the money in Laura's bank account: a total of $4,527. But it came with the stipulation that she must move out of the house and find an apartment in Richmond.

Christine sat stunned for a moment then burst into sobs.

"I don't understand. Why would Mama want me to move out of the house I've lived in all my life?"

Emory leaned his lanky frame against the back of the leather chair and gave a grunt of dissatisfaction.

"What in the world was Laura thinking? Christine's too young to be off on her own."

These reactions were exactly what Laura had warned Barkley about, so neither came as a surprise to him. He waited until the initial shock settled then said, "Go ahead and open the envelopes."

In Emory's envelope there was the deed to the house and a letter written in Laura's own hand.

"Daddy, this is my way of paying you back for all you have done for us over the years. You gave up your house to live with us, and although it is far from an even exchange I now give you mine. Please don't argue or challenge my choice. I made it with an open heart.

"I believe you will be happy here. You are an independent man with strength far beyond what I could ever understand. I know you can easily care for yourself, because after we lost Mama you did it for five years before coming to live with us. Now it's time for both you and Christine to have lives of your own. Please do that, Daddy. Christine loves you as much as I did and if you ask her to stay she will, but it is my dying wish that you don't ask.

"She is young and has so many years ahead of her. Let her go so that she can be free of these burdensome memories and find a love of her own, just as you and I once did.

"Your loving daughter, Laura."

IN CHRISTINE'S ENVELOPE THERE WAS a cashier's check for the amount Barkley had mentioned along with another handwritten letter. It spoke of how loved Christine was and what great joy she had given her mama during their years together.

"I know how much you love your granddaddy and me," Laura had written, "and that's precisely why I have chosen to do things this way. I don't want you to sit around mourning my death. You need to get out and experience life. Do all you can do, and be all you can be.

"You have a big heart, Christine, one that is capable of loving, and I want you to find someone as smart and wonderful as your daddy. You'll never do that if you remain here buried in worry and sorrow. Your granddaddy is a strong man, stronger than you or I. He can manage fine on his own, and once he no longer has to wipe away our tears he just might find a happiness of his own."

The letter concluded by saying she was to go to Richmond and discover new adventures for herself.

"Don't just do the things we did; instead find the magic of your own life."

She'd signed it, "Forever loving you, Mama."

AFTER THE READING OF THE will, Christine spent weeks sorting through her mama's personal belongings. Someone with less of an attachment could have done it in a day, possibly two, but Christine stopped to shed a tear over almost everything.

The lace-trimmed hankies brought a memory of how Laura dabbed them with a spot of lavender cologne before dropping them into her purse. A pair of worn slippers resurrected memories of an icy cold Christmas morning. Every dress was linked to an occasion, some special and some as ordinary as an afternoon of baking cookies. Even things like petticoats and bed socks had memories clinging to them.

It took almost three weeks before all of Laura's personal belongings were packed in bags or boxes and loaded into the car. That Sunday Christine walked into church carrying a shopping bag with the coat and hat Laura often wore to services.

"This is the last time I'll have a piece of you here with me, Mama," she murmured and placed the bag next to her in the pew. On Monday morning she added the shopping bag to the other packages in the trunk of her car and drove to Saint Michael's Thrift Shop.

That evening she told Emory it was time for her to leave and find an apartment in Richmond.

He knew this moment was coming but dreaded it. Pushing down the lump rising up in his throat he said, "It's for the best. Richmond is a fine place for a young person to live. Your mama had some of her happiest times there."

"Yes, but she had Daddy or me with her."

Emory set his fork to the side of his plate and looked into her eyes.

"You know you've always got me. If you need me, I'll be there. This is what your mama wanted, and I intend to respect her wishes."

He picked up the fork and carved off another chunk of the meatloaf she'd made.

"Why, if Laura looked down from heaven and saw me keeping you here, she'd send a bolt of lightning to fry my butt."

He gave a forced chuckle then stuffed the meatloaf in his mouth.

Christine looked down at her plate and pushed a mound of mashed potatoes to one side.

"So if I call and say I need you, you'll come to Richmond?" she asked.

He nodded. "If it's a genuine need, but don't be calling me for every little thing. Your mama wanted you to be independent and find yourself a happy life, and that's what I expect you to be doing."

Although Christine didn't say it, she seriously doubted happiness was a thing that could be found without her mama and granddaddy.

The Boarding House

Although it took Christine nearly three weeks to pack her mama's belongings, in a single day she stuffed everything she was going to take to Richmond into an unwieldy assortment of suitcases, boxes and bags. On Thursday morning she kissed her granddaddy goodbye, promised to call as soon as she'd found an apartment, then backed out of the driveway and started off.

Christine had no plans other than to arrive in Richmond; then she would figure out what to do. The Algonquin Hotel held fond memories but it was $26 a night, which was too pricey for her budget. With the things she'd brought from home rattling around the trunk of her mama's car, she drove up one street and down the next until halfway down Bailey Street she happened to spot a sign that read "Feeney's Boarding House, Rooms for Rent, $3 Daily, $15 Weekly." She pulled into the driveway and followed it around to the back of the house.

Christine parked the car then walked around to the front of the house and knocked at the door. After a short wait, a woman with red hair and a bridge of freckles across her nose opened the door.

"Missus Feeney?" Christine said.

"That I am," the woman said and gave a nod. "And who might you be?"

"Christine Wilkes. I'm looking for a room to rent."

Missus Feeney wrinkled her brow and eyed Christine head to toe.

"All my other boarders are gentlemen," she finally said. "I doubt you'd fit in."

The bright smile Christine had forced into place disappeared.

"It would only be for a short while," she pleaded. "Just long enough for me to find a job and get an apartment."

Irene Feeney thought back on the two female boarders she'd had the previous year. That had not worked out well. The girls hung stockings on the towel bars in the bathroom, smudged lipstick on the fresh-washed pillowcases and kept her up half the night with their giggling and chatter.

A look of trepidation tugged at the right side of her mouth.

"How long you figure that will take?" she asked.

"A week. Two at the most."

The desolate sound of Christine's voice weakened Irene Feeney's resolve. She pulled the door back and gestured for her to come inside.

"I'll give you two weeks, but that's it. Meals cost extra. It's twenty-five cents for breakfast, seventy-five for dinner."

"I don't mind paying extra," Christine said.

"Okay then. And there's to be no stockings left in the bathroom."

Christine shook her head. "You can be sure of that, ma'am."

Irene Feeney eyed Christine with a steely gaze.

"Like I said I've got all men boarders, so the language at the dinner table gets a bit salty at times. I hope you're not easily offended."

"No, ma'am," Christine replied. "I'm not, not at all."

She was none too certain exactly what salty language consisted of, but right now she was desperate for a place to stay so it didn't matter. She opened her purse and paid Irene Feeney $15 for the room plus $7 for seven days of breakfast and dinner. After that she sighed with relief.

"Well, at least I'm sure of a place to stay," she said.

"Temporarily," Missus Feeney reminded her.

"Yes, of course. Temporarily."

Christine returned to the car and carried in one suitcase, leaving everything else in the trunk. She was only going to be here for a short while, so there was little sense in unpacking everything. She pulled her blue dress from the suitcase and hung it in the closet. She would start looking for an apartment the very next day, and as soon as she was settled she'd go in search of a job.

That evening she met the other boarders at the dinner table, five men in varying shapes, sizes and ages. At the head of the table was Irene Feeney.

"Gentlemen," Missus Feeney said, "this young lady will be rooming with us for a short while, so I'm expecting that for the duration of her stay you will all keep a civil tongue in your heads."

One by one she introduced the men to Christine, and each in turn nodded at the mention of his name.

Whatever salty language Irene expected never came about. In fact, to a man, they were downright courteous. When Christine mentioned she'd be looking for a job, Lawrence Hawkins, the eldest of the group, offered to reach out to Hiram Mosley and ask if there were any openings at the Atlantic Savings and Loan.

"He's my associate and a supervisor," Hawkins boasted. "So if there's a job to be had, he'll know about it."

Edward, a small man with a round face and an even rounder stomach, rolled his eyes.

"Associate my foot," he quipped. "You left that job ten years ago."

"That doesn't mean I don't still have connections," Hawkins replied indignantly.

Christine spoke up quickly and said she'd appreciate any help they could give.

"Coming to Richmond was my mama's idea, and—"

This was the first time she'd had to explain about losing Laura, and the words stuck in her throat. Although her voice wobbled a bit, she told of all that had happened. Once the tale was finished she added, "So you see with being off on my own for the first time, I feel rather lost."

Before the table was cleared four of the five men were acting like doting uncles, offering directions, job suggestions and lists of places suitable for a young woman to live.

"Stay away from River Street," Edward said, and Hawkins agreed.

"South of Gerard, now that's a nice area," he advised.

A lanky young man called Stick said nothing. He kept his eyes focused on his plate, and the moment it was emptied he excused himself and left the table. Christine turned her head to watch him leave the room.

"Stick's not much of a talker," Edward explained; then he said if she took the crosstown trolley it would take her smack into the center of town.

"That's where you'll find a job."

THAT FIRST EVENING SEEMED SO promising, but after two weeks of looking Christine had found nothing. No apartment; no job.

Every evening her self-designated uncles arrived at the dinner table with a dozen more suggestions. A men's wear shop in town might be hiring. There'd been a rumor that the water company was looking for a receptionist. When Edward suggested the tavern where his lady friend worked, the others looked at him askew.

"Christine doesn't want to work in a tavern!" Lawrence said sharply.

"Actually, I'd be willing to consider it," Christine replied. "Mama's money won't last forever."

For the first time in the whole two weeks, Stick spoke up.

"The telephone company is looking for switchboard operators."

"Really?" Christine said.

Stick nodded and kept his eyes on his plate. "'Specially on the split shift."

"What's a split shift?"

"You work when it's peak calling times. Four hours in the morning and four in the evening."

Christine gave a bright grin. "I'd be willing to do that!"

"The thing is," Stick said, "Southern Atlantic Telephone is over on the far side of town. Five, maybe six blocks past the Algonquin Hotel."

Lawrence frowned. "She'd have to take the streetcar and the bus to get there! Doing that twice a day would be—"

"I wouldn't mind," Christine said. "During the afternoon break I could look for an apartment over in that area."

Missus Feeney said nothing, but her eyes darted back and forth as she watched the words coming from each of the roomers. A dozen different suggestions were offered up, and by the time coffee was served Christine had decided to apply for the job.

THE NEXT MORNING CHRISTINE CAME to breakfast wearing her blue rayon dress and a small hat with a cluster of cherries pinned to the side.

"You look lovely," Missus Feeney said. She set a plate of eggs and bacon in front of her.

"How come she gets eggs and bacon, and we get oatmeal?" Edward grumbled.

"Christine has a long day in front of her and needs nourishment."

"I got a long day too," Edward groused, but when Irene Feeney gave him a warning glare he stopped complaining and went back to the oatmeal.

That morning all of the men wished Christine good luck, and when she started for the door Irene Feeney pushed a brown bag into her hands.

"A ham sandwich," she said. "In case you get hungry."

ALTHOUGH BUSES NOW SHUTTLED PEOPLE from place to place in the downtown area of Richmond, in outlying areas such as Bailey Street people still rode the streetcar. Two blocks from Feeney's Boarding House, Christine caught the trolley and took it to the Clancy Street Station where she transferred to the downtown bus. She slid into an empty seat beside the window and watched as the houses gave way to shops and office buildings. Thirty minutes later when the bus passed by the Algonquin Hotel, Christine was reminded of her mama's letter.

"Find the magic," it had said.

She gave a sigh. "I'm trying, Mama. I'm honestly trying."

Two stops later she climbed down from the bus and walked four blocks west to the six-story building that housed the Southern Atlantic Telephone Company.

Christine hesitated a moment before entering, smoothed the wrinkles from the front of her skirt and brushed back a wispy curl that had slipped from beneath her hat. She pushed through the revolving glass door and saw it: a large chalkboard perched on a wooden easel. "Switchboard Operators Needed," it read. "No Experience Required."

Squaring her shoulders and summoning as much courage as she could muster, Christine approached the reception desk.

"I'd like to inquire about the switchboard operator position," she said.

The receptionist edged her glasses lower on her nose and peered over them.

"It's split shift," she said warily. "You okay with that?"

Christine nodded and answered with an enthusiastic yes.

After filling out the two-page application and taking what was called an aptitude qualification test, Christine met with Miss Forrester who asked a handful of questions and then passed her on to Florence Platt, the team leader. Miss Platt was a thin woman with a sharp nose and mousy brown hair pulled straight back into a bun.

"They tell you this is the split shift?" she asked.

Again Christine answered yes and said she had no problem with that.

"I'm happy to work split shift. Happy as can be."

Florence nodded. "Fine. Be here at nine o'clock Monday morning. The first week is training. You'll work nine to six. The next week you start split shift, six AM to ten AM, then six PM to ten PM. Now you sure you're okay with that?"

Christine gave a broad smile and again answered yes.

IT WAS NEARING THREE O'CLOCK by the time Christine left the telephone company. She glanced at her watch then turned and walked back toward the Algonquin. At the hotel she crossed the lobby, entered the grand salon and sat on one of the red velvet sofas she and Laura had often shared.

She ordered the same thing they had always ordered: rose hip tea and watercress sandwiches. The tiny sandwiches cut into triangles without a hint of crust had always been something to look forward to, but now they seemed tasteless and the tea was not nearly as sweet as she remembered. She stirred a second and then a third spoonful of sugar into her cup, but it didn't help.

Tears welled in her eyes, and in a whisper no louder than the flutter of a dove's wing she said, "I'm afraid, Mama. I'm afraid that without you I'll never be able to find the magic."

As she stood to leave, she felt the feathery touch of an arm circling her shoulders. She whirled around but no one was there.

"Mama?" she said, but there was no answer.

TRAINING CLASS

The Sunday evening before she was to start her new job, Christine was as fluttery as a robin in a snowstorm. She'd brought in the second suitcase and picked out five outfits for the coming week, a fresh one for each day. For Monday she selected a yellow suit with shoulder pads and a nipped-in waist. Hopefully it looked cheery but not too frivolous.

She remembered how her mama always claimed the first impression was a lasting one, yet try as she may she couldn't recall any specific instructions about what to wear, say or do. She did recall the one directive to look straight into a person's face and smile as she spoke, but that too was a problem. She couldn't seem to find a way to set her mouth in a smile when her lips were moving.

That evening at the supper table, she mentioned she was a bit nervous about her first day on the job. The gentlemen boarders, who by now had become friends of a sort, were quick to offer advice.

"Don't worry," Lawrence said. "You'll do fine. The key is to grab the upper hand and act as if you already know this stuff."

Christine frowned. "But I don't."

133

"You don't have to actually know it, just make them think you do."

"Don't listen to Mister Big Shot," Edward said. "He thinks he knows everything, but he don't know nothing. What you've gotta do is not chew gum, and answer 'Yes, ma'am' to whatever they say."

Irene Feeney stated that in her opinion having such a long workday necessitated a hearty meal and possibly an afternoon nap.

"Perhaps you should ask if they have a little lounge where you could rest in the afternoon," she suggested.

Christine gave an almost imperceptible shake of her head. "I doubt—"

"Just be yourself," Stick spoke up.

He gave a quick glance across the table, and when his eyes met Christine's he lowered his gaze back to his plate.

"You don't have to do nothing," he said softly. "They're gonna like you just because you're who you are."

Christine smiled and tucked his words away in her mind for safekeeping.

"Thank you, Stick," she said.

He glanced up, and again their eyes met.

ON THE DAY CHRISTINE HAD gone for the interview, the trip on the trolley and then the bus had taken one hour and twenty minutes. On Monday morning she allowed herself an extra twenty minutes. She left the house at 6:50 and arrived at the telephone company office a half-hour early. Following Florence Platt's directions, she entered the side door and took the elevator to the second floor.

"Good, you're early," Florence said. "Gives us time to get you settled."

She led the way to a back room where Christine was given a locker to store her purse and a coat or jacket in the wintertime.

"You might want to take off your suit jacket," Florence suggested. "Working a tandem board entails a lot of stretching and reaching."

Christine reopened the locker, hung her yellow jacket inside and then followed Florence back to the training room.

The class consisted of three women plus Christine. Each of them was given a headset that clipped across the crown of their head with an earphone on one side and a speaker circling around in front of their mouth.

"Make certain your headset is adjusted comfortably," Florence said. Then she seated them in front of a switchboard that stood six feet high with row after row of lights and holes. Once all four women were in position, Florence began her instructions.

"Each hole, or jack as they are called, represents a household. When the customer picks up their telephone receiver, a light flashes. When you see a flashing light, push the talk key open, pick up the back cord, plug it into the jack above the light and say, 'Number, please?'"

She eyed the four girls and asked, "Any questions so far?"

Angie, one of the trainees, grunted uh-uh, and Christine and the others shook their heads.

Florence smiled. "Okay then. Now, once they give you the number they're calling, locate it on the board, take the corresponding front cord, plug it into that number then close your talk key and move on to answer the next call."

In theory it sounded simple enough, but the tandem board was huge and the banks of jacks were stacked one on top of another until they stood as tall as a man. Just locating a specific number could take as long as five minutes.

All morning the women practiced connecting calls, sometimes tangling the cords before the lines could be plugged together.

"Don't worry," Florence said, "you've got a week to practice."

At ten-thirty the group took their first break.

"You've got precisely fifteen minutes," Florence said then disappeared into a back office.

The four trainees headed for the employee lounge. Eleanor, the woman who'd inadvertently listened in on two conversations because she'd forgotten to close the talk key, poured herself a cup of coffee and sat on a stiff wooden chair. With her shoulders slumped and her mouth turned down at the corners, she had the look of someone ready to give up.

"This is *not* as easy as I thought it would be," she said.

"It's not so bad," Christine replied, trying to make the situation sound a bit more positive. After three solid weeks of looking for work and finding nothing, she was determined to make a go of this job. "Once you start to remember how the numbers are arranged—"

"That's impossible," Barbara Ann cut in. "There's thousands of numbers in every panel."

"Yeah," Eleanor said with a sigh. "How are you supposed to remember that many? I'm starting to think this job ain't for me."

"I got two kids and a husband with a broken leg," Angie said. "I gotta have this job, or they ain't gonna eat."

The other three nodded and agreed such a situation was indeed tough. When the fifteen-minute buzzer sounded, the ladies hurried back to the training room.

Before lunch Eleanor crossed two cords and connected Herbert Green, who was calling Porky's Plumbing, to the maternity ward of Rosewood Hospital. Having also forgotten to close the talk key, she realized her mistake and disconnected them both. Herbert called back sputtering, stammering and complaining that she was the worst telephone operator he'd ever had the misfortune to work with. That's when Eleanor decided the job was definitely not for her. She unplugged her headset, handed it back to Florence and walked off.

Shortly after that the noon buzzer sounded, and Christine asked Florence how long they had for lunch.

"A total of one hour," she replied primly. "That means you are to be back at your station and ready to plug in your headset in sixty minutes."

Christine glanced at her watch then returned to the locker room along with the two remaining trainees. They all collected their purses and headed for the door.

"There's a coffee shop down the block," Angie said. "You gals wanna join me for lunch?"

Christine nodded, but Barbara Ann claimed she had something to do. Having overheard Herbert Green yelling at Eleanor had obviously unnerved her, and several tightly knotted ridges were stretched across her forehead. At a quarter of one, Barbara Ann called in and left a message that she wouldn't be returning.

"This job is much too stressful for a person like me," she said.

That left just Angie and Christine. With only the two of them working the board the practice session picked up pace, and before the day was out Christine felt fairly good about her progress.

BY THURSDAY, BOTH GIRLS KNEW they were ready. When a light flashed they were waiting with the plug in their hand.

"Number, please," they'd say smartly, and in a scant few seconds the front cord would be plugged into the appropriate jack.

Every day they went to lunch together, and when Angie talked about her two toddlers and Kenny, her brick-laying husband with the broken leg, Christine talked about Missus Feeney and the five gentlemen boarders.

"They're like uncles," she said. "Always giving advice and looking out for me."

"Maybe so," Angie replied, "but Bailey Street's a long commute when you're working split shift."

"Oh, I won't be going back there during the day. I plan to spend the afternoons looking for an apartment somewhere close by."

"What kind of apartment?"

"Something small." She hesitated a second then added, "It's just me. Alone."

Angie grinned. "You mind a loft for sleeping?"

"What do you mean?" Christine asked.

"An apartment. A studio actually, but you go up six or so steps to the loft, and there's a platform big enough for a bed and maybe one nightstand."

Christine's eyes brightened. "That sounds perfect!"

"It's Kenny's sister's place. She just got married and is looking to sublet it."

"How much?"

"That's the thing…" Angie grimaced. "She wants thirty-eight dollars a month, but she's willing to leave everything: furniture, linens, dishes, the whole kit and caboodle."

Christine chewed the last remaining crust of her toasted cheese sandwich and pondered the thought.

"That's almost two weeks' salary," she said. "More than I was planning on, but I guess if I don't have to buy any furniture…"

"It's ten minutes from here on the crosstown," Angie added. "You could walk to work if you wanted to."

Christine ran a bunch of numbers through her head, factoring in the interest on the savings account she'd opened and the fact that she could walk to work once or twice a day instead of spending money for the bus. In the end she decided it might be a stretch, but it was definitely worth looking into.

FRIDAY AFTERNOON WHEN THEY FINISHED their last day of training, Angie took Christine to see the apartment. They walked from the office to the apartment building then climbed the single flight of stairs. Angie unlocked the door, and they stepped inside.

Christine could see the entire apartment, including the doorway that led to the bathroom. It was a tiny place but beautifully decorated. She gave a sigh of delight then walked deeper into the room. Trailing her fingers along the smooth maple surface of the coffee table, she smiled and dropped down onto the nubby plaid sofa.

She leaned into the cushions and said, "Comfy."

"I thought you was gonna like it," Angie replied. "Kenny's sister is a real pill, but one thing I gotta give her is that she keeps a nice house. You ain't gonna find a speck of dirt in this place."

"I can see that."

Christine had been set to try and negotiate a somewhat lower price, but she'd already fallen in love with the place.

"How soon will it be available?" she asked.

"Right now. Anne Marie and Wayne were married last Sunday."

Christine crossed the room, climbed the few steps and peered into the sleeping loft. She could already imagine the picture of her mama and daddy sitting atop the maple nightstand.

"I'll take it," she said.

"Anne Marie told me whoever rents it has gotta pay one month's rent and one month's security up front," Angie warned.

Christine sat in the small desk chair with her purse on her lap and opened her wallet. She counted the bills then said, "I've only got fifty-eight dollars. Can I give you fifty now and the other twenty-six when we get paid next Wednesday?"

Angie nodded. "I guess that'll be okay. Anne Marie and Wayne don't get back from their honeymoon until Friday."

She pulled three keys off of her key ring and handed them to Christine. "This is the downstairs entry door. This one's the mailbox, and this is the apartment door."

"Can I move in this weekend?"

Angie shrugged. "Sure, if you want to."

THAT EVENING CHRISTINE WAS LATE to supper, and when she arrived back at the boarding house Missus Feeney was wearing a frown.

"Supper is supposed to be at eight." She glanced over at the clock and stated the obvious. "It's twenty past."

"I'm sorry," Christine said apologetically. "But you'll be glad to know I've finally found an apartment."

"An apartment?" Missus Feeney repeated. Her voice had the sound of disappointment threaded through the words. "I rather thought you might decide to stay."

"But you said this is basically a gentleman's boarding house."

"Well, yes. But that was before you came. Since you've been here the men have been on their best behavior, so if you want to stay…"

Christine moved closer to Missus Feeney and wrapped her arms around the chubby little woman.

"How can I ever thank you?" she said. "I love it here and I do hate to leave, but with working a split shift the commute would be impossible."

"I understand," Missus Feeney said sadly. "But if you'd like to come for dinner on Saturday or Sunday, there'd be no charge.

"I'd love to come for dinner," Christine replied.

THAT EVENING THE CONVERSATION AROUND the supper table was all about Christine's new apartment. She glowingly described the ecru-colored drapes, the lacquered desk, the sleeping loft and a dozen other features.

"Of course I'll miss everyone."

She gave a saddened sigh; then her voice brightened when she added that she would be coming back for dinner every so often.

"It's not like I'm moving to the other end of the earth," she said. "The apartment is just across town."

Momentarily allowing his eyes to look directly into hers, Stick said, "Would it be okay for some of us to stop by if we're ever on that side of town?"

"Well, of course it would," Christine answered, but by then Stick had already lowered his eyes and was back to looking down at his plate.

CHRISTINE

O h, what I wouldn't give for Mama to see my new apartment. She'd love it, I know she would.

This evening after I finished telling the boarders about the sleeping loft and how nicely everything was decorated, I started thinking about my last trip with Mama. When we passed by those little apartment buildings, I remember how she looked back at them so longingly. At the time I thought maybe she was wishing she could live there, but after all that's happened I've come to understand it was what she wanted for me. Day by day I'm finding little bits of happiness here in Richmond; it's not the magic Mama spoke of but an easier peace of mind.

When Mister Barkley first read her will, I couldn't see myself ever being happy here. I even asked Granddaddy if perhaps I shouldn't just stay in Wyattsville. I told him I could cook for him and keep house, but he shook his head and said no.

"Your mama always had a way of knowing what was right for you," he said, "and I've got to believe this situation is no different."

Of course I disagreed and argued him seven ways 'til Sunday, but he stood firm. In a way, I'm glad he did.

I'd like to say I'm one hundred percent happy, but I'm not. Missus Feeney and the fellows here at the boarding house have been wonderful to me, but I still miss Mama more than you'd believe possible. When I walk by a place where we've been together, my heart aches with wishing she were here with me.

When something good happens—like finding a job or that cute little apartment—I keep wishing I could tell Mama about it. Having good stuff happen when you have nobody to share it with is kind of sad. It's like opening up a beautifully wrapped present and discovering the box is empty.

Times when I feel like that, I remember Mama saying, "Just wait, and one day you'll find the magic meant for you."

I'm starting to think maybe she was right.

THE STRIKE

On Saturday morning Christine left Missus Feeney's Boarding House and moved into the small studio apartment. She spent the afternoon unpacking her clothes, smoothing the wrinkles from her dresses and hanging them in the closet. She set shoes side by side in a row along the floor of the closet, shoved a small box of heavy sweaters onto the top shelf and then filled the drawers of the highboy.

Once everything was put away and arranged to her liking, she dropped down on the sofa and sat there looking around. Already the place felt like home. Christine felt confident that despite the rent being more than she'd planned on spending, she'd made the right decision.

That afternoon she pulled on a lightweight jacket and began exploring the neighborhood. She walked up and down the crooked little streets, looking in shop windows and nodding amicably to passersby. Four blocks east of the building she happened upon a Friendly's Grocery Store and went in. With only eight dollars to last until payday, she held back on buying anything extravagant and stuck to the necessities: eggs, milk, bread, bologna and one small bag of chocolate chip cookies.

That evening for supper Christine fixed herself a scrambled egg sandwich. Oddly enough, it tasted almost as good as Missus Feeney's homemade stew.

ON MONDAY MORNING, CHRISTINE WOKE a half hour earlier than necessary. She dressed quickly and was out the door with plenty of time for walking to work. Retracing the path she and Angie had taken on Friday, she walked with a bounce in her step and her handbag swinging back and forth.

The walk took twenty minutes, and when she passed the shoemaker on Clinton Street she caught sight of her reflection in the store window. For a moment it seemed not to be her. The girl in the glass had squared-back shoulders and a broad grin. The girl in the glass was who Christine wanted to be, not who she was. As she passed by the Laundromat, she sneaked a second glance and saw it was indeed her. The new her.

She had somehow become a person who could discover the magic her mama spoke of.

CHRISTINE'S FIRST WEEK OF ACTUALLY working the switchboard flew by, and with each day she became more adept and faster at answering callers. In addition to saying "Number, please" and "Thank you," she took to adding an occasional "Have a lovely day."

She had hoped to be working side by side with Angie as she had in training. But Angie had children who needed care and a husband with a still-broken leg, so she'd been excused from the split shift and temporarily assigned days.

On Wednesday after Christine cashed her paycheck and took a bit extra from the savings account, she met Angie in the break room and handed her the remainder of the rent.

"I'm loving the apartment," she said and smiled.

It was true. Not only did she love the apartment, she also loved the neighborhood, the friendly shopkeepers, the invigorating walks back and forth to work, and the newfound independence she was growing into. By the time Friday rolled around she had made three new friends and joined the bowling league. On Saturday she telephoned Emory and told him the good news.

"I've got a terrific job," she said, "and a lovely apartment."

"That's great," he replied. "Tell me all about it."

She did, explaining how she'd met Angie and through Angie sublet the apartment.

"It's a whole new feeling," she added. "I wake up in the morning and can't wait to jump out of bed."

Saying nothing about how empty the house felt without her or how a dinner alone was something he'd come to dread, Emory said, "Your mama would be proud of you. She believed you could do it, and it looks like you're proving her right."

There was a brief moment of silence; then he added, "Just remember, if you ever need anything I'm here for you. You have only to call."

"Thank you, Granddaddy, but you don't have to worry. I'm doing great. And it makes me feel good to know I'm doing what Mama wanted."

THE SECOND WEEK OF WORKING at the Southern Atlantic Telephone Company started out just fine. On Wednesday Christine went in, worked the morning shift as she always did, then walked back to the apartment and tidied up. That afternoon she carried a load of clothes to the Laundromat, washed, dried and folded them, then returned home. After a quick sandwich, she applied a fresh coat of lipstick and headed back to the telephone company for the second half of her shift.

When she arrived at the building, there was a large group of women milling around outside. They were waving signs and chanting, "No raise, no work!" The women were pushed up against one another and standing five deep. Angie was smack in the middle of the crowd. Christine eased past two girls with their fists in the air and tugged on Angie's shoulder.

"What's going on?" she asked.

"It's a strike. Nobody works unless they agree to our demands."

Christine wrinkled her brow. "What demands?"

"Haven't you been going to the union meetings?" Angie said. "They're trying to get us better pay, more vacation and pension benefits. The company is playing hardball, so the union called a strike."

"Fine for you," Christine said, "but I've got to go in. I'm working split shift."

Angie turned and gave a warning glare. "Are you crazy? Do you know what will happen if you try to cross the line?"

Christine shook her head.

"They'll crucify you! You won't have a friend left in the entire company!"

"Oh, dear." A look of dismay settled on Christine's face. "I really can't afford to get fired because I didn't show up for work."

A middle-aged woman with a gray bun pinned atop her head turned.

"That's what the union is for. Stick with us, and you can't get fired." She handed Christine a sign. "Here, move up front to where those policemen are and start waving this."

"I don't feel comfortable doing that," Christine replied

apprehensively. "Can't I do something else? Something less conspicuous?"

"Okay." The woman yanked the sign back and handed Christine a five-dollar bill. "Run down to the A&P and get ten cartons of eggs."

"Ten cartons? But what—"

"I don't have time for questions, just go!"

Angie nudged Christine's back and whispered, "Go. Gertrude's our union rep. She knows what she's doing."

Feeling more than a little bit intimidated, Christine turned and started toward the grocery store. Eggs didn't make a whole lot of sense, but maybe the union was planning to feed the strikers.

It took almost twenty minutes to walk to the A&P and return with the two sacks of eggs. When Christine approached the crowd, she saw Angie but couldn't find Gertrude.

The crowd was thicker now and louder. Christine tried to maneuver her way through to Angie, but it was impossible. She was trying to squeeze past the brunette waving a sign that read "Unfair Wages" when Gertrude spotted her.

"Hey, kid, over here!"

Gertrude raised her arm and motioned to the crowd. "Let the kid through."

The strikers pushed back to make an opening wide enough for Christine to move through to the front of the line where Gertrude was standing. As soon as she squeezed by, the crowd closed up and went back to waving signs and hollering.

Christine handed over both bags. Gertrude grabbed them and started passing out cartons of eggs to everybody on the front line.

"Give it to 'em!" she yelled.

The eggs began flying through the air, hitting the glass entrance of the Southern Atlantic Telephone Company, splattering the front of the building and ultimately bombarding the handful of policemen who rushed the crowd trying to stop the melee. A beefy looking sergeant raised his arm and waggled a finger in Christine's direction.

"Get the girl with the ponytail! She's the troublemaker who brought the eggs!"

Christine turned and tried to disappear back into the crowd, but it was impenetrable. Seconds later a strong hand latched onto her elbow and lead her away.

"I'm sorry," she said apologetically. "I didn't know that's what they were going to do. I wasn't trying to be a troublemaker."

She mumbled a feeble explanation about the eggs not being her idea, but by then it was too late. Jack Mahoney was already loading her into the patrol car.

Only two people were taken to the station house that day: Christine Wilkes and Gertrude Hamm.

PATROLMAN JACK MAHONEY HAD BEEN on the force for less than a year. He was hoping to make detective someday, so he volunteered for the duty assignments no one else wanted. Maintaining crowd control with the striking switchboard operators was just such an assignment. When he arrived at the station house with a tearful Christine Wilkes in tow he intended to turn her over to Sergeant Hastings for interrogation, but there had been a jewelry store robbery on Lambert Street and the precinct was two men short.

Having lost patience with hauling in people who would walk free in an hour or two, the captain told Jack to handle it himself.

"This is small potatoes," he said. "Give her a warning then cut her loose."

Following orders, Jack led Christine into an interrogation room, sat her at the table and removed the handcuffs.

"Sorry about that," he said.

"Sorry?" she replied, rubbing her chafed wrists. "I should think you would be. I told you I wasn't part of that group. If you wanted to arrest someone, why didn't you arrest the people throwing eggs?"

"The others didn't bring the eggs to the demonstration; you did."

"I didn't exactly *bring* them," she said. "I went back to the A&P and bought them because that's what I was told to do. How was I supposed to know what they were planning?"

"Didn't you think *ten dozen* eggs was a rather strange request?"

Christine hesitated for a moment, wondering if perhaps she had known what was going to happen. She gave a pensive sigh then said, "I can't honestly say whether or not I suspected they'd throw the eggs. I didn't know what they were planning, but I didn't think it through either."

The genuineness of her statement caused the corners of Jack's mouth to curl. Granted he'd had less than a year's experience, but this girl had none of the earmarks of a rabble-rouser.

Changing tactics, he asked, "Do you want something to drink? Water? Coffee?"

"A glass of water, please," she replied.

Leaving her at the table, he disappeared out the door and returned a few minutes later with a glass of water and two bottles of Coke.

"I thought you might enjoy this," he said and handed her a bottle.

"Thanks."

"It's nothing," Jack said nonchalantly. He lowered himself back into the chair and downed a long swig of soda before he asked his next question.

"When the union rep spoke to the group and discussed the strike, was there any mention of egging the building?"

"I told you before, I'm not part of the union group," Christine said. "I didn't even know there was going to be a strike. I was on my way back to work when I ran into the crowd in front of the building."

"On your way back to work? Are you working split shift?"

"Yes," she said with a weary nod. "Or at least I was. I imagine there's a possibility I'll get fired because I didn't show up for work this evening, and then..."

"You won't get fired," Jack assured her. "The telephone company is trying to make peace with the union. They're not about to bicker over somebody willing or not willing to cross the picket line."

Jack asked a string of questions, mostly to prolong the conversation rather than obtain information. He asked if she knew the organizers of the rally, if she could name any of the participants and how long had she been working at the telephone company. Her answers were no and no; then she explained.

"This is only my third week on the job. I moved here from Wyattsville."

"So you're new in town?" Jack gave a warm smile. "Well, other than the inside of a police station, have you seen much of the city?"

"Not recently." Christine returned the smile and found herself liking him despite the situation. "Mama and I used to come to Richmond, but then she got sick and..."

"She's better now?"

"No." Christine shook her head sadly. "She died. Now she's with Daddy."

They sat and talked for a while longer—not about unions, or demonstrations, or egg throwing, but about life and the unfairness it sometimes brings. In time Jack excused himself and left the room again. When he came back, he told Christine she was free to go and he'd be happy to drive her home.

"Thanks," Christine said, "but I'd better go back to work so I don't get fired."

Jack frowned and shook his head. "Not a good idea. The demonstrators are still out there. Go home, and when you go in tomorrow just tell your boss you couldn't get past the picket line."

"But that's not the truth."

He gave her a playful grin. "It's close enough."

WHEN THEY LEFT THE STATIONHOUSE, Jack dropped her back at her apartment building and returned to finish his assignment working crowd control at the Southern Atlantic Telephone Company. The funny thing was that as he scanned the shifting crowd of faces, he kept seeing hers.

GETTING TO KNOW YOU

On Thursday morning the Southern Atlantic Telephone Company agreed to return to the bargaining table, and the strike was called off. The switchboard operators resumed work that afternoon, and there were no further ramifications. With one exception.

Florence was on the management team pulled in to handle calls the previous day, which rankled her to no end. Usually the supervisor strolled back and forth behind the row of girls at the switchboard and gave a gentle tap on the shoulder and a suggestion for improvement. The hard click of Florence's heels against the linoleum and the bristly tone of her voice told of her frustration at being pulled back to the switchboard during the strike.

When Christine returned for the Thursday evening segment of her shift, she hurried to her station and plugged herself in. She was in the middle of connecting 57834 to a number in the Pikestown area when Florence tapped her on the shoulder.

"I'm expecting you to work the split shift on Saturday to make up for lost time," she said sharply. "Otherwise you'll be docked."

Saturday was the day Christine planned to have supper

with Missus Feeney and the gentlemen at the boarding house.

"Can I do Sunday instead?" she asked.

"Do you not like your job?" Florence snapped. "Your shenanigans caused me a great deal of inconvenience, and—"

"I'm sorry," Christine cut in. "I'll be happy to do Saturday."

At eight o'clock when she took her fifteen-minute break, Christine called Missus Feeney and explained the situation.

"Would it be okay if I come on Sunday?" she asked.

"Certainly," Missus Feeney replied. "Just remember Sunday supper is early, so be here by five."

"Five it is," Christine replied brightly. She asked how all of the men were doing and said she missed everybody.

"We miss you too," Missus Feeney replied. "Stick's asked me three times when you're coming to dinner, and Lawrence has got a copy of Sinclair Lewis's new book for you."

They chatted for a few minutes; then she hung up and returned to work. As Christine stepped back onto the switchboard platform, something warm settled inside of her. Less than two months earlier she'd come to Richmond feeling lost and alone; now she had a life. She had a job, an apartment and friends. Angie and the girls she worked with, Missus Feeney, Lawrence, Edward, Stick.

She pictured Stick with his kind words and shy smile. It would be good to see Stick again.

By Friday everything was back to normal at the telephone company. Christine arrived at 6AM and worked until 10AM. With eight hours before she had to return for the evening shift, she hurried from the building and pulled the list of errands from her pocket. First she would stop at the dry cleaner and after that...

She didn't see Jack until he touched his hand to her arm.

"Hi, there."

Christine jerked back. "Oh, my gosh, you startled me."

"I'm sorry. I wanted to catch you when you came off your shift, but you shot by so quickly—"

She laughed. "I guess I was concentrating on today's to-do list."

"I hope egg buying isn't on that list," Jack said.

He laughed, and she laughed with him.

"Don't tell me you're planning to arrest me again."

"Absolutely not."

He gave a sheepish grin, and his eyes crinkled at the corners. He was wearing his uniform, and she caught the faint smell of a leathery aftershave.

"This is my regular beat," he said. "I just thought I'd stop by to make sure you're okay. You know, make certain there were no problems with the job."

"No problems. They didn't fire anybody, but our supervisor let us know she was not happy."

Jack glanced at his watch then said, "I was about to take a break. Want to join me for a cup of coffee?"

A warm, glowing feeling settled in Christine's chest as she began to suspect she was the reason he'd decided to take a break at this very moment. She smiled and tucked the list back into her pocket.

"Sure," she said, "I'd love to."

They bypassed the crowded luncheonette a few doors down from the telephone company and walked three blocks to the Brown Bean. With his hand barely touching her elbow, Jack guided Christine to one of the red leather booths in the back of the shop. He stood and waited until she slid in then took off his hat and slid in on the opposite side. He handed her the menu lying on the table and looked across as if he were studying her face.

Until now Christine hadn't noticed the soft hazel color of his eyes, greenish almost but with a touch of gray. His hair, brown and tousled from wearing the hat, was sun-streaked in places. He had a strong jawline and an easy smile, and he looked handsomer than she remembered him being.

"You mentioned you're new in town," he said. "So what brought you to Richmond?"

"It's what my mama wanted."

Christine looked down at the hands in her lap as she told him of the will and the granddaddy living back in Wyattsville.

"After Daddy died, Mama and I somehow seemed happier when we were here in Richmond. I think she wanted to believe I'd come here and find that kind of happiness again."

"Have you?" Jack asked.

She looked up and allowed her gaze to meet his.

"I'm starting to," she said and smiled.

There was no awkwardness in their conversation. It shifted back and forth easily with each statement leading into the next one. She told him about leaving Wyattsville and moving into Missus Feeney's Boarding House, and he told her he'd lived in Richmond all his life.

"What made you decide to become a policeman?" she asked.

Jack chuckled. "Gus Barnes. He was a cop who lived down the street from us. Gus liked to fix things: broken bicycles, bent roller skates, toys of any kind. At Christmastime Gus would put on a Santa suit and deliver those toys to kids whose families couldn't afford to buy presents. It was during the Depression and everybody was struggling, but when Gus showed up we all knew we'd get something."

Close up Christine could see Jack's mouth was just a tiny bit crooked, higher on the right side than the left, but the imperfection made him look all the more handsome. Moving her thoughts back to the story, she leaned in and smiled.

"Gus sounds like a swell guy."

"Yeah, he was."

"Was?"

Jack nodded. "Gus was killed five years ago. My dad and I cried when we heard the news. Saint Agatha's had a mass, and so many people came they overflowed the church. Everybody loved the guy."

Without pausing to think about it, Christine stretched her arm across the table and covered his hand with hers.

"That's so touching..." she murmured with sympathy.

He saw her small hand atop his and felt the warmth of it. Turning his hand palm up he twined his fingers around her wrist and remained there for a few moments. Jack wanted to stay. He wanted to sit there having cup after cup of coffee and talk for hours, but he had a job to do.

"I've got to get back to work now," he said. "Can we continue this conversation tomorrow over supper?"

"I'd love to," she answered, "but I have to work."

"On a Saturday?"

"It's my penance for the strike."

"Sunday then?"

She tilted her head and gave an apologetic shrug. "Afraid not. I promised Missus Feeney I'd come for supper."

"Oh." Jack's disappointment was obvious. He released his hold on her hand. "Maybe some other time?"

"I'd like that."

They left the coffee shop and walked together for three blocks. When she turned onto Mason Street, he remained on Gerard.

"See you soon," he said and gave a wave.

"Yes, soon," she answered. Partway down Mason she turned to see if he was watching her. He wasn't.

SATURDAY WAS A SLOW DAY at the switchboard. The busyness of weekdays was missing, and the time dragged by. The morning

157

hours brought less than a dozen flashing call lights and there were seven girls working, three strikers and four regulars.

Angie, also working the split shift to make up for strike time, leaned toward Christine and whispered, "I am so bored I could scream. I suppose this is Flo's idea of payback."

Christine giggled at the thought of calling the stern supervisor "Flo." She gave a nod and rolled her eyes. "And I had to turn down a terrific date for this."

Angie grinned. "With who?"

"That cute policeman who arrested me the day of the strike."

Angie guffawed, and within seconds the click of Florence's heels was right behind her.

"There is no socializing while you are at your work station!" she bellowed. "Do you understand that?"

"Yes, ma'am," they both replied.

WHEN CHRISTINE LEFT FOR THE afternoon, she did some of the errands she'd put off the day before but with less exuberance. She picked up the dry cleaning, shopped at Friendly's Market then on the way home bought a bouquet of flowers for Missus Feeney. She was hoping perhaps Jack would call but then realized he hadn't even asked for her telephone number.

When he said, "Maybe some other time," she'd said, "I'd like that." Was that definite enough? Was he looking for something more? Should she have suggested next weekend?

No, she thought, *that would have been much too bold.*

Luckily when she returned to work for the evening shift, the switchboard was a bit busier. Not busy enough to stop her from thinking about him but busy enough so the hours didn't drag on as they had that morning. At ten o'clock she unplugged her headset from the workstation, returned to the locker room, gathered her purse and left the building.

One thing Christine did not like about working split shift was walking home in the dark. Weeknights there were usually a few businessmen still closing up shop, but this night was exceptionally quiet. She glanced right then left. The street was empty. She started down Gerard then heard footsteps behind her and quickened her pace.

"Hey, wait up!"

She recognized the voice, turned and saw Jack Mahoney, not in his uniform but wearing a yellow sweater and brown slacks.

"I thought you might like some company for your walk home," he said.

"Where'd you come from?"

"The bench across the street. I was waiting for you."

He fell into step and walked alongside of her.

"Next Saturday the Richmond Colts are playing the Roanoke Red Sox. It's not major league, but Roanoke won the league championship last year. The stadium hot dogs are good and the beer is cold, so I was wondering—"

"I'd love to."

Jack blinked once or twice. "No buts this time?"

She smiled and looped her arm through his. "No buts."

ON SUNDAY CHRISTINE DROVE CROSSTOWN to Bailey Street, parked in back of the boardinghouse then walked around to the front door and knocked. It was several minutes before Missus Feeney tugged the door open.

"Good grief," she said through heaving breaths, "why didn't you just come through the kitchen instead of making me run all this way?"

"Well, I thought since I don't live here anymore..."

"For you this will always be home, and you'd best not forget it."

Irene Feeney stopped in the center hall and called up the stairs for Lawrence to get a move on.

"Supper's ready, and Christine's here," she called.

When they settled at the table, Lawrence was first to ask about the job. Christine began by telling how the job that once seemed so difficult was now easy enough for her to do it blindfolded.

"Well, not actually blindfolded," she added with a chuckle, "because I still have to see the numbers."

She talked about the apartment and the new friends she'd made then segued into the story of the strike.

"I hadn't been to a single union meeting, but I was still the one arrested."

Everyone laughed as she told about buying the eggs and carrying them back for the demonstrators to toss at the building.

"It was very embarrassing to be carted off in a patrol car, but one good thing did come of it," she said. "I met a really nice policeman named Jack Mahoney."

She told how he was waiting for her when she left work Saturday night and had walked her home. With a happy but rather goofy looking grin she added, "He's taking me to a baseball game next Saturday."

"Don't you think we ought to meet him first?" Lawrence asked.

"Yeah," Edward said. "Him being a policeman don't mean he won't try to take advantage of you."

"How old is this chap?" Missus Feeney asked. Without waiting for Christine to answer, she tossed out several more questions about his family and income.

"Those things don't matter," Christine replied defensively. "It's only a date."

"For now," Missus Feeney said.

She leaned back in the chair and folded her arms across her chest, but her tone left the implication it was more than a date. A momentary lull slid into the conversation.

Finally Stick mumbled, "Christine's a smart girl, so leave her alone. She knows what she's doing."

Before he had time to look away, Christine's eyes met his and she smiled.

"Thank you, Stick," she said.

"Welcome," he replied and ducked his head.

THE BALL GAME

Saturday dawned with a sunny sky and a forecast for temperatures in the high eighties. Christine took a white sundress from the closet, pulled it over her head then checked her reflection in the mirror. The narrow straps flattered her shoulders, and the full skirt made her waist look even tinier than it was.

The last time she'd worn the dress was when she and Laura stayed at the Algonquin. Looking back, she could picture her mama, thinner than usual, but still happy and full of life. They'd had brunch at the Lady Anne Tea Shoppe then walked to the far end of Gerard Street. The day started out sunny, but in the afternoon it clouded up and there was a chill in the air.

They'd passed a small boutique and seen the blue cardigan in the window.

"It's perfect," her mama said and pulled Christine into the store.

The sweater was more than they should have spent, but her mama insisted she have it.

"It's the exact blue of your eyes," she said.

Christine reached into the closet now, pulled out the sweater and shrugged it over her shoulders. She smiled at her reflection and whispered, "Thank you, Mama."

The lobby buzzer sounded at precisely eleven o'clock. She hurried out the door and down the steps.

Peering through the glass door, Jack caught sight of her as she descended the staircase. When she came through the door, he raised an eyebrow and gave a grin of appreciation.

"Wow," he said, "you look fantastic!"

"Thanks." She eyed Jack in his tan slacks and white sport shirt then added, "You look pretty good yourself."

In the bright light of day and without his uniform, he looked younger, more boyish, less intimidating.

IT WAS A FAIRLY SHORT drive to Mooer's Field, so they arrived with almost an hour to spare. They made their way down to the seats, but before Jack sat he suggested getting some hot dogs and beer.

"Better do it before the stand gets too crowded."

As he made his way back up the stairs, Christine settled into her seat. The seats were low along the first base line and just above the Colts' dugout. She could hear bits and pieces of conversation. Curious, she leaned over to look down.

A young man in a Colts cap smiled up at her. She returned the smile then sat back in her seat. This day was going to be a hot one; already she felt warm in the sweater. She took it off and folded it across the back of her seat.

Players from both teams were warming up on the field. Pitchers on the sidelines tossed the ball back and forth; outfielders stretched their legs and swung weighted bats. Before long Jack returned carrying a cardboard carton filled with hot dogs, beer, peanuts and candy. He slid into the seat next to Christine.

"Mustard or no mustard?" he asked.

"Mustard."

He laughed. "I knew it. You're my kind of gal."

He took one of the mustard covered hot dogs and handed it to her. Jack bit into his hot dog then waggled a finger at one of the pitchers tossing the ball.

"That's Sam Lowry. He's pitching today."

He moved on, pointing out one player and another, talking about how they might or might not do this, that or the other thing. Christine knew little if anything about baseball, but she enjoyed the sound of his voice and the way he leaned closer to her when he spoke, making each word meaningful, something special in its own right.

The ability to make small talk without it sounding like small talk was just one of the things she liked about Jack. There were other things…many other things. The fondness with which he remembered Gus; the gentleness that was so evident in his eyes.

When Christine finished the last of her hot dog, he leaned into her and wiped a smudge of mustard from the side of her mouth. For a brief moment she thought he was going to kiss her, but he didn't. Had he tried, she would have let him.

"Peanuts or candy?" he asked.

"Candy."

He grinned. "I knew it."

He handed her the package of M&Ms then leaned back and casually placed his arm on the back of her seat. Before the candy was gone his hand was curled around her bare shoulder.

Christine couldn't say if it was the pleasant giddiness of the beer, the warmth of the sun or the feel of his hand against her skin, but she felt something she had never felt before. A tingling that stirred her heart and made her wish the day would never end.

All too quickly the afternoon was gone. It had been a fast game with the Richmond Colts not scoring a single run. A pitcher's battle, Jack called it. The score remained 0-0 until the top of the ninth when Lowry walked the Red Sox first baseman; then Ray Allen got a double that brought the man home. The Colts were last at bat with three straight strikeouts, and that ended the game.

As they pulled out of the Mooer's Field parking lot, Christine scooted across the seat closer to Jack.

"I had a great time," she said.

"So did I," he replied.

It all happened so easily, every little piece falling into place exactly as it should. After the game, Jack parked the car on one of the downtown side streets and they walked hand in hand in much the same way Christine and her mama once did. Christine remembered how they would spend time browsing shop windows, talking about first one thing and then another, and after a while deciding on what to eat and where to go for dinner.

"Are you up for something new?" Jack asked.

She nodded. "Everything we've done today has been new for me."

She meant the ballgame, but beneath that meaning there was another one; one she herself was almost afraid to believe.

"There's a great roadhouse just outside of town," he said. "Good steaks, good music and dancing."

She looked up at him picturing how it would feel to rest her head on his shoulder and float across the dance floor in his arms.

"Sounds wonderful," she said.

THAT EVENING THEY SHARED A bottle of red wine, held hands across the table, talked as if they'd known each other all their life and danced one dance after another. When the trio played *For Sentimental Reasons,* Jack tightened his arm around her waist and she nuzzled her head against his chest.

It was near dawn when they arrived back at her apartment. He kissed her goodnight in the vestibule, not once but several times. When he left she stepped inside the apartment and could swear that on the street below she heard someone whistling the first few bars of *Sentimental Reasons.*

Such foolishness, she thought, but the sound of that whistling remained in her head even as she drifted off to sleep.

IN THE WEEKS THAT FOLLOWED, Christine and Jack dated often. On days when she worked split shift, they met for lunch or coffee or a leisurely walk home.

"You shouldn't be walking alone in the dark," Jack said, and even though they had no plans to meet she'd find him sitting on the bench across the street each evening when she started for home.

That summer they picnicked in the park alongside the Franklin River, went to three more baseball games, dined in countless restaurants and danced until near dawn. On evenings when the heat of the day lingered past supper they took in a movie, and if the air conditioning chilled her shoulders he wrapped his arm around her. Afterward they'd drop by Schumann's Drugstore, sit in a booth and order ice cream sodas as they looked back on the antics of Walter Mitty's secret life or speculated on whether or not it was possible for Mrs. Muir to actually fall in love with a ghost.

Twice they had supper at Irene Feeney's Boarding House. On the second visit, Lawrence took Christine aside and told her he wholeheartedly approved of Mister Jack Mahoney.

Before the leaves of the oak trees began to turn, Christine knew this was indeed the magic her mama had wished for her.

CHRISTINE

If last December you'd told me I was going to be madly in love and feel this happy, I would have figured you were crazy. Back then the only thing I could feel was a heartache so huge it was almost suffocating. Standing at Mama's grave, I was certain my next breath would be my last one. I couldn't imagine an hour, let alone a day or a week or a month without Mama.

I thought having Granddaddy close was about the only thing I had left in my life. Then when Mister Barkley told me about the will I cried for days, because I couldn't understand why my own mama would do such a thing to me.

Now I understand. Mama was trying to give me the kind of happiness she had with Daddy. All those years when I listened to her talk about him as she did, he was like the prince in a fairy tale: handsome, kind and loving. I dated boys in high school, but never once did I find one that was even remotely like that. They were nice guys but ordinary. Up until I met Jack, I figured God only created one man as wonderful as my daddy.

Jack treats me the way I imagine Daddy treated Mama. He shows how much he loves me in a zillion different ways. Not just with words and kisses but with all the other things he does, like going out of his way to walk me home. Every evening he's waiting for me when I get out of work. One night it was pouring rain and I figured he'd surely not come, but I was wrong. He was standing in the doorway of the building with a big black umbrella.

Lord how I wish Mama was here to meet Jack. She'd love him; I know she would. I pray she's looking down on me and can see how happy I am. Knowing Mama, I'm certain that my being happy would make her happy.

AT THE ALGONQUIN

O n the third Saturday of October, Christine took the blue
silk dress from the back of the closet and pulled it over
her head. She had a feeling tonight was going to be the
night she'd been waiting for. Earlier in the week Jack had dropped
subtle hints about a surprise and suggested she wear something
special.

When the buzzer rang at seven o'clock, she was ready. She
hurried down the stairs and slid into his arms as had become their
custom.

"Now are you ready to tell me where we're going?" she asked.

He touched his finger to her nose, trailed it down to her lips,
then leaned in and kissed her.

"Not yet," he said playfully.

They walked to the car. He opened the door for her, waited
until she sat then circled around and climbed in on the driver's
side. The drive was short, and when he parked across from the
Algonquin Hotel her eyes lit up.

"This is it?"

He nodded. "Do you like my choice?"

"Love it," she said.

BETTE LEE CROSBY

The maître d' led them to a table that sat slightly apart from the others. It was nestled in a vine-covered arch with candles lighting the table.

"Beautiful," she murmured.

He gave a smile of satisfaction and tightened his grip on her waist. As soon as they were seated he gave the waiter a nod, and a bottle of champagne was delivered to the table. Once the glasses were filled, they touched them one to another and Jack said, "To us."

She smiled and lifted the glass to her lips.

They talked about the way they'd come together: the luck of him being on duty the afternoon of the strike, the silliness of her handing over all those eggs, the scent of lavender shampoo he'd caught as she'd climbed into the patrol car. He leaned his cheek on his fist and fixed his eyes on hers.

"Before we got back to the stationhouse, I knew I wanted to see you again."

A faint smile played at the corner of her mouth. "You didn't need to arrest me; you could have just asked for a date."

"I was buying time to plead my case," he said with a gentle laugh. "I thought there was a chance you might say no."

"I wouldn't have," she replied and lifted the glass to her lips.

They moved from talk of things familiar to other things, things they had yet to learn about one another. She spoke of a carousel ride she remembered from her childhood; he told a story of his grandfather. As they spoke, the champagne bubbles filled her head with thoughts of a thousand wonderful possibilities.

At eight o'clock the band began to play. Jack took Christine's hand and led her onto the floor. She slid easily into his arms, and they moved to the music. When she felt the heat of his hand against her back, she lowered her head onto his chest and sighed. For a brief moment she closed her eyes and saw the youthful figures of her mama and daddy, as happy and as much in love as she and Jack were at this moment.

When they returned to the table, dinner was served without ordering. It was as if everything was planned, sprinkled with magic and offered up for her pleasure. The waiter lifted the silver dome covering the plate and beneath it was roasted chicken, exactly what she would have selected if given the choice.

"How did you know?" she asked.

Jack smiled. "How could I not know?"

Over the months they'd dated, he'd listened to her every word. Her dreams had become his dreams. He was in love with her. Not a little in love, but hopelessly in love. He nervously slid his hand into his jacket to check the small box was still there. It was.

Once they'd finished eating, the waiter reappeared. He refilled their glasses, gave Jack a sly nod and then carried away their plates. When they were once again alone, Jack stretched his arm across the table and took her hand in his.

With his eyes looking deep into hers, he said, "I am crazy in love with you, Christine, so much so that I can't stand the thought of being apart. When we're together I want the evening to never end, and when I'm not with you I think of you every minute of the day. I want your face to be the last thing I see at night and the first thing I see in the morning..."

He fumbled in his pocket, pulled out the small box and thumbed it open.

"Say you'll marry me, and I'll spend the rest of my life making you happy."

He held out the box and offered it to her.

Christine looked at the sparkling diamond ring and tears welled in her eyes.

"Yes," she said softly. "A thousand times yes. Nothing would make me happier than being your wife."

He stood, came around the table, lifted her from the chair into his arms and kissed her as she had never been kissed before. As if on cue, the band began playing *For Sentimental Reasons,* and he slid the ring on her finger.

They stayed and danced until the last note of the last song had fallen away. When they left, Jack drove Christine home and they lingered in the vestibule for nearly an hour.

"I want you to meet Granddaddy," she said. "He'll probably give you the third degree, but it's only because he loves me. Once he sees how happy I am, I know he'll be happy for me."

"I want you to meet my parents also," Jack replied, and then he kissed her for what could have been the thousandth time that evening.

"Why don't we do what we did tonight?" he suggested. "Invite all three of them to a celebration dinner at the Algonquin Hotel."

"Perfect," she said.

And so it was that they began to plan for just such an event.

THE FOLLOWING WEEK CHRISTINE CALLED Emory and gave him the news. For a moment there was only silence on the other end of the telephone.

"Granddaddy?"

He gave a labored sigh then asked, "Aren't you kind of young to be thinking of marriage?"

"Mama was younger than me when she married Daddy."

"Times were different then, and Franklin was a very responsible man."

"Jack's responsible. Good grief, he's a policeman. You can't get any more responsible than that."

Emory drew in a sharp breath. "A policeman?"

"What's wrong with being a policeman?"

"It's dangerous. With a job like that, a man can get himself killed easy as not."

"Daddy had a safe job, and look what happened to him."

"I hope you're not comparing this Jack Mahoney to your daddy."

"Yes, I am. Judging from the stories Mama told me, Jack is a lot like Daddy."

Emory gave a grunt of displeasure. "Your daddy was a businessman, not a policeman. He was a respectful man, someone to be proud of."

"Jack is respectful and someone to be proud of also. When you meet him you'll see, Granddaddy."

"He's not all that respectful," Emory replied, "or he'd have spoken with me before asking you to marry him."

"Granddaddy! You're in Wyattsville, and he's here in Richmond. It's not right around the corner you know."

"It's not at the far end of the earth either," Emory said.

No matter what Christine said Emory saw it from a different angle, but in the end he agreed to come for the family dinner party.

"My apartment only has one bed, so we're going to reserve a room for you at the hotel," Christine said.

"There's no need," Emory replied. "I'll come home afterwards."

"It's not safe for you to drive so far at night. Anyway, Jack insisted, and he's paying for the room."

Insisted? Such a word felt overbearing to Emory.

"I'll pay for my own room," he said begrudgingly.

WHEN EMORY HUNG UP THE telephone, he paced back and forth

across the living room. All along he'd thought Christine would spend a year or two in Richmond, have her fun, then return to Wyattsville. He expected she'd marry one of the local fellows and, like her mama, live somewhere within walking distance.

This Richmond fellow changed everything.

He was working himself into a state of anger when he remembered Rose's words.

"Don't be so judgmental," she'd said when he'd voiced the exact same complaints about Franklin.

He'd listened to her warning, and as it turned out Franklin was more than a good husband. He'd been a *great* husband. He'd been a friend, somebody Emory could respect. An equal.

Emory didn't have the same high hopes for this Jack Mahoney, but he'd wait and give the lad a chance to prove himself.

THE DINNER PARTY

On the Saturday of the dinner party, Emory was up before dawn. He pulled the dark suit he used to wear for work from the back of the closet and packed it into a bag along with a crisp white shirt and red tie. His car was already gassed up and ready to go. He took one last look in the mirror, fingered the edge of his beard then walked out and closed the door behind him.

The drive to Richmond was a good four hours, more if there was traffic. Emory drove slowly with thoughts of Jack Mahoney needling him. He'd told himself not to be judgmental, but saying it was considerably easier than doing it.

As far as he was concerned, Mahoney already had a number of strikes against him. Christine was too young. The boy hadn't sought his permission before proposing marriage. It was insulting to assume he couldn't pay for his own hotel room.

In comparing thoughts of Jack Mahoney to his memories of Franklin, the lad fell short. Way short. Being a policeman was not the same as being a stockbroker. A policeman could end up dead, and then what? Like Laura, Christine would be left a widow. She'd face a life of loneliness just as her mama did. Didn't his granddaughter deserve better?

175

Emory arrived at the Algonquin Hotel a few minutes before two, parked his car in the small lot behind the building and walked in carrying one small suitcase. At the registration desk, the girl smiled and handed him the note Christine had left. He recognized the handwriting but didn't open the envelope until he got to his room.

"Call me when you get in," she'd written, "and I'll hurry on over so we can spend some time visiting before dinner."

He lifted the telephone and gave the operator Christine's number. She answered on the first ring.

"Are you here, Granddaddy?" she asked.

Her voice had the sound of happiness woven through it. Emory found that in itself a bit grating. It was as if she was moving ahead without waiting for his approval.

"I'm here," he replied sullenly.

"I'll be there in fifteen minutes," she said and hung up the receiver.

WHEN CHRISTINE ARRIVED AT THE hotel she looked around the lobby, half-expecting Emory to be downstairs waiting for her. Not seeing him, she went to his room, rapped on the door and called, "Granddaddy, are you there?"

"Coming," he called back.

The minute he opened the door, she threw her arms around his neck and kissed his cheek.

"I've missed you so much," she said.

Still burdened by the thoughts he'd had on the drive over, he tugged himself free and turned back into the room.

"I guess you didn't miss me that much, or you'd have come for a visit."

She followed at his heels. "I've been busy with my new job."

"Is it the job or this Mahoney fellow that keeps you so busy?"

Christine gave a sigh of exasperation. "Oh, Granddaddy, let's not argue at a time like this. We've got so much to be happy about..."

She told of what a wonderful evening it was going to be, but by then Emory's thoughts had drifted off. In his mind there was little to be happy about. Christine was the last of his family, and now he was losing her just as he'd lost Laura, Rose and Franklin. How could a man left with nothing be happy?

A sense of melancholy settled over him like a black cloak, but Christine failed to notice. She took his arm, guided him out of the room and down through the elegantly decorated lobby.

"We'll take a walk together," she said and pushed through the glass doors leading to the street.

As they walked, she pointed out one thing after another.

"Here's the Brown Bean. It's where Jack and I had our first sort-of date. It was only a coffee break, but even then I knew. And that tall building is the Southern Atlantic Telephone Company where I work. Jack sits on that bench across the street and waits for me every night."

Emory gave a nod to one thing and another but said nothing. He found the mere mention of Jack Mahoney grating on his nerves.

As they passed the Federated Bank building, Christine looked up at the big clock.

"Oh, my goodness," she said. "It's almost six. We need to get going; Jack will be waiting for us."

Emory slowed his steps and stopped to look in three different shop windows as they headed back.

JACK WAS SITTING IN THE lobby when they arrived. He spotted Christine at a distance, then stood and walked toward them. As he neared Emory, he broke into a wide smile.

"You must be Christine's granddaddy."

He stuck out his arm, grabbed Emory's hand and pumped it vigorously.

"It's a pleasure, Mister Hawthorne," he said. "A true pleasure."

"Same," Emory replied without changing his sour expression.

Jack had been forewarned that Emory could be "a bit difficult," as Christine had so tactfully phrased it, but he was determined. He asked if Emory had a pleasant trip, if the room was to his liking and if he had a preference for beef or chicken.

"Both are good here," Jack said. "I personally prefer the Beef Wellington. It's the best you'll ever taste."

"Think I'll stay with chicken," Emory replied.

This was proving more difficult than Jack thought. He nervously eyed his watch then glanced toward the front entrance.

Emory gave a scornful look. "Have you got someplace else to be?"

"No," Jack said, "not at all. I'm just keeping an eye out for my parents."

Moments later his mama came through the door.

"Ah, here they are now."

Jack hurried over to greet them. As he brushed a kiss across his mama's cheek, he whispered a word of warning.

"Please be patient with Mister Hawthorne. I don't think he's too happy about Christine and me getting engaged."

Irene Mahoney laughed. "Nonsense. Why would he not—"

Having never met Christine or her granddaddy before, Irene was on top of them before she realized it.

"Mom, Dad," Jack said, "this is Emory Hawthorne, Christine's granddaddy." He then turned to Emory. "Mister Hawthorne, my parents, Irene and Frank Mahoney."

Irene flashed a smile wider than Jack's.

"A pleasure," Frank said.

"Same," Emory repeated, not changing his stone-faced expression.

Jack felt a fluttering sensation in his stomach and reached into his pocket for the packet of antacids he carried.

"Why don't we go in to dinner?" he suggested.

Walking behind everyone else, he popped a tablet into his mouth.

AS THEY GATHERED AT THE table, Christine leaned over and whispered in Emory's ear.

"Granddaddy, be nice."

"You don't have to tell me that," Emory replied.

His words were louder than they should have been, and Christine gave an apologetic shrug. Trying to move past the awkwardness of the moment, she began talking about an early spring wedding.

"We're thinking March or maybe April," she said. "Granddaddy, is that okay with you?"

"It's a little late to be asking my opinion," he answered.

"Granddaddy!" Christine's voice had a disapproving chord threaded through it. "I'm asking because I want you to give me away."

"Give you away? Why would I—"

Emory stopped mid-sentence and thought back on when Franklin had come to him and asked for Laura's hand in marriage. That was how it was supposed to be done. With Franklin it was man to man. They'd spoken honestly, and he'd been upfront about it. There was no slipping behind his back and deciding to get married before permission had been granted.

"Spring's fine," Emory said.

By then he'd decided he wasn't all that hungry and pushed his plate back.

ONCE THE DINNER WAS OVER and everyone stood to leave, Jack breathed a sigh of relief. It hadn't been amicable but at least there had been no harsh words, no flaring tempers, and for now that was enough. He said goodbye to his parents as Christine walked her granddaddy back to the elevator.

"For my sake, please try to be nice to Jack," she said as she hugged Emory. "Give him a chance. I'm sure you'll love him when you get to know him."

"We'll see," he said doubtfully.

"Promise me you'll try," she urged. "Jack and I will be back at nine tomorrow morning, and we'll all go to church together. Afterward we can go to the Brown Bean. They have the best pancakes ever."

Emory stepped into the elevator, and as the doors slid closed Christine gave him one last smile and mouthed the word, "Please."

EMORY

There's an unfairness to life that, for the love of me, I simply can't understand. Is it wrong for a man to want to protect his family?

I'd like to be happy for Christine, but I've got a truckload of worries on my mind. Granted, some of them are selfish in that I was hoping she'd come back to Wyattsville and live close by. But beyond that, I'm concerned about her future.

I can see she looks at this Jack the same way Laura looked at Franklin, which is good and not good. The lad is a policeman for God's sake. You'd be hard-pressed to find a job more dangerous than that.

I watched Laura spend the best years of her life mourning Franklin's death; I don't want to see Christine go through the same thing. Besides, she's still so young. It would seem she ought to experience a bit more life before she settles down and starts having babies.

I know it should seem that way, but when a young woman is in love she's blind to reality and deaf to reasoning.

Times like this I miss Rose something fierce. She had the kind of wisdom I seem to be lacking. She knew how to glide over the rough spots of life and settle into the comfortable places. If I could go back to those days when we'd sit in the parlor and talk, I'd do it in a heartbeat.

181

Unfortunately, life is what it is. We don't get to relive the part we enjoyed most.

In the letter Laura left, she said Christine and I should both find a life of our own. Maybe the reason I'm so angry about Christine marrying Jack is that she's found that life, and I haven't.

It's a hard thing to do, but I'm going to have to put my pride and selfishness aside and be happy for Christine. It's either that or lose her for good, and that's not something I'm willing to do.

The Elks Club

The next morning when Christine and Jack arrived at the hotel, Emory was waiting in the lobby.

"Good morning, Granddaddy," she said and kissed his cheek.

Given Emory's mood of the night before, Jack was uncertain what to do. He settled for a manly half-hug, which was somewhere between a handshake and a pat on the back.

"Good to see you again, Mister Hawthorne," he said.

His tongue stumbled over the "Mister Hawthorne" part, but he was hesitant to try any anything more familiar.

"Morning," Emory replied. While he didn't look particularly happy, the crackle of tension that had been there the previous night was gone.

There was little conversation as they walked to church and then later from there to the Brown Bean. They settled into a booth with Jack and Christine on one side of the table and Emory on the other.

Sitting as they were facing Emory, Christine and Jack made a valiant attempt at small talk. They avoided anything controversial or subject to argument. He asked about the time it took to drive from Wyattsville, and she chatted about her job. After the orders were placed and coffee served Emory interrupted them, stating he had something to say.

"As you both know, I think Christine is too young to be getting married," he said, "but I thought the same when Franklin asked me for Laura's hand. I figured a girl her age couldn't possibly know what love is, but I was wrong. The way Laura and Franklin felt about each other was something special."

He let his eyes meet Christine's. "It was the kind of love your grandma and I had."

He hesitated a moment, blinked back the tears dampening his lashes then looked at both of them.

"Seeing you two together last night, I was reminded of Laura and Franklin. Back then Rose was there to save me from a foolish decision, and I'd like to think maybe some of her wisdom has rubbed off."

"Granddaddy, are you saying—"

"Jack, if you can swear to me that you love Christine as much as I do," Emory cut in, his voice a bit gruff, "you'll have my blessing."

"Oh, I do, sir," Jack said. "I absolutely do!"

Christine reached across the table, took Emory's hand in hers then bent and dropped a kiss into his palm.

"Thank you, Granddaddy," she said.

"Don't thank me," he grumbled. "Thank your mama and grandma."

ON THE DRIVE HOME, EMORY began thinking about his own life. Christine wasn't coming back. She wasn't going to live down the street or around the corner. She was going to live in Richmond.

She and Jack both worked there; it was the sensible thing to do. Painful for him but sensible for them.

He thought about his lonely existence. At times the house seemed so quiet he could hear himself think. At night when he sat in the chair and leafed through the newspaper, there was no one to read to, no one to comment on an interesting article or challenge his biased opinion.

Back when he worked all day and came home weary he welcomed the relaxation of a quiet evening, but not now. Not when the daylight hours led to long nights of boredom. He thought about the countless times he had gone for nearly a week without speaking to anyone, the radio being the only other voice he heard.

One thought led to another, and before long he remembered Laura's letter and her words. "Time for you to have a life of your own." But after so many years of living a life built around his family, how was he to start one for himself?

As if he were flipping back the pages of a calendar, Emory ran through the years of his life. He tried to remember when he was last happy and what made him so. Of course there was Laura. She'd stepped into her mama's shoes and would just as willingly listen as he read from the newspaper or stated his opinion on one thing or another.

He'd also gotten a certain amount of pleasure from doing the odd jobs that needed doing. He pictured himself painting the bedroom and putting a new door on the cellar, but once he thought it through he crossed those jobs off his list. There was no pleasure in doing something when no one was there to notice and say, "Well done."

Then there had been the years when Laura worked at the steel factory and he'd kept a close eye on Christine's comings and goings, making sure the boys she dated were not lotharios who would tarnish her reputation. Those had been good years, not only because of watching over Christine but also the victory gardens he tended. Every housewife on the block looked to him to stock their refrigerators with tomatoes, lettuce, cucumbers and…

Emory stopped there. He remembered how Harriett Winthrop used to invite him in for a cup of coffee, and they'd sit and talk for an hour. And the young wife in the grey house — Iris something or another — she'd brought lemonade to the garden and stayed, handing him the tools as he called for them.

Gardening was something that didn't have to end when the war did. People still enjoyed those vegetables, but now they plunked down good money to buy them at Safeway or the farm stand out on Route 9. Was there a woman in the world who wouldn't welcome a lovely garden in her backyard? He thought not.

Emory snapped on the car radio and twisted the dial. When he came to a station playing *Across the Alley from the Alamo*, he left it there and started singing along.

THE DAY AFTER HE RETURNED from Richmond, Emory went up and down the street asking whether people would be interested in having him plant a vegetable garden in their backyard.

"Free of charge," he said.

The widow in the corner house claimed she was thinking of selling the place and didn't want the backyard torn up. Two doors down, a mother of twins who were at that crawly stage said once the boys were four or five she might entertain such an idea, but for now her hands were full.

"You wouldn't have to do a thing," Emory replied, but by then one of the twins started squalling and she had to go see what was wrong.

Iris had moved away and a family called Johansson had moved in. Otto answered the door and when Emory explained what he wanted to do, Otto said he doubted that Hilda would go for such a thing. Instead he invited Emory in for a beer. Figuring he'd done enough for one day, Emory accepted.

Once they got to talking Emory discovered that Otto, like himself, was retired.

"You know that haberdashery on the far end of Broad?" Otto said. "Well, I used to own it. Last year my son-in-law bought me out."

"No kidding."

"God's honest truth." Otto gulped down a swig of beer and set the bottle back on the counter. "Retail's tough. Long hours, and you're on your feet all day."

"So what do you do now?" Emory asked.

"Nothing. I'm retired."

"Don't you get bored just sitting around all day?"

Otto shook his head. "If I got nothing else to do, I go play cards or shoot pool with the guys at the club. Then I stay for dinner."

"What about Hilda? Doesn't she mind?"

"She's only here on Thursday, so my going to the club is no skin off her nose."

"You've got a wife who's only home on Thursday?"

Otto twitched his brow and gave Emory a strange look.

"Marjorie's been dead some twenty-two years," he said. "Hilda's the woman my son-in-law sends over to clean up a bit and stick a casserole in the oven."

He leaned in and whispered as if he were telling a secret. "Hilda's cooking is terrible, which is why I eat at the club more often than not. Sixty cents for the daily special, and it's way better than Hilda's cooking."

Emory laughed. "Sounds like you've got it made."

"Listen, I worked long and hard to get here, so whatever fun I get I've got coming."

He finished his beer and stood. "I'm gonna have another; how about you?"

Emory grinned. "Yeah, think I'll join you."

When they finished the second beer, Otto said he was off to the club for dinner and asked if Emory would like to join him. That evening the club special was short ribs and Emory declared it so good he asked for seconds, which were free. It was the first of many nights that he and Otto would spend at the Elks Club.

The Following Months

In the months that came, Christine and Jack drove to Wyattsville several times to spend the weekend visiting Emory. While Christine was off in the kitchen fixing dinner, Jack sat in the parlor with Emory listening to stories of things that once were. Emory told how during the war Laura worked as a stamper at the steel mill and he'd planted victory gardens for every woman on the block.

"It might not seem like it, but those were good times," he said. "Not for everybody because there were a lot of gold stars hanging in the windows."

"Was that how Christine's daddy died?" Jack asked.

Emory shook his head in the most sorrowful way imaginable. He leaned forward with his shoulders hunched and his knobby hands dropped down between his knees. Then he began to tell the story of Franklin's death.

"Those were tough years. A lot of people lost money; some lost everything. But what happened wasn't Franklin's fault. He told people to take their money out of the market while they still could. Unfortunately, most of them didn't listen. The way things were going you could almost see trouble coming."

Jack leaned closer and asked, "How was Franklin involved?"

"He was a stockbroker," Emory replied. "One of the best. When the market dipped the first time and then bounced back, he told George Feldman to get out. George refused. Instead he put more money in, thinking he'd make a killing."

"I take it he didn't," Jack said.

"Right. The company went belly up, and he lost everything. A week later Franklin was working late, and Feldman found him in the office. He stood there and fired six shots into Franklin's chest."

Jack's jaw dropped open. "Dear God."

Deep crevices lined Emory's face, and he took on a look older than his years.

"I was the one who found Franklin. That night I swore I'd find the killer and make him pay, but I never did. The police didn't either."

"But didn't they know it was this George Feldman?"

"They knew, but by then the man had left town. Vanished off the face of the earth. Sergeant Carroll followed up every lead, but nothing ever came of it. After three or four years, they stopped looking."

"It would seem there was some way—"

"You might think," Emory said. "But the country was in the middle of a depression, and people were struggling to put food on the table. Following up on a murder that happened years earlier wasn't all that important."

Eventually they moved on to other topics of conversation but the thought of such an injustice got stuck in Jack's head, and he continued to think about it.

From time to time he would ask questions, and months later Emory pulled the briefcase from beneath his bed to show the newspaper clippings that told of the story. A glassy-eyed George Feldman was featured on the front page of the *Wyattsville Register*.

OVER THE MONTHS, EMORY CAME to feel about Jack as he did

Franklin. He never was happy with the thought of his being a policeman but consoled himself with the knowledge that unlike Franklin, at least Jack had a gun to protect himself. Although Emory was not an avid churchgoer he believed in the power of prayer, and every morning he asked that both Jack and Christine be kept from harm.

"Our family's already seen enough tragedy," he'd say, then close with an amen.

WHEN CHRISTINE AND JACK SAID they'd selected April eleventh as the date for their wedding, Emory insisted on paying for the reception.

"Oh, Granddaddy," Christine said, "that's way too much money for you to be spending."

"Nonsense," he huffed. "At my age I've got little else to spend it on, and you and Jack are the only family I have."

By then Emory had joined the Wyattsville Elks Club, and the Exalted Ruler, who'd taken a liking to him, was more than happy to make arrangements for the affair to be held in the Richmond clubhouse. The Elks Club in Richmond was nearly three times the size of the one in Wyattsville, so Emory told them to invite as many friends as they wanted.

"This is my treat," he said and insisted on paying for everything, even Christine's dress.

"I can't let you do that, Granddaddy. I'm working and I can afford to buy—"

Emory pinched his brows together and squared his jaw. "Would you deny an old man the pleasure of doing for his family?"

Seeing the look of determination stretched across his face, Christine laughed.

"No, sir," she said. "I wouldn't dream of doing that."

THE MONTH OF MARCH FLEW by as preparations were made. Angie, now Christine's closest friend, helped her shop for a wedding gown. Once a favorite was picked, she telephoned Emory and asked him to come to Richmond to put his stamp of approval on the selection.

That Saturday they went to the bridal shop together. She stepped into the dressing room, and when she reappeared wearing a white satin dress fitted at the top with a billowing skirt, long white gloves and a small beaded crown, Emory eyed her with a look of adoration.

"Beautiful," he said and brushed away a tear with the back of his hand.

Afterward they went back to her apartment, and Jack joined them.

"You're a lucky man," Emory told him.

Jack wrapped an arm around Christine's waist and planted a kiss on her cheek.

"Don't I know it," he said and smiled.

That evening the three of them squeezed around the tiny kitchen table to eat the spaghetti and meatballs Christine made.

"I guess this is kind of crowded," she said apologetically.

Emory laughed. "It's what your mama would have called intimate."

He launched into telling of the cold water flat he and Rose lived in.

"Now that apartment was small. It had one little bedroom, and Laura slept in the alcove on a built-in bed." He gave a chuckle of fond remembrance. "It wasn't even a real bed, just a bunch of boards I'd hammered together."

That night Christine insisted he stay over, and Emory did.

He slept on the sofa. As he lay there, he thought back on how far the family had come since the days of living in that apartment. He could still remember the day they'd received the letter saying his daddy had left him all that money. What a difference it had made in their lives. Emory had some money in the bank, but given the increased price of things it was nowhere near as much as his daddy had. He lay there wishing he could do for Christine what his daddy had done for him.

That's when he came up with the plan.

THE WEDDING

April eleventh dawned with a clear blue sky and the fragrance of jasmine floating on the air. Christine knew the moment she opened her eyes it was going to be a glorious day. She was just setting the coffee on to brew when the telephone rang.

"Are you excited?" Angie said.

"Beyond belief," Christine answered. "Poor Granddaddy slept on the sofa again last night, so I hope he's not too cramped to walk me down the aisle."

"I heard that," Emory called out jokingly.

Christine laughed. "I've gotta go fix breakfast. See you at the church."

"In the vestry, four o'clock, right?"

"Right," Christine echoed. "Should I call and remind the other girls?"

"I'll do it," Angie replied and hung up.

IT HAD BEEN MONTHS IN the planning, but now every last detail had been taken care of. The flowers would be delivered to the church, and the Elks Club had set out tables and chairs to accommodate 200 guests. On each table there was a small arrangement of roses and baby's breath.

Emory purchased a new suit and tie for the event even though he doubted he'd have occasion to wear it again. And the previous afternoon before arriving at Christine's, he'd stopped by the club to check on the set-up. Everything was ready; the only thing left to do was to enjoy the party.

AT PRECISELY FIVE O'CLOCK, THE organist pumped down on the pedals and began the prelude. By then most of the guests were seated. Jack's parents beamed from the front row with an empty seat beside them awaiting Emory's arrival. Behind them was a row of guests from the Wyattsville Elks Club: Otto, two middle-aged bachelors and the Exalted Ruler with his wife.

All the other seats were taken, filled by the girls from the telephone company, off-duty policemen, friends, neighbors and even a distant cousin of Jack's who'd come all the way from Kentucky. Jack and Walter Preston, a fellow officer he'd chosen as his best man, walked down the aisle, stepped to the side and waited. Other than the sound of the organ, the church was silent.

Jack shifted nervously, listening for the sound that had become familiar. The few minutes he waited seemed like hours. Then he heard it: the click of her high heels against the marble floor. After so many nights of sitting on the bench and waiting for her to come from the telephone company building, he knew the sound of her step. He craned his neck and looked toward the foyer, and at that moment the organist broke into *Here Comes the Bride*.

Everyone stood and turned to look toward the foyer. Angie

was first down the aisle. She wore a pink princess cut dress that hung long and swished across the floor with each step she took. When she reached the end of the aisle, Angie stepped to the right and stood beside Walter.

Christine appeared in the entranceway standing arm in arm with her granddaddy. Seconds before they started down the aisle, Emory leaned over and whispered in her ear.

"You look as beautiful as your mama did," he said.

Christine turned to him and touched her hand to his face.

"Thank you, Granddaddy," she replied.

They walked as they had rehearsed, with slow measured steps. At the end of the aisle, Emory lifted the veil from her face, kissed her cheek and then turned to Jack.

"I am giving you my greatest treasure," he said. "See that you care for her as I would."

"You can trust that I will," Jack said solemnly.

He stepped in beside Christine and took her hand in his as Emory moved back to sit alongside Jack's parents.

"We are gathered here today..." Pastor Reed began. He continued and read from Corinthians, reminding them that love is patient and kind. That it keeps no record of wrongs and is not easily angered.

"In the end," he said, "we are left with three things: faith, hope and love. And the greatest of these is love."

He asked if Christine would take Jack Mahoney to be her lawfully wedded husband.

She smiled and answered, "I do."

He turned and asked Jack if he would forever love, honor and cherish Christine, but it seemed almost an unnecessary question. The look on Jack's face foretold the answer.

Once they were pronounced husband and wife, Jack took Christine in his arms and kissed her. The organ, which had remained silent throughout the ceremony, came to life with a rousing rendition of *The Wedding March*, and they started back down the aisle.

THE RECEPTION TURNED OUT TO be a gala such as the Elks Club had never before seen. When a spring breeze lifted the sound of the music into the air and carried it through the streets of Richmond, folks sitting on their front porches began tapping their feet and humming along. The happiness of that day bubbled over. Although it was not something that anyone could have predicted, before the year was out three of the young policemen were engaged to the telephone company girls they met that evening.

The band was hired to play for three hours but stayed until the last guest wandered off, which was sometime close to midnight, and they didn't charge a dime extra. At the end of the evening, no one could say exactly when Jack and Christine left the party except Emory. A few minutes before ten they'd taken him aside and thanked him.

"It was the most wonderful wedding ever," Christine said and threw her arms around his neck. "And you're the best granddaddy in all the world!"

Jack said pretty much the same thing; then he hugged Emory to his chest.

As Emory stood there watching them slip away, he couldn't help but think how much Jack Mahoney reminded him of Franklin.

It's odd I didn't see that right off, he thought.

Feeling good about life, he wiped away the smudge of lipstick she'd left on his cheek then returned to the reception. They say before the night was over Emory Hawthorne danced with every young woman at the party, and no one young or old had a better time than he did.

NEW BEGINNING

Jack and Christine spent the first night of their honeymoon at the Algonquin Hotel. Somehow it seemed only fitting.

Jack was the one who'd suggested it, and, remembering that her mama and daddy had also began their married life here, Christine was thrilled with the idea. When they arrived in the bridal suite, there was a bottle of chilled champagne waiting for them. Jack popped the cork and filled both glasses. He handed one to Christine, then touched his glass to hers.

"A toast," he said. "To our forever."

At the reception it had been a whirlwind of conversations with family and old and new friends, drifting dreamily across the floor to the soft strains of *There's a Tree in the Meadow* and then kicking up their heels to the lindy hop. Now it was a quiet time; a time for just the two of them.

Jack took her in his arms and kissed her mouth, first tenderly then hungrily.

"I love you more than you could possibly know," he whispered as he slowly undid each button along the back of her gown.

"I love you just as much," she replied as she gave herself to him.

They made love, not frantically but slowly and sweetly, each touch meaningful and in the right place at the right time. He breathed in the scent of gardenia on her skin, and she ran her hands across the sinewy muscles of his back. Afterward they fell back against the pile of pillows, their bodies spent but their souls united.

The next morning they drove to New York City and spent three nights at the Essex House in a room overlooking Central Park. Each morning they slept late then called downstairs to have coffee and pastries sent to their room.

New York was a city of a million pleasures. Christine said she had always wanted to see Radio City Music Hall so they went to see *A Date with Judy* and sat in the third balcony, which was so high it made her feel almost dizzy. When they left the theatre she all but danced along the sidewalk singing *It's a Most Unusual Day*.

The days flew by as they strolled Fifth Avenue, browsing the shop windows of stores such as Saks and Tiffany. They did all the things tourists usually do, including a visit to the top of the Empire State Building and a lunch of hot dogs from the mustached man with an umbrella cart.

On the last evening they went dancing at the Starlight Ballroom, and Christine wore the brand new silk dress she'd splurged on at Lord and Taylor. It was the blue of her eyes and had a stylish cinched waist with a full skirt. After she'd slipped it over her head and announced she was ready to go, Jack gave a low wolf whistle.

"You look like a movie star," he said.

"I feel like one in this dress," she replied then twirled around like a ballerina.

He caught her in his arms and kissed her.

If Christine had to pick the one night of her life that was perfect beyond her wildest dreams, it would be that night. They drank champagne, had dinner and danced atop the Waldorf

Astoria beneath a sky filled with stars. On that last night as they were lying in the bed, giddy with the romance of the evening and exhausted from all they'd done, Christine's thoughts flickered back to the years she'd spent with her mama. She moved closer and snuggled deeper into his arms.

"Promise me one thing," she said.

"Anything," Jack replied.

"Promise me you will never leave me to face life alone."

They'd spoken of this before. It was the one thing she feared. For a policeman danger was a constant. It hid in the shadows like an ominous stranger. Always waiting. Always threatening.

Jack knew what she wanted to hear and was painfully aware such a promise was not his to give. He gave a wistful sigh and tried to offer an alternative that would put her heart at ease.

"Tomorrow is a guarantee only God can give," he said. "But this I can promise: I will always be with you in this life and beyond."

A shiver ran up Christine's spine. It was almost the same thing her daddy had told her mama.

"Oh, Jack," she said and buried her face against his chest.

Jack put his hand to the back of her head and held her close.

"Don't waste today worrying about tomorrow," he said. "I'm working to make detective, and that job is a lot less dangerous than being a beat cop."

That was the one and only time they talked about the danger of his job, but not a day went by that Christine didn't think of it and remember the tragedy of her daddy's death.

WHEN EMORY RETURNED HOME FROM the wedding, he knew what he wanted to do. The idea had been bouncing around in his head for the past two months, but he was unsettled on how he would handle his end of it. Once he'd seen Seth Porter's apartment, everything became clear as day.

Emory met Seth a month or so after he joined the Elks Club. Seth was one of the regulars who came to play cards and have dinner. Like Emory, he was a widower. Before long the welcoming pinochle games evolved into a good-natured friendship.

On a night when the club served pork roast as the daily special, Emory went back for a second helping. As he scooped the last forkful into his mouth, he said, "You're never going to find a meal better than this."

"Not true," Seth replied. "Last week I had a corned beef and cabbage dinner that was way better than this pork."

Emory eyed him suspiciously. It was a known fact that most of the men in their pinochle group could barely boil water, never mind cooking a dish like corned beef and cabbage.

"Who you trying to kid?" Emory said. "The club hasn't had corned beef since Saint Patty's Day."

"I didn't have it here," Seth replied smugly.

"You asking me to believe you cooked up a pot of corned beef yourself?"

Seth shook his head. "I'm not asking you to believe anything of the sort. I didn't cook it; Clara did. She made it special for me."

"I thought you said you weren't married."

"I'm not."

Emory remembered his earlier experience with Otto. "I get it, Clara's your cleaning lady, right?"

Seth chuckled. "Clara'd have a fit if she heard you call her that. She's a neighbor and a friend."

Emory thought about the nights when he was home alone. He had to open up a can of beef stew or spaghetti. No one brought him a homemade dinner.

With his brows still hooding his eyes, he asked, "So this Clara's husband, is he okay with her cooking dinner for you?"

Seth laughed. "Clara ain't married. There're only a handful of married folks in the building. They're mostly all widows or widowers like us. That's what makes it a good place to live. You don't feel like an outsider. Most everybody's in the same pickle you're in."

"It's not an old age home or something like that, is it?"

"Shoot, no," Seth said. "It's a nice apartment building. You got neighbors and friends. It's way better than living in a big house all alone."

The thought of that settled comfortably in Emory's head, and after a few minutes he asked, "What's it cost to buy a place like that?"

"You don't buy it," Seth replied. "You rent it by the month."

Once Emory showed an interest in the place, Seth said he was having the boys in for a game of cards on Tuesday night and asked if Emory wanted to join them.

"Poker, two cents a hand," he said.

"I can do two cents," Emory replied and took down the address.

TUESDAY NIGHT WAS THE FIRST time Emory ever visited the Wyattsville Arms, but he found the evening so pleasurable that he stayed until almost midnight. Then, figuring he might be too tired to drive home, he spent the night on Seth Porter's overstuffed sofa, which was considerably more comfortable than the tiny sofa in Christine's apartment.

CHRISTINE

I'd like to tell you I'm not going to worry about Jack, but I know I will. When you love someone as much as I love him, it's impossible not to worry.

Sometimes when I think about Mama and how she loved Daddy right up until the day she died, I have to wonder if she ever regretted marrying a man who got himself killed. I don't believe she did. She used to say six years of being loved by Daddy was more happiness than some people get in an entire lifetime. I'm a born worrier, but I'm determined not to let it spoil our life.

If it were up to me, we would have never taken that wonderful honeymoon. I would have kept the money in the bank to save for a house. Jack is the one who planned the whole thing. He said, We'll only have one honeymoon, so I want it to be memorable. And it certainly was.

I thought maybe once we got home and he moved into my tiny apartment he'd regret spending all that money in New York, but he doesn't. Not even when he stands upright in the loft and bonks his head. The ceiling up there is only a little over five feet. It's fine for me, but Jack's over six feet tall.

I suggested we find a bigger apartment with a real bedroom, but Jack *said as long as I'm working split shift he wants to live close by where it's convenient for me.*

The truth is that if we had to live in a closet, I'd still be happy about being married to Jack. I'm happier than I've ever been, and I'm trying to see the future one day at a time. Every day of happiness that passes is one day more than I had before.

I'm determined to keep thinking this way.

The Big Move

Once Emory discovered the group at the Wyattsville Arms, he went back time and time again. That summer there was a round of parties that ran for almost a week straight. After he'd slept on Seth Porter's sofa for three consecutive nights, Seth suggested he think about getting an apartment in the building.

"It ain't that I mind your company," Seth said, "but sleeping on a sofa's bad for a man's back."

"That's the God's honest truth," Emory replied as he twisted his torso trying to work a kink loose. "Do you know if they've got an apartment available?"

Seth shrugged. "Can't say. You've got to talk to Clara."

"She's the building manager?"

"No, but she knows most everything going on here. If there's an apartment available, she'll help you get it."

Seth explained that all of the apartments at Wyattsville Arms were reasonably priced and more often than not snapped up before the "Apartment For Rent" sign could be posted.

"You're gonna need Clara's help to get one," he said.

THAT AFTERNOON EMORY WALKED OVER to the florist, bought a bouquet of gladiolas, then returned to the building and rang Clara's doorbell.

"If you've got a few minutes, there's something I'd like to talk to you about," he said and handed her flowers.

As they sat there on Clara's sofa, Emory ran through the entire story of how the daddy he never knew left him money and how after almost thirty years of marriage he'd lost Rose.

"Now with Laura and Christine both gone, I'm living in a house that's way too big and too empty," he said. "So I'm thinking maybe it's time to pass along the blessings I've been given."

As he explained his plan, the look in Clara's eyes softened. She reached across and patted his knee.

"You're a good man, Emory," she said. "A real good man. We'd be glad to have you in the building."

The way Clara spoke you might think she owned the place, but technically she was a tenant like everyone else. The difference was that Clara had a way of making things happen, so it was never a wise move to cross her. Donald Dwyer, the building manager, knew this and such a thought irked him to no end.

AS SOON AS EMORY WAS out the door, Clara telephoned Donald.

"I have a friend looking for an apartment in the building," she said.

With a get-even tone of gleefulness he answered, "There's no vacancies."

"Not yet, but one might be coming up."

"No one has given notice," Donald replied sharply.

"Well, in the event someone does, mark down that Emory Hawthorne is to get the apartment, okay?"

"Okay," he answered begrudgingly. Judging by the confident tone of her voice, he had a feeling Clara knew exactly which apartment was going to become available.

LATER THAT AFTERNOON CLARA WRAPPED the tiny sweater she'd crocheted for Gloria Wilkinson's grandchild in gift paper and stopped by her apartment.

"This is for that new grandbaby you're expecting," she said and handed her the box.

Gloria was a weepy woman to begin with, and the thought of her daughter living alone had been tearing at her heart ever since she'd learned there was a baby on the way. The mere mention of the baby caused her eyes to well up.

"I don't know how the poor child is going to survive with a mama who works all the time," she said. "Eloise insists she's not going to quit modeling. Claims she worked too long and hard to get where she is and is not giving it up now."

Clara gave a pinched look of concern. "I can't imagine how the girl can keep working as a model with a newborn."

"I'll tell you how," Gloria replied testily. "She'll have a perfect stranger move in to care for the baby, that's how! Imagine, an irresponsible stranger caring for my only grandchild."

Clara gave a discouraged sounding sigh.

"I've just about made up my mind to take the job myself," Gloria huffed. "I'd be a lot more loving than a stranger. If it wasn't for having this apartment and all this furniture…"

"That's the only thing holding you back?"

Gloria nodded. "Eloise is so fussy about her house. She claims everything has to match and won't even consider letting me bring my own furniture."

She squeezed her forehead into a worried looking knot and gave a sigh. "I know my things aren't worth much, but after all these years I can't bear the thought of setting them out on the curb for the trash man."

Clara smiled. "What if I was to tell you I know of a good man who's in need of a furnished apartment?"

Gloria blinked back the tears threatening to overflow her eyes and said, "You know such a person?"

Clara leaned in and told her about Emory. The truth was he'd said nothing about the apartment needing to be furnished. He'd said only that he wanted an apartment, but as far as she was concerned it was a minor point. Certainly not a bone of contention. And it was an opportunity to give two people the happiness they each deserved.

By the time Clara got back to her apartment and called Emory with the good news, he'd already started whitewashing the fence.

"A house sells better when it's in tip-top shape," he said.

BEFORE THE MONTH WAS OUT, Emory had the house shined up like a new penny. Christine commented on it both times she and Jack came to visit. Emory acknowledged that the house was indeed looking good and grinned, but he didn't mention the "For Sale" sign waiting to be staked in the front yard.

THE WEEK BEFORE LABOR DAY, Emory set out the sign and placed an ad in the *Wyattsville Register*. That weekend five different families came to look at the house, and by Monday evening he had an offer for twice as much as he'd gotten for the Chester Street house.

Gloria Wilkinson was scheduled to move out the following week, so Emory hurried over to the Wyattsville Arms, met with Donald Dwyer and gave him a check for the deposit and first month's rent.

"I'll be moving in October first," he said.

In the weeks that followed, he filled boxes with the personal treasures that once belonged to Rose and afterward to Laura: the music box on Laura's dresser, the embroidered hand towels, the potholder Christine made at camp, photo albums and framed pictures, Franklin's ash tray. Each item was wrapped in tissue paper and carefully packed away. When the boxes were filled, he carried them over to the Wyattsville Arms and stacked them in the storage room. In time he would sort through everything and pull out the pictures and souvenirs he knew Christine would want to set on her mantle, but for now he'd keep them stored—at least until she and Jack had a place of their own.

EMORY

You might think I'm sad to be leaving the house, but I'm not. The truth is that it feels like a burden lifted off my back. It's one thing to keep memories in your head where you can pick and choose to hold on to the good ones and let go of the others, but it's quite another to be living in the middle of them. I've come to realize you can't move forward if you're stuck in the past.

In this house it's just me, alone with the ghosts of yesteryear. At the Wyattsville Arms it's different. I have friends, people like me who have time to sit and chat or play a few hands of cards. Such things might seem trivial to a young person, but to someone my age it's reason enough to wake up in the morning and look forward to the day.

Everything in life has its own time. When I was younger my family was my world; now everyone is gone or moved on so my friends have become my family. This doesn't mean that I love Christine less. Quite the contrary; it means that I love her enough to give her the freedom to live her own life. Looking back, I can see that's exactly what Laura intended when she wrote her will.

One advantage of growing older is that you learn to see with your heart rather than your eyes. When you're young your eyesight is sharp and focused. You look at the world and think, we'll need this, that or the other thing. You see the future and plan for having a family and a home where you can raise those babies.

I'm not saying that's wrong; it's as it should be. But when you get to be my age and there's nobody but yourself to look after, you start to realize how truly little you do need.

If I can spend the rest of my days knowing I have a place to sleep, food to eat and friends to share the day, I'll be a happy man. You can't ask more of life than that.

ALL GOOD THINGS

On October first Emory finalized the sale of the house, deposited a check for a little over $6000 into his bank account and then into moved into the Wyattsville Arms.

Claiming he'd help get things straightened up, Otto came along. With every last piece of Gloria Wilkinson's furniture still sitting in its rightful place, it turned out there was very little to straighten. Once Emory hung his clothes in the closet and plunked his underwear into the dresser drawer, he and Otto went down to the recreation room for a bottle of beer and a few hands of cards. After Otto won the first two hands, he said there was no way he was leaving.

"I'm on a lucky streak," he said and raised the pot a penny.

When it got close to dinnertime, Fred McGinty suggested he get the cheese and sausage from his refrigerator so they could have snacks and keep playing. By then Otto had lost as many hands as he'd won, but he, like everyone else, was in favor of the idea. Harry Hornsby even said he'd contribute some crackers and pretzels. After everyone grabbed a beer, they sat down and dealt another hand.

Later that evening, Maggie Swift from 7B came in with a chocolate cake that was high on one side and low on the other.

"I was making cakes for the church bake sale," she said, "but this one came out rather lopsided, so I thought maybe you fellows would like to have it."

"Sure thing," McGinty said and pulled some dishes from the clubroom cupboard.

When the game finally ended it was close to midnight, and rather than drive Otto home Emory suggested he spend the night on the sofa.

THE NEXT AFTERNOON, EMORY WAITED until the time between Christine's split shift hours then telephoned.

"If you and Jack aren't busy, I'd like to come for a visit this weekend," he said.

"What a coincidence, Granddaddy," she replied laughingly. "I was just going to call you and say we'd like come to Wyattsville this weekend."

Without giving such a thought time to settle Emory replied, "No, this time it's better for me to come there."

"But isn't it uncomfortable for you sleeping on the sofa?"

"Actually I've gotten rather used to it."

"Why would you be—"

"It's a long story," he cut in, "and I've got a lot to tell you, but let's hold it until the weekend."

"Okay."

Christine hung up the telephone and stood there with a smug grin.

Granddaddy might have something to tell me, she thought, *but wait until he hears what I have to tell him.*

EMORY ARRIVED AT THE APARTMENT shortly before noon, and

when he got to the apartment Christine was packing the last of the sandwiches into a wicker basket.

"Jack has the day off, and since it's so beautiful we thought it would be fun to have a picnic lunch in the park. Is that okay with you, Granddaddy?"

"Perfect," Emory replied. "This apartment is way too small for two people, never mind three."

"It's small, but we're managing fine," Jack said. He could have added they'd be getting a bigger apartment soon but didn't want to spoil Christine's surprise.

As they walked the five blocks to the park, Emory noticed the bounce in Christine's step; she seemed healthier and happier than he remembered.

"You look mighty chipper," he said.

She flashed a grin and said, "I guess it's all this beautiful weather we've been having."

In an area that was just a stone's throw from the pond, they stopped and spread the blanket on the ground. It was a day as perfect as you might ever wish for with the sky a clear blue, the smell of fall in the air and the oaks ablaze with color. Once they were settled, Jack pulled a bottle of champagne and three glasses from the basket.

Figuring there was no way they could know what he had to say, Emory asked, "Are we celebrating something?"

Christine gave a giggle and nodded. "You're going to be a great granddaddy."

Not catching on right away, Emory replied, "I thought I already was a great granddaddy."

"No." Christine rubbed her tummy playfully. "I mean you are really going to be a great granddaddy."

Emory's eyes grew wide, and he started to grin. "You're having a baby?"

Jack and Christine both nodded proudly. Then everyone

began to talk at once, and questions and answers flew back and forth. When was the baby due? How was she feeling? Had they picked out names? Did Jack's parents know yet?

"The doctor just confirmed it three days ago, so we're taking it one step at a time for now," Jack said. "Next month we're going to start looking for a larger apartment."

A wide grin settled on Emory's face. "Why would you do that?"

Christine eyed him with a curious look. "It seems obvious. The apartment is barely big enough for the two of us. We'd never have room for—"

"I realize you need more space," Emory cut in, "but why not a house?"

"In a few years we should be able to afford a house, but not right now," Jack answered.

"I'm using the money Mama left me to buy furniture," Christine added.

The big silly-looking grin remained on Emory's face as he reached into his vest pocket, pulled out a check for $5000 and handed it to them.

"This rightfully belongs to you, Christine. It's from the sale of your mama's house—"

"But, Granddaddy, aren't you living in it?"

"No more," Emory said proudly. "I've got a nice little apartment of my own."

"Oh, Granddaddy..." Christine gave a solemn sigh. "You shouldn't have."

"I absolutely should have!" Emory interrupted with that grin still stuck to his face. "I'm doing what I want to do, and I'm happier for it."

He went on to explain how he'd moved to an apartment building where there was a lot to do and friends to keep him company.

"An old man like me doesn't need a big house or a lot of things," he said. "I think when your mama left me that house, she knew I'd come to this conclusion sooner or later." He laughed. "I only wish it had been sooner."

Christine passed the check back to him. "You don't need to give me this, Granddaddy. Keep it so you'll have money to live on."

"I've got all that I need."

He folded the check into her hand and pushed it away.

"This is what your mama would have wanted. She used to say 'Life is like a carousel; what goes around, comes around.' Well, this is life coming around. Franklin paid for that house, so it's his money. Just as my daddy left me money to buy a house, I'm passing along your daddy's money so you can buy a house."

Christine's eyes filled with tears, and her lower lip quivered. Jack spoke because she couldn't.

"This is such a huge gift, neither of us know what to say."

Emory chuckled. "You don't have to say a thing, but once you do get that house I'm hoping it has a guest bedroom because I'll be coming to visit."

"Rest assured it will," Jack said emphatically.

A FAMILY LIFE

In early December, Jack and Christine found a lovely three-bedroom Cape Cod that was less than a mile from Missus Feeney's Boarding House. It needed a coat of paint and a new porch railing but the price was right, and with the money Emory had given them the mortgage payment was small enough that they'd be able to save a bit even with Christine no longer working.

Alexander Street was a place where young families came to settle and raise children. In many ways it was like the street where Christine had grown up. Children played outside. Wash was hung on the clothesline in the backyard. Husbands mowed the grass on Saturday. And neighbors seldom passed by one another without stopping to chat.

The day they moved in, Jan McGee came over with a chicken and dumpling casserole for their dinner. She handed Christine the dish and said, "Moving day is so hectic. Hopefully not having to fix dinner will make it a bit easier."

Once the dishes were stacked in the cupboard and the clothes hung in the closet, Christine dished up the casserole and sat across the table from Jack. After only a few mouthfuls she gave a sigh of contentment and said, "I just know I'm going to love living here."

And she did.

During the months of fixing up the house, stitching curtains and hanging pictures, she came to know every one of her neighbors. Jan and Ed McGee on the right had one child, five-year-old Stacy. Donna and John Rollins on the left had three boys who were like stair steps; the eldest was only four years old. Directly opposite was Jenny and George LaGrange, a young couple, both of them still working.

The week after Jack Junior was born, Donna came over with a basket of freshly-washed baby clothes.

"Billy has outgrown these," she said, "but they'll be perfect for Jack next summer."

ON THE SATURDAY THAT JACK started painting the house, Ed McGee and George LaGrange both came by. Jack had not asked for help, but they'd seen him out there with a paint brush and hurried over.

"Looks like you could use a hand," Ed said and picked up a brush.

The three of them finished the entire house that weekend, and on Sunday evening they sat out back in lawn chairs enjoying a cold beer and the warmth of each other's friendship.

That night when Christine and Jack climbed into bed, she snuggled up to him and said, "I can't think of anything more perfect than living right here."

That's how it was on Alexander Street. Jack and Christine hadn't simply bought a house. They'd become part of a community.

EMORY SETTLED INTO HIS LIFE at the Wyattsville Arms in much the same way. Before long he was a regular for both the Tuesday night poker game and the Thursday canasta club. He remained a member of the Elks Club and joined Otto and Seth for the dinner special three or four times a week until the following year when the Elks raised the price from sixty cents to ninety-five. Thinking that outrageous, he stayed at home a little more often. But even then he almost always had some tasty treat one of the neighbors had shared.

After the second year he quit buying canned beef stew altogether. He gathered up all the canned food he'd accumulated in the pantry and donated it to the Holy Trinity food drive. That same year he organized a garden club to plant tomatoes and zucchini in the lot behind the parking area.

STAYING TRUE TO HIS PROMISE, Emory visited Jack and Christine. At first it was once every few months, but after Jack Junior came along he was there at least once a month and sometimes twice. He'd park himself in the large overstuffed chair with the baby on his lap looking as contented as can be.

"This little fellow's got your mama's eyes," he'd say then segue into a story of when Laura was that age.

As soon as Jack Junior started to babble Christine tried to teach him to say granddaddy, but all he got from it was the "daddy" part so he took to calling Emory Da-da.

"Granddaddy," Christine repeated over and over again with no success.

When that didn't work she tried to teach him to say "Pop-pop" but that came out sounding like "pup," which was what he called Boomer, the Saint Bernard they now had. Finally she worked on getting him to say "G-G," meaning "Great Granddaddy," and that was something Jack Junior could handle.

Once he began calling Emory "G-G" it stuck, and when Chrissie came along two years later it was inevitable that she would latch on to the name. By that time Jack Junior was trailing after Emory like a shadow.

CHRISSIE WAS BORN THE YEAR Jack got yet another raise and was assigned to squad car duty. Anxious to keep moving up the ladder toward detective, Jack often worked odd hours and got home long after it turned dark.

Jack Junior had been an easy baby. He napped during the day and slept straight through the night. On the rare occasion when he did wake early, he'd lie in the crib kicking his chubby legs in the air and cooing playfully.

Chrissie was just the opposite. She woke up wailing and seemed impossible to quiet. With Jack Junior at the age where he was into everything, it was more than Christine could handle. Knowing the boy's affection for G-G, she called Emory and asked if maybe he could come to lend a hand.

"At least until Chrissie gets over this colic," she said.

Looking pleased as punch, Emory told Seth Porter he'd have to pass on this year's poker tournament because he was needed to help out with his grandson. He came to Richmond that August and stayed until mid-September.

All month long Jack climbed up onto his great granddaddy's lap and listened as he read the newspaper. The day Emory read about gas prices going up to twenty cents a gallon, Junior sat there shaking his head in the same worrisome way his great granddaddy did.

"This boy's smart as a whip," Emory said proudly; then he went right back to reading about the situation in Korea.

When Junior wasn't listening to Emory read the newspaper, they sat side by side watching television. While Emory listened to Dave Garroway's comments on the world at large, Junior laughed at the antics of the chimpanzee, J. Fred Muggs. In the afternoon,

Christine was able to nurse the baby and start dinner while the two of them sat watching Buffalo Bob and his freckle-faced sidekick Howdy Doody.

VISITING WITH JACK AND CHRISTINE was the one thing Emory enjoyed as much as he did his friends at Wyattsville Arms. Over the years he'd grown as fond of Jack as he'd once been of Franklin. One evening while Christine was upstairs tucking Chrissie into bed, Emory started thinking how much she and Jack reminded him of Laura and Franklin.

"It's a shame you never knew Christine's daddy," he told Jack. "You would have liked him a lot."

"I'm sure I would have," Jack replied.

He waited, knowing there would be yet another story about Franklin. There was. One story led to another, and in time Emory's voice took on a melancholy sound as he told of Franklin's murder and the inequity of never having caught George Feldman.

By then Jack had begun studying criminal law and cold case behavior patterns, so he asked question after question about Feldman. Did he have relatives? What kind of work did he do? Was there any follow up? Of course very few of these questions had answers.

"Don't forget it was twenty-five years ago," Emory said. "Back then people disappeared without a trace, and there was no way of finding them. After a while, the police quit looking."

"But it was a murder case," Jack argued. "Murder is a capital offense; on something like that there's no statute of limitations."

Emory gave a weary nod. "Maybe so, but things were different back then. We were in the middle of a depression. The police did what they could and when they couldn't find even a trace of Feldman, they moved on."

In time they set the conversation aside and switched over to something less troubling, but the thought of such an injustice remained in Jack's mind.

JUNIOR WAS FIVE AND CHRISSIE three when Frankie was born. He was christened Franklin, but right from the start everyone called him Frankie.

By then Jack was third in line for a detective spot on the Richmond force. He had all the qualifications, but there hadn't been an opening on the squad for over a year. With a number of the detectives being young men his age, it didn't look any too promising going forward.

After a year of waiting, Jack spoke to Captain Hennessey.

"I've got a family to think about," Jack said, "and it doesn't look like anything is going to be opening up on the squad. Is it possible I can make detective if I transfer to South Richmond?"

"I'll look into it and get back to you," Hennessey replied.

An Overdue Opportunity

When nearly a month passed without another word from Hennessey, it was beginning to seem as if Jack's request had been forgotten. Then the first Tuesday in June, Jack was called into the office and Hennessey closed the door.

"Have a seat," he said and motioned to the chair in front of his desk.

The conversation started off with a few pleasantries. Hennessey asked about the family and congratulated Jack on the new baby.

"Frankie is six months old already," Jack said proudly. He thought about showing the baby picture in his wallet but moved past the idea. Obviously that wasn't what he was here for.

After an awkward few moments of pushing papers from one side of his desk to the other, Hennessey glanced up and looked Jack square in the face.

"I spoke to South Richmond, and they're in the same spot we're in. The detective squad is mostly young guys. The first foreseeable opening would be Sam Berman's spot, and he's ten years from retirement."

Jack let out a whoosh of disappointment.

"You're a good guy," Hennessey went on. "You're dependable

and thorough. You're somebody to be counted on, and that's worth something. Even though there's nothing available, I agree that you deserve to move up."

Uncertain of where this was going, Jack mumbled, "Thanks."

"So I called around, put out feelers, made a few inquiries. What I came up with is a senior detective spot, two grades higher than you are now, with a nice bump in pay."

A look of interest settled on his face, and Jack leaned forward. "Sounds good."

"Good or not depends on you," Hennessey said. "This opening is on the Wyattsville force. That means relocating."

Jack winced, and Hennessey held his palm up.

"I know, I know," he said apologetically. "Jack Junior goes to school with my Eddie, so I realize what this means. It's a big move. You've got to uproot your family, sell your house—"

"Christine is happy where we are. She's got friends—"

Hennessey gave a sympathetic shrug. "Trust me, I understand. But before you make a decision, think it over carefully. This is a great opportunity, and you're pretty much a shoo-in for the position. I told Captain Rogers you're one of my best men. He wants to meet you."

"I appreciate what you've done," Jack said, "but I'd like to discuss this with Christine before I talk with Captain Rogers."

"Fine. Take a couple of days and get back to me."

Hennessy closed the folder on his desk then looked up. Seldom did he play favorites but Jack reminded him of Eddie, the kid brother shot to death by a crazed drunk. The memory of that flashed through Hennessey's mind.

With a serious expression he said, "Consider this opportunity very carefully. Compared to Richmond, Wyattsville has a really low crime rate and it's a good place to raise a family."

"We're familiar with the town," Jack said. "Christine's granddaddy lives there. It's where she grew up."

"Well, then, she probably won't mind moving…"

Hennessey didn't notice the doubtful look stretched across Jack's face.

JACK WAITED UNTIL THE KIDS were in bed; then he sat on the sofa alongside Christine.

"There's something we need to talk about," he said.

Given the expression on his face, she knew it was something serious. She could still remember how her mama had seemed perfectly fine until all of a sudden she was dying.

"Oh, Jack," she said, anxiety in her voice, "please tell me you're not sick."

"It's nothing like that. It's about my job—"

With his furrowed forehead and the downturn of his mouth, Christine knew it was not good.

"You didn't get the detective spot?"

"Yes and no," Jack answered. He went on to tell of his conversation with Hennessey.

"Ten-year statistics indicate Wyattsville has a low incidence of violent crime, and the pay grade is good for thirty percent more than I'm making now."

Everything about the job sounded wonderful…except the part about it being in Wyattsville.

We'd have to leave here. Move away.

Christine let out a disheartened sigh.

"So if you don't take it," she said, "does that mean it could be another ten years before you make detective?"

"Unless something unexpected happens."

"Unexpected?"

He nodded. "If one of the detectives currently on the squad is injured, killed or decides to quit the force." He took her hand in his. "I know how you feel about living here, and I want you to be happy. This isn't just about me; it affects our whole family. It's a decision we have to make together."

Christine gave a saddened nod. The thought of leaving Alexander Street brought tears to her eyes.

"We don't need to do this tonight," Jack said. "Let's sleep on it, think it over and talk about it again in a day or so."

SLEEP WAS ALMOST IMPOSSIBLE TO come by that night. Christine tossed and turned, thinking of the ramifications involved with moving. They would have to leave this house they'd so lovingly restored. They'd have to leave their friends, neighbors who were always willing to lend a helping hand, people who were now like family.

Jack Junior was in kindergarten; the move would mean a new school, new friends. And the price of homes was higher now; they might not be lucky enough to find another house quite so perfect on a street that welcomed them with open arms. It seemed there was a thousand reasons for staying, and one big reason for going.

Wyattsville is safer.

She thought back on last year's robbery of the jewelry store in the center of town. It happened two blocks from the telephone company. The young officer working Jack's old beat was shot and killed.

Thinking back on the early years of their marriage, Christine remembered how Jack insisted on meeting her every evening she worked split shift. He never allowed her to walk home alone. "It's not safe," he'd said.

Wyattsville was a town. Richmond was a city; a place where transients came and went. A place where crimes were an everyday occurrence.

Sure, Alexander Street was nothing like that, but it was on the far edge of Richmond, in an area where policemen were seldom needed. The nearest stationhouse was almost ten miles away. Jack didn't work in a neighborhood of well-intentioned people; he worked downtown where anything could and sometimes did happen.

Wyattsville is safer.

CHRISTINE WAS UP EARLY THE next morning. Jack was working second shift, so he didn't have to be in until eleven o'clock. By the time he got up, all the kids had been dressed, fed and, with the exception of Frankie, shuffled out the door. Junior was at Donna's house playing with Billy, and Chrissie was next door with Stacy.

Here we have neighbors willing to lend a hand.

Christine was standing at the sink with her back to the door when Jack came into the room. She turned, and he kissed her mouth.

"Good morning, beautiful," he said.

He was wearing his uniform. Although he was now a daddy with three children, Christine couldn't help but notice how he still had the look of a young man. There were a few crinkles at the corners of his eyes, but his waist was still narrow, his shoulders broad and his smile filled with the mischief she'd loved from the start.

"I've made my decision," she said.

"So soon?"

She nodded. "I think you should go for it. It's more money, it's what you've been working for and the possibility of waiting another ten years…"

She rattled off a list of reasons for him taking the job in Wyattsville but never mentioned the one that had been her deciding factor.

Wyattsville is safer.

CHRISTINE

The thought of moving just about breaks my heart. Our friends are here; our children's friends are here. We've been living on Alexander Street for over seven years. It's not a lifetime, but it seems like a lifetime to me.

I remember how happy we were the day we moved into this house. I thought we'd live here for the rest of our lives. I imagined our children growing up, moving off and us one day turning the spare bedroom into a sewing room or a place to sit and watch TV.

A dozen or more times Jan and I have laughed about how it's likely we'll still be chatting across the back fence when we're old and gray. Now none of those things are going to happen.

I realize I could have told Jack I don't want to move, and given how much he loves me he would have accepted my answer. But I love him too much to do that. Before we had any of this we had each other, and I'd like to believe that long after it's all gone we'll still have each other.

Nothing in the entire world is more important to me than Jack and the children. When I feel the overwhelming sadness that will come when we leave this place, that's what I have to remember.

Moving to Wyattsville isn't all bad; there are some advantages to it. One is that we'll be closer to Granddaddy. Now that he's getting on in *years, it's not good for him to be driving such long distances. And if you go by what Captain Hennessey says, violent crimes aren't something that happen in Wyattsville. There's a lot less on-the-job risk working in a place like that.*

Plus Jack will be doing what he's wanted to do for a long time. I know he'll make a good detective, because he has an analytical mind. He sorts things out and sees tiny little details nobody else bothers with. Wyattsville is lucky to be getting a man like him.

The bottom line to all of this is that when it comes to my being happy here or Jack being safer on the job, it's not even a choice. I'll do for him what I know he'd do for me.

TRADING PLACES

Jack waited until Thursday to tell Captain Hennessey of his decision. Seeing the office door open, he rapped on the wooden frame to get the captain's attention.

"Got a moment?" he asked.

Hennessey looked up, waved Jack in and motioned for him to sit.

"I take it you've made a decision?"

Jack smiled and gave an affirmative nod. "Christine and I talked it over, and she's okay with going to Wyattsville."

"Good. It's a smart move."

Hennessy picked up the telephone and asked the stationhouse switchboard operator to get Captain Rogers on the phone. Minutes later Jack had an appointment to see the Wyattsville captain at eleven o'clock the following day. Hennessey briefed Jack on what to expect.

"Be sure to tell him you worked the Bowers case," he said, "and mention you've worked third watch. It shows you're a team player."

As Jack stood to leave, Hennessey gave a rare smile and said, "Good luck."

"Thanks," Jack replied. "I'm going to need it."

JACK ARRIVED IN WYATTSVILLE A full twenty minutes before his interview. He circled the stationhouse and parked his car in the back lot. He sat there for a few minutes remembering Captain Hennessey's suggestions, then pulled two antacid tablets from his pocket and popped them into his mouth.

The stationhouse was quiet compared to Richmond. A uniformed sergeant sat at the front desk.

"Can I help you?" he asked.

"Mahoney," Jack replied. "I have an appointment with Captain Rogers."

CAPTAIN ROGERS WAS A FAIRLY short man with a graying beard and a strong handshake. Just as Hennessey had warned, he fired off a string of pointed questions and expected quick answers.

"We've got a small five-man squad," he said, "so you'll be working whatever comes along. Could be homicide, could be B and E. Any problem with that?"

"No, sir, not at all."

Jack talked about the diversity of the cases he'd worked in Richmond.

"I was first on the scene for the Bowers murder," he said, "and did the collar on the Wellington case."

"Impressive."

Rogers leaned forward and continued the questions. After well over an hour, he pushed back in his chair and gave what could be considered a smile.

"You've got good qualifications and Hennessey says you're the best there is, so that's enough for me. The job is yours if you want it."

IT WAS AFTER SIX WHEN Jack got home. The kids were already eating dinner, Junior and Chrissie at the table, Frankie in his highchair.

Hearing Jack come through the door, Christine looked up but didn't need to ask if he'd gotten the job. The answer was in the grin on his face. He circled the table, kissed each of the kids as he always did then bent and kissed Christine.

"I got it," he whispered.

ONCE THE CHILDREN WERE IN bed, Jack pulled two cold beers from the refrigerator; then he and Christine sat on the lawn chairs in the backyard. It was a balmy night, warm but not hot, the kind of weather that came before a sweltering summer.

Christine wiggled her toes in the grass then leaned back in her chair. She knew her days of being here in this place she loved were numbered. Breathing in the faint scent of lavender and sage, she sighed.

"I don't remember it being this peaceful in Wyattsville."

"You were much younger," Jack said. "Youth doesn't look for peaceful. Youth looks for fun and excitement."

She laughed. "You're right. The moment I was out the door, I jumped on my bicycle and headed for a friend's house or the soda shop."

He stood and moved his chair closer to hers.

"We'll find a place as lovely as this in Wyattsville," he said. "It's a promise."

Christine tried not to let her sadness show through. She smiled, took his hand in hers and kissed his knuckles.

"Thank you," she whispered affectionately.

"Next week I have to be in Wyattsville for indoctrination. Why don't you and the kids come with me, and we'll start looking for a house?"

She scrunched her nose and shook her head. "It wouldn't be fair to Junior. Wednesday is the last day of school, and he's looking forward to the class party."

Jack gave a nod of acceptance.

"Anyway," she said, "there's a lot to do here. I have to call a realtor, get the house listed and start packing."

"Don't worry about packing, I'll help when I get back."

"I can handle the packing, but while you're in Wyattsville why don't you start looking around for a house?"

It was a suggestion, not a question. The truth was that Christine had no desire to go from place to place looking at other houses, oohing and awing over a spacious room, high ceilings or fenced-in backyards. She knew it would be impossible for her to fall in love with another house when her heart was tied to this one.

"Remember how long it took us to find this place?" she said. "If you pre-screened some places and narrowed it down to just a few houses, it would be easier to make a decision when we get there."

Jack agreed, and they began to discuss what he'd be looking for.

"We need four bedrooms," she said, "so we'll have a place for your parents when they come to visit."

"And a good-size backyard," Jack added.

When they'd finished listing all the things they wanted

and didn't want, Christine knew they'd described a house exactly like theirs on a road that was a replica of Alexander Street.

ON FRIDAY, CHRISTINE CALLED EMORY.

"Granddaddy, I've got good news."

Emory was as familiar with Christine's ways as he'd been with Laura's, and he could tell when bad news was being disguised as good.

"It doesn't sound like good news," he said.

"Oh, it is." Christine hiked the register of her voice and pushed in the sound of happiness. "Jack is being promoted to a detective spot on the Wyattsville force. We're moving back home."

As the words rolled off her tongue Christine couldn't help thinking although Wyattsville was at one time home, it was no longer true. Alexander Street was home.

"When?" Emory asked.

She explained that Jack would be there the following week, but they wouldn't be moving back until the first of July.

"We might actually get there a few days earlier so we can find a place to stay until we settle on a house."

"You can stay here," he replied. "I'll bunk with Seth, and you can use my apartment."

"Granddaddy!" Christine said, laughing. "You have a one-bedroom apartment. We've got three kids and a big dog."

"I'm sure you can make do," he replied, miffed. "People do what they've got to do. We lived in a third-floor cold water flat when your mama was a little girl, and she slept in an alcove."

Christine gave a sigh of resignation. "Okay. Hopefully we'll find a house soon and not be in your way for too long."

"You won't be in my way at all," Emory said. "I'll be happy to have you."

THAT AFTERNOON CHRISTINE TUCKED FRANKIE into his stroller; then she and Chrissie walked up and down Alexander Street telling friends and neighbors about their plans to move. She left Jan McGee for last.

Over the years Jan had become her best friend. Their children had grown up together. She and Jan had exchanged recipes and whispered secret thoughts not shared with anyone else. As Christine explained about Jack's transfer, tears cascaded down Jan's face.

"I'm going to miss you something fierce," she said through her sobs.

Trying her best not to cry, Christine said, "You and Ed can come to visit. Wyattsville is only a four-hour drive. Virginia is putting in a highway that cuts straight across the state. Then it'll be even faster."

"It won't be the same as having you next door."

"I know," Christine echoed sadly.

She pulled Jan into her arms and for a long while the two women stood there holding on to one another, perhaps counting the handful of times they had left to share moments such as this.

CHRISTINE DREADED THE THOUGHT OF telling the children about the move. They were happy here; they had their friends and their day-to-day routines. They didn't like change any more than she did. In fact, they flat out resisted it. She could still recall the ruckus Junior raised when he had to give up his crib and move to a big boy bed. She waited until the last possible moment then picked the one positive she could find and focused on that.

"We're moving closer to G-G," she said, making it sound like a special adventure.

She braced for a tantrum or at the very least an argument and some serious pouting. It didn't happen.

Junior jumped around joyfully. "Yay, we're going to see G-G!"

Although Chrissie had a look of uncertainty stretched across her face, she followed his lead and let out a quiet, "Yay."

Surprised at their reactions, Christine said, "This is not just for a visit. We're moving to Wyattsville and not coming back."

Such a statement didn't dampen their enthusiasm one bit. In fact they couldn't wait to get going. That same evening Junior insisted on calling Emory to ask if he could come for a sleepover.

"Well, of course you can," Emory replied. "I can't wait for you to get here."

Such an answer made Junior all the more anxious to get going. The next morning he took the cardboard box Christine had set aside for blankets, filled it with toys and announced he was ready to go. Seeing him so anxious to leave a place she thought for sure he'd loved boggled Christine's mind.

"Aren't you sad to be leaving your friends?" she asked.

He gave an innocent shrug. "I'll find new friends."

For a few moments she stood there looking at her six-year-old son and wishing she could have the same mindset. Unfortunately she didn't.

On the day a young couple returned to see the house for a second time, Christine felt her heart sink to the pit of her stomach. The wife, who was quite obviously expecting, poked her head into cupboards, peeked out of windows, checked the faucets and then peppered Christine with questions about the schools and the neighborhood.

"The schools are wonderful," she said sadly, "and the neighbors will make you feel so welcome you'll never want to leave."

Christine went on to tell of Donna's boys and Jan's daughter, Stacy, who was almost old enough to babysit. As painful as leaving was, she was determined to find comfort in the thought of another young family taking their place.

That day Suzanne, the realtor, whispered in Christine's ear that she was fairly certain they were going to make an offer.

THE WEEK WENT BY IN a flurry of activity. Christine sorted, cleaned and packed almost every moment of every day. Staying busy was the only thing that could keep the sadness at bay. If she stopped to enjoy a cup of coffee or chat across the backyard fence, she'd start to remember all the things she'd be leaving behind and the tears would fall.

By the time Jack returned from Wyattsville, all of the winter clothes, good china, knick-knacks and extra linens were already packed in boxes.

"I've got good news," she said glumly. "We've got an offer on the house."

"Did we get our asking price?"

Still looking rather solemn, she shook her head then slowly gave way to a partial smile.

"We got more than our asking price. Suzanne had two bids and one young couple really wanted the house, so they upped theirs."

Jack pulled Christine into his arms and danced her around. In the middle of a turn he stopped and asked, "Did they say when they want to close?"

She smiled again. "They're a cash buyer. She's expecting a baby in August so they'd like to move in tomorrow, but I told them the best we could do is July first."

Jack spotted the boxes lined up against the wall. "Looks like you're almost finished with the packing."

Hearing his daddy's voice, Junior came thundering down the stairs.

"Guess what, Daddy?" he shouted. Before there was time for an answer he added, "We're moving to G-G's house!"

"Not house," Christine corrected. "Apartment." She gave a weary shrug and added, "I can't imagine how the five of us are going to manage in a one-bedroom apartment, but Granddaddy insisted."

"We may not have to manage for long," Jack said. "I found three really nice houses for you to look at."

He went on to explain one was standing empty and ready to move in, a second one would be available in early August and the last one on September first.

"They're all nice, but my favorite was the one that's available now."

"I like the thought of sooner better than later," Christine replied.

"You'll like the house too," Jack said. "It's older than the other two and needs a bit of fixing up, but it's in the most beautiful section of town and very well built. It's a two-story colonial with a wide center hall, four bedrooms and a great backyard. There's a large oak in back of the house that would be perfect for hanging a swing."

Christine liked such a thought because it brought back her own childhood memories. "Where's it located?"

"About a block off of Broad on the west side of town."

"That is a nice area," she said. "My grandparents lived over there before Granddaddy came to live with Mama and me."

"I spoke to the moving company today," Jack said. "Once we're ready, they'll send a truck to pick up our stuff and store it until we've found a house. We can leave as soon as we're ready."

Christine doubted she'd ever truly be ready to leave this place. She gave a weary sigh.

"With your help I think we can finish up packing by the end of next week."

"Great," Jack replied, not noticing the sadness in her eyes.

APARTMENT DWELLING

The following Saturday the Allied moving van pulled up in front of the house, and two burly men began carrying out furniture and boxes. It seemed as though it had taken years to get everything placed in just the right spot, but in a matter of hours the rooms were bare. It was like a puzzle painstakingly put together and then swept from the table. The only things left behind were an old broom, a potted ivy on the kitchen windowsill and dust mites that had been hiding beneath the furniture.

Christine swept the rooms, watered the ivy and then herded everyone into the Buick. Boomer was pushed into the back with Junior and Chrissie. The Saint Bernard took up most of the seat. Christine sat in the front and held Frankie on her lap. Once everyone was settled, Jack pulled out of the driveway and turned toward the highway.

In the side mirror Christine watched the house she loved get smaller and smaller until it was the size of a freckle; then it faded from view. She bit her lip to keep from crying.

Before they turned onto the highway, Chrissie started complaining Boomer was squashing her.

"He can't help it; he's a big dog," Christine replied. "Just scoot over a bit."

That was only the start of it. All the way to Wyattsville it was one thing after another. Chrissie's shoe got caught under the seat. Junior was hungry, and then twenty minutes later he was thirsty. Frankie needed a diaper change. Jack wanted to grab a container of coffee.

In all they made nine stops, and it was almost dark by the time they arrived at the Wyattsville Arms. That perhaps was better since Emory had warned the building didn't allow dogs, and Christine would have to slip him in without being noticed.

"I think we should just look for a motel in the area," she said. "I doubt it's possible to bring a Saint Bernard in without being noticed."

Jack shrugged. "Just be discreet."

Fortunately the elevator was empty, and they made it to the apartment without encountering anyone. Before she rang the bell, Christine heard the sound of voices but figured it to be the television. Latched onto Boomer's leash and Chrissie's hand, she wiggled a finger free and pressed the buzzer. The door swung open immediately.

"You're late," Emory said. "We were beginning to worry."

"We?"

Before Christine could ask who "we" were, Clara squealed, "Oh, isn't he precious!" and lifted Frankie out of Jack's arms.

"Didn't I tell you they were cute?" Emory said proudly.

When Christine looked around, there were four people besides her granddaddy waiting to greet them.

"I thought you said…"

Emory laughed. "Don't worry about the little stuff. These are my friends, and after all the bragging I've done they wanted to meet you."

One by one he introduced Clara, Seth, Fred and Otto who by then had his own apartment on the fourth floor.

"Come eat." Clara waved a hand toward the dinette table spread with what appeared to be enough food for a week.

"You shouldn't have," Christine said. "The kids ate hamburgers on the way over and—"

"Nonsense," Clara cut in. "After a long trip you always have to eat. It takes the edge off."

Jack eyed the table. "That potato salad looks great."

"Homemade," Clara said. "My mother's recipe." She set Frankie down on the floor and headed for the table. He crawled after her.

Once everyone began talking, Emory poured glasses of iced tea and Jack fixed plates for the kids. Not long after they'd eaten the day began to take its toll, and their little eyelids drooped.

"I've got sleeping bags for the kids," Emory said, "and I borrowed a crib for Frankie."

Although Christine had arrived with every nerve stretched thin, now she felt reasonably calm. She kissed Emory's cheek, whispered a thank you and led the kids off for their nightly routine of teeth brushing, prayers and kisses.

As she stood there listening to Junior ask God to bless everyone including Boomer and the lady who made potato salad, she marveled at how pleasantly the evening had turned out. They'd met Otto at their wedding, but this was the first time she'd met the others and it was impossible not to like them. They were a warm and welcoming group. It was easy to understand why her granddaddy had chosen to give up the house and come to live here.

By the time Christine returned to the living room, the table was cleared and the guests gone.

"Where is everyone?" she asked.

Emory smiled. "After a long day they thought you might be

anxious to get some rest." He gave her a hug then turned toward the door. "Seth's waiting for me. You get a good night's sleep, and we'll see you in the morning."

That night as she and Jack settled into the darkness of the unfamiliar bedroom, Christine whispered, "I don't think our staying here is going to be nearly as difficult as I thought."

THE NEXT MORNING CLARA INVITED everyone to her apartment for pancakes, which it seemed was her specialty. She also volunteered to help Emory babysit the children while Jack and Christine went to look at houses.

They met Robert Lansing, the realtor, at his office, and he suggested they start with the house Jack favored.

"Could be you'll like that one so much you'll want to stop there."

Remembering how they'd looked at more than twenty houses before they found the house on Alexander Street, Christine chuckled. "That's pretty optimistic."

"Oh, I don't know," Robert said. "This house is a beauty. If you don't mind putting in a bit of work to get it fixed up…"

"We can look at it, but…" As Christine climbed into the back seat of Robert's car, she mumbled something about three kids and no time for restoring old houses.

Jack caught her words and said, "When Robert talks about it needing work, he means small stuff; nothing major."

"Okay," she replied absently.

It was a short ten-minute drive, but when Robert pulled up to the curb Christine was fishing through her purse and wondering if she'd left Frankie's pacifier at the apartment. She didn't see the house until she stepped out of the car. When she did she gasped.

She turned to Jack wide-eyed and asked, "What street is this?"

"Chester," Robert answered.

For a moment she said nothing as she stood there looking up at the house.

Noting her reaction, Robert asked, "Is something wrong?"

Christine shook her head. "No." She then turned to Jack, "This was Granddaddy's house before he came to live with us."

"I'm sorry," Jack stuttered. "I didn't know—"

"There's nothing to be sorry about; I love this house." She caught hold of his hand and started up the walkway.

THE MINUTE THEY STEPPED INSIDE Christine felt it. Although the house was devoid of furniture, she saw it the way it was all those many years ago. She lovingly traced her hand across the oak mantle and along windowsills that had gathered a thin layer of dust.

"I was a kid the last time I was here," she said. "Granddaddy and I used to sit in this room listening to the radio. On winter evenings when there was a chill in the air, he'd make a fire so we could toast marshmallows and we'd laugh ourselves silly listening to Amos and Andy."

She led the way from room to room, remembering family dinners in the big dining room and the squeaky step on the staircase.

"This railing needs to be polished," she said as they mounted the stairs.

Robert trailed along behind Jack and Christine. "If you want something that doesn't need a speck of work, I've got a brand new ranch I can show you. It's down on Baker Street—"

Jack turned and waved him off. He knew what Christine liked, and a sprawling ranch wasn't on the list.

Still holding on to Jack's hand she said, "I can't believe you picked this house. Did you know?"

He shook his head. "I had no idea. When we started coming to see your granddaddy, he lived in that Cape Cod on Madison Street."

Christine laughed. "That was Mama's house. She made Granddaddy come to live with us after Grandma died." She gave a wistful sigh as the memories resurfaced.

"At first Granddaddy argued and fussed, saying he could take care of himself just fine. Then Mama told him maybe he could, but we couldn't. That's when he finally gave in. It was the Depression years and things were tight, so he sold this house and made Mama take the money."

"If we bought this house, do you think he'd be upset? You know, because of the memories?"

Christine pictured her granddaddy with his snow-white hair and the cane he used from time to time. Like her, he'd held on to the good memories and left the sorrowful ones in the past. He'd moved on and found friends and a new life at the Wyattsville Arms. He looked at life in much the same way Junior did, trusting that tomorrow would bring its own bounty of goodness.

She smiled. "I think he'd be happy about it, but let's ask him to make sure."

As they left the house and headed back down the walkway, Robert said, "There's a great two-story colonial over on Belfry—"

"Let's not bother," Christine said. "We've found the house we want."

EMORY

Yesterday afternoon Christine came and asked if I'd be upset were she and Jack to buy the old house on Chester Street. Of course I told her no. I can't imagine why she'd even think such a thing.

Knowing my granddaughter and Jack will raise their family in that house gives me nothing but pure pleasure, and I believe Rosie would be just as happy. Thinking back on how she used to love that house, I wouldn't doubt she's the reason they found it. Some people don't believe in heaven and guardian angels, but the older I've gotten the more I've come to believe. Sometimes there's no other explanation for the way things happen.

I'm not saying it's always fair, because it's not. Franklin being killed for example; there's no justice in that. And certainly none in the fact that his killer was never made to pay for his sin. But just as I've got my ways God has got his, and I don't expect Him to offer up any excuses.

Losing Franklin as she did Laura had a tough life, but she did a good job raising their daughter. Christine's grown up to be a fine woman and a wonderful mama. She's a lot like Laura.

Once she knew for certain they were buying that house, she asked if maybe I'd like to move in with them. I said absolutely not. I figured it *best to put a lid on that thought right away. I told her,* Your mama got away with saying she needed me because of not having your daddy, but you've got Jack and he's a darn fine husband.

I had to laugh, because I looked over and caught Jack grinning ear to ear when I said that.

I've got a good life here and I'm not looking to go anywhere, except maybe heaven so I can be with my Rosie again. When that time comes, it comes. Until then I'm just gonna sit back and enjoy this life I've got.

A PLACE CALLED HOME

As it turned out, staying in Emory's one-bedroom apartment was not much of a problem. A week after the Mahoney family moved in to Emory's place they moved out, taking all three children and Boomer. Since the Chester Street house was empty anyway, they were allowed to move in two weeks before the actual closing.

On moving day when the big Allied truck pulled up in front of the house and the men began carrying in their furniture, Christine knew exactly where each piece was to go. The sofa got pushed in the spot where it always was, and the breakfast set went in the bumped-out bay window overlooking the backyard. Piece by piece they settled in, each table, chair or dresser in exactly the right spot. By the end of the day when everything was in place, it looked as if each item of furniture had been purchased with precisely that spot in mind.

Two days after they moved in the next-door neighbor, Brenda Hofstadter, knocked on the front door.

"Aren't you Christine Wilkes?" she asked.

Christine laughed. "I used to be. Now I'm Christine Mahoney."

"I'm Brenda Garth, Mister Pinkerton's biology class!"

"Well, good gracious!" Christine exclaimed. "Shame on me for not recognizing you right off."

Brenda shook her head, and her blond curls bounced from side to side.

"Nobody does," she said with a chuckle. "It's the hair. It used to be that mousy brown color."

Christine had been in the middle of cleaning the upstairs windows but she left the pail sitting on the landing and tugged Brenda inside, insisting that she stay for a cup of coffee.

After downing two cups and sharing a slightly stale cheese Danish, Christine realized this actually was home. The girls she'd known in high school were now mamas just like her. Why, she wondered, hadn't she remembered how wonderful Wyattsville was?

"I can't wait until the girls learn you're back in town," Brenda said excitedly. "Tuesday is book club at my house, so please say you'll come."

Of course Christine did, and she slid right back into her group of friends as if she'd never been gone.

IN LATE SEPTEMBER, AFTER JACK had given the banister a new coat of varnish, replaced the broken hinge on the back door and changed the front door back to its original burgundy color, they invited Emory to a celebratory dinner.

"Kind of a belated housewarming," Christine said.

By then she'd gotten a bit nervous about her granddaddy driving, so the plan was for Jack to pick up Emory and have him spend the night.

On the way over the two men had been chatting, and Emory wasn't really watching as Jack pulled to the curb. When he stepped out of the car and looked up at the house, a smile came to his face. The house looked as it did in the years when Rose tended the garden. A bed of yellow chrysanthemums bordered the walkway, and to the side of the front porch pansies and snapdragons blossomed in a perfusion of color.

"It looks every bit as good as it did the first time I saw it," Emory said.

THAT EVENING THEY ATE SUPPER in the dining room, and the table was set with the good china that had once belonged to Rose. It had been handed down first to Laura and then to Christine. With it came a lifetime of good memories: festive family dinners, special holidays and celebrations.

After dinner they sat in what was always called the front parlor, the only big difference being that a television set had replaced the radio. On this night, the television was not turned on. Instead they sat and talked.

"It was right here in this very room that your daddy came and asked me for your mama's hand in marriage," Emory said. "He was a fine man, your daddy."

When Christine took the children upstairs to get ready for bed, the two men continued to talk.

"You remind me of Franklin," Emory told Jack. "Not so much in looks, but personality. You've got his love of family and dedication to duty."

He gave a saddened sigh of regret then continued. "Of course in Franklin's case that dedication was what probably cost him his life. If he hadn't been in the office that night..." Emory let the rest of his thought drift away. It was one of those things that not even time could change.

Understanding the pain of such a thought, Jack said, "Sometimes a thing is destined to happen, and there's nothing anyone can do to prevent it. If Feldman hadn't found Franklin in the office that night, he most likely would have come back the next day or, worse yet, gone to his house. Then only God knows what might have happened."

Emory gave a nod of agreement. "I know. The truth is that I should let go of this resentment, but thinking about Feldman getting away with what he did weighs heavy on my heart."

Jack sat there saying nothing for a long minute before he asked if Emory had held on to the file folder of newspaper clippings about the incident.

"Of course," Emory replied. "I keep thinking maybe someday..."

"Want me to take a look at it?" Jack asked. "After all these years there's probably nothing new, but it wouldn't hurt to check."

When Christine returned to the room, they changed the topic of conversation.

"I'm thinking the Washington Senators will have a better season next year," Emory said.

Jack, a hard-core Yankees fan, picked up on it right away. "They're at the bottom of the league now. What makes you think they'll be any better next year?"

There was no further mention of Franklin or the tragedy of that night.

IT WAS CLOSE TO MIDNIGHT when they finally went to bed, and even though it had been a long day Jack found sleep impossible to come by. Two seconds after he kissed Christine, she turned on her side and fell fast asleep. But for him that was impossible. He kept coming back to thoughts of the earlier conversation.

He pictured Franklin's face as it was in the picture when he stood beside Christine on the carousel. Franklin was a young father, a man doing no wrong, a man simply trying to provide for his family. He was Christine's daddy.

Jack thought of how his own father had been there for him throughout the years of the Depression. It hadn't always been easy, but he'd been there. He'd been someone Jack could turn to for guidance. He'd sat alongside Jack's mama at the football games and at his graduation. Even in the lean years he was there every night, sitting at the head of the table saying grace and promising to take care of his family.

Christine had had none of that.

COLD CASE

Jack had planned to simply drop Emory off on his way to work the next morning, but instead he parked the car and followed him upstairs.

"Mind if I take that folder of clippings now?" he asked.

Emory pulled the file from the shelf of the hall closet and handed it to him. "Do you really think there's a chance…?"

Jack gave a doubtful shrug. "It's been over twenty-five years; that's an awfully long time, but you never know." He grinned. "One lucky break, and we might have ourselves a case."

He turned and started toward the door. As he disappeared into the hallway, Emory barely whispered, "God willing," but Jack never heard it.

AT THE STATIONHOUSE JACK CHECKED his messages, and when there was nothing new he sat at his desk and began browsing through the folder. The newsprint had faded and the paper yellowed with age, but it was all there. A picture of Franklin in a business suit, looking as young as he did on the carousel. The photo of George Feldman said it had been taken from the employee files at the Reliable Steel Company. At the time he had a round face, thinning hair and a look of anger that at first glance marked him as problematic.

Jack read through the interviews where co-workers called Feldman an ill-tempered fellow who blamed the world for his misfortune. According to Ed Ruppert, the foreman at Reliable Steel at the time, Feldman flew into a rage when told his station was slowing down the line.

"He turned red in the face and looked like he was going to explode," Ruppert said. "I was afraid he'd do something to sabotage the whole operation, so I moved him over to the finishing line where a slow-down didn't affect others."

The next-door neighbor was quoted as saying, "Feldman was a man who'd snap off the hand that fed him. Hated the bank; blamed them for causing the crash."

Bertha Paulson, who lived directly across the street, said that in her mind George was the reason Anna Feldman was dead.

As he continued to read, Jack came across the stories of how Franklin was considered fair in every sense of the word. A dozen different people said he'd warned them that the market was extremely volatile the first time it took a dip.

"To be perfectly honest, Howard and I thought Mister Wilkes was overly cautious," Emily Dougherty said, "but later on we were mighty glad we'd listened to his advice."

In the back of the folder was the small clipping of an obituary saying that Franklin was survived by his wife Laura, a five-year-old daughter and his parents. There was no mention of Emory.

Jack closed the folder and sat there for several minutes thinking over all he'd read.

The murder had happened twenty-five years ago. Witnesses move, get married, get divorced, remarry and sometimes die.

Even back then when the trail was fresh and everyone was optimistic, George Feldman could not be found and brought to justice. Their efforts had proven fruitless. Yet...

Jack looked across the desk to Leon Schulte. "How long have you been on the Wyattsville squad?"

"Eleven years in January. Why?"

"I wanted to ask about a cold case; see if maybe you remembered it."

"So ask."

"This one was before your time. It's a 1930 homicide."

Leon laughed. "Lots of luck. The only person here that long is Captain Rogers. Did he assign you the case?"

Jack shook his head. "This is personal. I promised somebody I'd look into it."

"Check Rogers. If he's got anything, he'll tell you."

Reopening the folder Jack began browsing through the articles again, this time not so much reading as studying faces. He was the new guy on the force, still unproven. How risky was it to take on a case they couldn't close back then and were less likely to close now that twenty-five years had gone by?

He thought back on the words Emory had spoken as they'd sat in the dim light of the front parlor.

"Franklin deserves better."

Jack picked up the folder, walked across the room and rapped on the door of Captain Rogers's office.

"Got a minute?" he asked.

Captain Rogers waved him in and said to have a seat. It was his experience that detectives seldom came knocking at his door when there wasn't a problem.

"Anything wrong?" he asked.

"Not wrong," Jack said, "but probably challenging." He handed the folder of news clippings across the desk. "This belongs to my wife's granddaddy. Franklin Wilkes, the victim, would have been my father-in-law."

Rogers glanced up with a look of surprise. "Wilkes? The stockbroker?"

Jack nodded. "I promised that I'd—"

"That case is twenty-five years old!"

"I know," Jack said, "but I was hoping I could look into it. I thought maybe I could poke around a bit and see if Feldman has resurfaced."

Rogers gave a tight-lipped look of doubt. "The Wilkes homicide was one of the worst we've had here in Wyattsville. I was a rookie patrolman back then, so I didn't work the case." He handed the folder back to Jack. "I can't promise we've still got the files, but given that it was such a high profile homicide my bet is we do."

"Do I have your okay to look into it?"

Rogers nodded. "Take Schulte with you and check the Harbor Street warehouse. If we've got the files, that's where you'll find them."

"Thanks, Captain," Jack said and disappeared out the door.

THE HARBOR STREET WAREHOUSE WAS on the far side of Dorchester. It was a building with bars on the windows and a padlock on the door but no watchman.

Schulte unlocked the door, and they stepped inside. The cement building had the musty smell of old paper and years of dust. Ahead of them were rows of metal shelving stacked floor to ceiling with cardboard boxes.

"Are these alphabetical or by year?" Jack asked.

Schulte chuckled. "There's no system. This is the last stop, a holding bin before files are destroyed. Because of the way they're hauled over here, it's likely the oldest cases are somewhere further back."

Jack walked halfway down the center aisle and brushed a layer of dust from the label on the front of a box. It read "Crimmins – March 1948."

He moved two rows back and found files from 1936 and 1937. He was near the end of the last aisle when Schulte hollered, "I got it!"

The carton marked "Wilkes – January 1930" was on the rack marked Do Not Destroy. It was a large box with considerable weight. They tugged it from the shelf, loaded it into the trunk of the car and headed back to the stationhouse.

INSIDE THE BOX

For the next two days, Jack sat at his desk reading through witness statements and police reports.

It appeared that John Carroll, the officer in charge of the investigation, had interviewed everyone with even the remotest connection to George Feldman. Jack read through the statements of neighbors, coworkers, the Reliable plant foreman, an aunt who lived in New Jersey and even a woman who worked in the luncheonette where he was seen earlier in the day. No one had even the slightest inkling of where George Feldman would have gone.

"He wasn't a very likeable man," the foreman said, "and far as I know he didn't have any friends. At least none here at the plant."

Two coworkers claimed they'd seen him with a girlfriend on occasion. One described the woman as a tall blonde; the other said she was redhead. Neither of them knew the woman's name or her whereabouts.

The summation report indicated that the house where Feldman lived with Anna Feldman, his mother, was repossessed by the bank. Anna died the same day as the shooting. Albert

Feldman, his father, had disappeared years earlier and since that time had no contact with his wife or George. The report listed Albert Feldman as an electrician by trade but with no known employment.

Each statement seemed to lead to a dead end. The aunt had not seen George since he was a teenager. There was no trace of the girlfriend nor was there proof one ever existed. Based on the fingerprint evidence, a warrant was issued for George Feldman's arrest. A wanted poster was issued, and along with departmental distribution it went out to all steel mills. At the time it was believed George might look for employment in the industry since he was an experienced cinder-pit man and metal wheeler.

The last entry in the file was in July of 1935 when Bertha Paulson reported that she thought she'd seen George lurking around the Feldman house.

"If it's not him then it's someone who looks remarkably like him," she said.

Two uniformed officers investigated the report and found footprints in the mud behind the house and the lock on the back door broken. However they did not find George Feldman inside or anywhere in the vicinity. The house, which was still empty at that time, burned to the ground that night. There was evidence of arson but no suspect other than the possibility George Feldman had indeed torched his own home.

Jack went through folder after folder of reports and statements, but in the end he had very little to go on. He jotted down the most relevant names and addresses, figuring he would start by again interviewing the people who had known George.

First on the list was Bertha Paulson. There was no telephone listing, so Jack and Schulte drove out to the house. The woman answering the door said to the best of her knowledge Bertha had passed away in early 1941.

"We bought the house from her son that November, and she was already dead then," she said.

After thanking her for her time, they moved on.

"As long as we're out here, let's canvass the neighborhood and see if we can find anyone else who might have known Feldman," Jack said.

"I'll take the houses on this side." Schulte waved a hand toward the other side of the street. "You get those."

Jack crossed over and rang the doorbell of the house that had been rebuilt on the Feldman lot. A middle-aged woman answered. Jack flashed his badge then asked how long she'd been there and who she'd bought the property from.

"What's this about?" she asked suspiciously.

"We're just following up on a 1930 homicide."

"That's twenty-five years ago! We didn't even buy the lot until nineteen forty-two, and it was nineteen forty-three before the house was finished."

"The man we're looking for lived in the house that burned down," Jack explained. "Sometimes when a suspect believes you're no longer looking for them, they come back to an area they're familiar with. Over the years have you noticed anyone hanging around, maybe asking questions about how you got the house?"

"Not until now," she said. "Are we in some kind of danger?"

"No, no," Jack replied. "Nothing like that."

"If we are then you've got to tell me, because I have two girls in high school—"

"This is a cold case. There's no danger, I can assure you."

"Well, if there's no danger, then I would think you'd have better things to do than go around scaring people half to death!"

She abruptly closed the door and left Jack standing on the front porch.

It was a similar story up and down the block. Almost all of the people living on the street had moved in during the late 1940s when there were more jobs to be had and better pay. The only resident left from 1930 was Wilbur Ross. He'd been in his early twenties at the time of Wilkes murder but remembered reading about it in the newspapers.

"I wasn't none too surprised, 'cause George was always kind of strange. He had a look in his eye that made you think maybe he was a little off."

Wilbur wriggled a finger toward his skull indicating crazy.

"I was about ten when his daddy ran off and left them. George was older than me, but I remember how he used to sit on the front steps all the time looking like he thought his daddy would be coming back any minute. Even a fool would have known that man wasn't ever coming back."

"What about since then?" Jack asked. "Have you seen him? Maybe a few years after his mama died?"

Wilbur shook his head. "Missus Paulson said she saw him, but I never did."

Once the interviews were concluded, they returned to the stationhouse. Again reviewing the twenty-five-year-old statements, Jack pulled out the telephone number for the aunt in New Jersey and placed a call. A man answered.

"May I please speak with Debra Feldman?"

"There's no Debra here."

"Is this Central 6-4723?"

"Yep, but there's no Debra here."

Jack glanced down at the statement form then asked, "Are you located at 220 Back River Street, Hackensack?"

"I don't think that's any of your business," the man snapped. "Now—"

Jack jumped in. "I should have introduced myself. Detective Mahoney, Wyattsville, Virginia, police department. I'm trying to locate Debra Feldman in regard to a cold case homicide."

"Sorry, mac, I can't help you. I've had the same telephone number for over six years and never heard of this Feldman woman."

When Jack hung up he penciled "NG" alongside the telephone number on the statement then called information and asked for a Debra Feldman in Hackensack.

No listing.

"Try Bergen County," he said.

They had a listing for the name in Leonia. Jack took down the number and called it.

After a lengthy and somewhat confusing conversation, it was determined that the woman was the only child of Harriett and Benjamin Feldman of Rochester. It was sheer coincidence that her name happened to be the same, but she was in no way related to George Feldman.

Another dead end.

THE NEXT DAY JACK MAHONEY drove out to the Reliable plant alone. Instead of rolled railroad tracks, they were once again manufacturing sheets of steel to be used for refrigerators. He sat across the desk from Ken Gardiner, the personnel manager, and explained that he was looking for information on George Feldman who worked at the plant back in 1930.

"Ed Ruppert was the foreman back then," Gardiner said, "but he retired back in forty-nine."

Jack rattled off the names of the co-workers who had been interviewed at the time. Not one of them was still working at the plant.

"Reliable had a lot of layoffs during the Depression years," Gardiner said. "Very few of those men ever came back."

After nearly two hours of searching through old records and names that didn't have a scrap of familiarity, the only thing Gardiner could provide was Ed Ruppert's address and he couldn't say whether the man was still alive. When Jack left the mill, he stopped at a phone booth and called the office.

"Have you got anything more on any of those names?" he asked Schulte.

"Nope," Leon answered. "Came up dry on all of them."

"The only thing I got was the foreman's address," Jack replied. "It's in town, so I'll stop there on my way in."

MAHONEY RANG THE BELL AND waited. After several minutes, a thin silver-haired man wearing a bathrobe opened the door.

"Sorry to keep you waiting," he said.

"Ed Ruppert?"

The man nodded. "What can I do for you?"

Again flashing his badge, Jack introduced himself then explained that he was investigating a homicide that took place in 1930.

Ed gave a nod of recognition. "I don't recall the name, but I bet I know who you're talking about. The guy was a real wacko."

"Feldman, George Feldman," Jack said. "He worked at Reliable when you were the foreman—"

Ed cut in. "Yeah, that's him. A nut case. Wanted a job but didn't want to work. I should've never hired him. You see a man with that look in his eye, you'd best run the other way. He suckered me in. Said his mama was sick and he needed a job, so I gave him a chance."

"You ever get to know anything else about him? His friends maybe? Or a girlfriend?"

Ed shook his head. "I doubt anyone knew anything about him. I only heard him talk about his mama, and it was never anything good."

"Was he friendly with any of the other employees? A co-worker, the janitor or maybe a secretary?"

"Nope," Ed said and again shook his head.

After fifteen minutes of questioning, Ed said he'd already told the investigators everything he knew about Feldman.

"I thought there might be a chance you'd remember something you'd forgotten to mention during the original investigation," Jack said.

Ed laughed. "From twenty-five years ago? Not likely."

Jack Mahoney

I've hardly gotten any sleep for two nights. I go to bed exhausted; then before I close my eyes I start thinking about this case again. Christine asked me if something was wrong, but I told her no. I'm deliberately not telling her or Emory, because I don't want them to get their hopes up.

After going through the evidence box and looking at the crime scene photos, I assure you I'll never let Christine see them. Emory was the one who found Franklin that night, and now I know why it left such a mark on his heart. Franklin's chest was torn open from the impact of the bullets. George Feldman had to be standing less than five feet from him when he emptied the gun into his chest. What kind of a monster does something like that?

Tomorrow I plan to track down the people who were in the building that night: the janitor and a woman who was in one of the offices on the fourth floor. Chances are that after twenty-five years they're no longer there, but if they're still alive I'll find them. Maybe Feldman had a connection in the building, someone who opened the downstairs door and let him in.

Schulte thinks this is a lost cause. He's come up with a dozen different reasons why the case is never going to be solved. Time of course is the big factor. Witnesses forget what they might have once known, and the evidence trail grows cold. George Feldman is older; his appearance has no doubt changed, and he was obviously a loner. It would appear the man didn't have a close connection to anyone other than his mother, but I don't buy into that. Somewhere there's someone who knows something about George Feldman; it's just that we haven't yet found it.

Even in a case like this there's always a loose thread left dangling, a seemingly meaningless thing that was overlooked in the past. A connection no one else saw. It's my job to find the tail end of that thread. Once I've got it, one tug and everything starts to unravel.

At least that's what I'm praying will happen.

Looking at it realistically, I know there's a very slim chance I'll come up with something but I'm sticking with it. Emory deserves to have closure, and the truth is I couldn't live with myself if I didn't give it everything I've got.

NEEDLE IN A HAYSTACK

The next morning Jack went directly to the Morgenstern building. Before he'd gotten through the first question the building manager, a narrow-faced fellow in his twenties, said he'd only been on the job a year and couldn't be held responsible for any prior problems. When told the questions were in reference to a homicide, he put his hand to his mouth and started chewing on his fingernails.

"Is this a security issue?" he asked.

"Not currently," Jack replied. "The homicide occurred back in 1930. We're looking into it to make sure nothing was overlooked or missed the first time."

"Good grief, don't tell me somebody is looking to sue."

"Absolutely not. This is just a routine investigation."

The young manager pinched his brows together and gave a suspicious looking frown. "A routine investigation? After twenty-five years?"

"Sort of a double check," Jack said. "Before we close the books."

After a good fifteen minutes of going back and forth, the manager finally agreed to check the archives.

"Just don't get your hopes up," he said and disappeared into the back room.

He was gone for well over a half hour, and when he finally did return he said, "We've got nothing on a janitor named Abraham Porter."

"What about Brentwood Accounting, Margery Kramer's firm?"

"They declared bankruptcy and defaulted on the lease in 1933."

After wasting another hour, Jack left with nothing more than he already had. Twenty-five years was a long time. Perhaps too long.

BACK AT THE STATIONHOUSE, JACK again opened the evidence box and started rereading the statements. So far all he was doing was getting the same or less than what was contained in the statements of 25 years ago. There had to be something else, something not seen last time. He pulled a sheet of paper from the drawer and started mapping out what would have been George Feldman's world.

In the center of the page was a square labeled "George." Surrounding that box were boxes for the others who played a part in the original investigation. In one box Jack wrote "Mama Feldman"; beneath her name he wrote "deceased."

One by one he filled in the other names: coworkers, neighbors, aunt, father, possible girlfriend. As he traced and retraced the connections, he marked an X across those that had already resulted in a dead end. He also crossed out the ones who were deceased. After nearly two hours of checking the earlier statements and reports, he was left with only two loose ends: the mysterious girlfriend and the unheard-from father.

He had nothing to go on about the girlfriend and very little on the father whose name was Norman Feldman. Up until the day he walked off and left his wife and son to fend for themselves, he'd worked as an electrician. The only description was a tall man with dark hair. There was no photo.

Jack sat there for a long while looking at that square. Twice he started to cross off the father because reports stated the man hadn't seen his son for the ten years prior to the murder. Each time he thought better of it. Jack knew if he were in trouble, the first one he'd turn to would be his dad or Emory who was like a dad. Maybe, just maybe, George felt the same way and found a way to get in touch with his father.

How?

Suddenly it dawned on him there was a chance that if Norman Feldman continued to work as an electrician, he would have joined a union when the big push to unionize started in '38.

Jack called across to Schulte. "Hey, Leon, you know if there's a union for electricians?"

Schulte grinned. "I ought to; Jenny's brother belongs to it."

THE INTERNATIONAL BROTHERHOOD OF ELECTRICAL Workers was broken out by state, so Schulte started with Local 103 out of Richmond. When he found no Norman Feldman, he continued on until he'd contacted every local chapter in the state of Virginia. Looking back to Jack, he gave a single shoulder shrug.

"Good hunch, but there's no Norman Feldman in Virginia."

"Try New Jersey," Jack replied.

Back in 1930 Debra Feldman lived in New Jersey, so it was likely that Norman, probably her brother, would have gone there when he left Virginia.

After another six or seven phone calls, Schulte hung up the receiver then grinned and said, "Bingo. We've got him. Hudson County Local 409."

He then briefed Jack on what he'd found. "Norman Feldman was a member of IBEW until seven years ago when he retired. Here's the last known address and phone number."

SINCE JACK STARTED HIS SEARCH he'd learned something: people had a reluctance to talk about anything involving criminal activity. He suspected that most everybody had some little thing they wanted to hide. And the minute he mentioned homicide, he could virtually see the hair on the backs of their necks rising up. This time he was going to take a different approach.

He went into one of the smaller offices, closed the door and dialed the New Jersey number he'd been given. A man answered.

"Good afternoon," Jack replied, acting as if he had all the time in the world. "May I ask if you are Norman Feldman?"

"Yeah. Who're you?"

"My name is Mahoney. I represent Reliable Steel. We'd like to get in touch with your son, George, regarding his pension plan."

"Pension plan? You gotta be kidding. George hasn't worked since God knows when."

Mahoney forced a chuckle, trying to sound like this was nothing more than a casual follow through.

"Yes, I know. I have his employment records right in front of me. But his plan was set up back in twenty-nine, and now that he's nearing the official retirement age we're legally obligated to pay it out." He hesitated a moment then added, "Unless he's deceased."

"He ain't deceased," Norman said, "but he ain't here either."

"Do you have an address where we can get in touch with him?"

For a long moment there was only silence on the other end of the phone.

Sensing his indecision, Jack said, "George will need to sign these forms before we can start issuing checks."

"How much money are we talking about?" Norman asked.

"Well, George was only in the plan for two years, but with compounding it should come in somewhere about thirty-eight dollars a month."

"George could sure use that money." Norman gave a sigh of reluctance. "I haven't seen the boy in a long while, but last I heard he was staying with my sister in Richmond."

"Can you give me her address and phone number?"

"Debra Hettinger. I don't know that she's got a phone, but the address is 721 Butcher Street. And, uh…do me a favor, will ya?"

"Of course."

"Tell the kid I'm glad something good is finally happening for him."

"Sure," Jack replied, feeling a bit of sympathy for Norman. It was easy to be judgmental, but being a parent was no easy task.

JACK'S NEXT CALL WAS TO Captain Hennessy over at the Richmond precinct. He explained the situation and asked if he could have one of the local guys ride with him in case he found George Feldman there.

"After coming this far, I don't want to drop the ball on this because of a jurisdictional problem."

END OF THE ROAD

Before Mahoney and Schulte left the stationhouse, Jack called Christine and told her he'd be late getting home.

"Don't wait dinner," he said. "I'll grab something on the road."

It was a four-hour drive to Richmond, but on this particular afternoon they made it in three-and-a-half. The first stop was at the Richmond East stationhouse where they picked up Ed Boyden, the detective who was to work with them. Having worked the Richmond precinct, Jack was familiar with Ed. He was the senior detective on the squad, well known and well liked.

"Is this your first case on the Wyattsville squad?" Ed asked.

"Not my first," Jack said, "but the first homicide."

"I understand this is a 1930 cold case," Ed said. "They must think a lot of you to assign a toughie like this to a newcomer."

"Captain Rogers didn't exactly assign it," Jack said and told of how he'd asked for the case because of the promise he'd made to Emory.

BUTCHER STREET WAS IN A run-down neighborhood of grayed

town houses pushed up against each other. They were all pretty much the same. No grass or flowers, just a cement square bordered by a three-foot high iron fence and garbage cans chained in place to prevent thievery. A low hanging door squeezed in beneath the stoop led to what was most likely the basement. The stoop rose above the cement yard with five or six steps leading up to the front door. Number 721 was no better or worse than the others.

When they got out of the car, Jack stepped back and suggested Boyden take the lead.

"I don't want to blow this because of inexperience," he said.

"I'll cover the back," Schulte said and circled around to the alley behind the houses.

Jack stealthily climbed the fence and stood next to the basement door with his back pressed to the wall. Once Schulte was in place, he gave a nod and Boyden climbed the front steps and bonged the doorbell. A woman wearing a flowered housecoat opened the door.

"I'm looking for George Feldman," Boyden said.

"Why?"

He caught the smell of whiskey on her breath. "How about we go inside and talk about it?"

She narrowed her eyes and looked him up and down. "You a cop?"

Boyden laughed. "Do I look like a cop?"

With an expressionless look she gave a shrug.

"Look, I've been told George has money coming to him. If he's not interested, that's fine by me." Boyden turned as if he were going to walk off.

"Wait," she called and pulled the door open. "I'll get him."

She turned toward the back of the house. Boyden followed her partway across the living room then stopped and watched. The house was a string of railroad-style rooms, and from where he stood he could see back to the kitchen. In there he heard a door click open, and she called down.

"Hey, Georgie, you got company."

A man's voice answered. "I ain't expecting no company."

"Come on up, it's about some money you're owed," she said.

George Feldman knew better. He lost every last dime he had to Broadhurst, and with it he'd lost the opportunity to ever hope for anything more.

"Bullshit!" he yelled then bolted for the basement door.

Before he was clear of the doorjamb, Jack was on top of him. Hearing the scuffle, Boyden ran from the house but by that time Jack had George face down on the cement.

"Need bracelets?" Boyden asked with a grin.

"Nope." Jack pulled a pair of handcuffs from his back pocket, clicked the first one onto Feldman's right wrist then pulled his arms back and clicked the left in place.

"You're under arrest for the murder of Franklin Wilkes," Jack said as he pulled Feldman to his feet. By then Debra Hettinger was scurrying down the front stairs.

"What the hell is going on here?" she screamed. "You said you wasn't a cop!"

Without addressing the charge, Boyden replied, "Your nephew is being arrested for murder."

"Georgie never murdered nobody! He owed money to some thugs. You arresting him for owing money?"

Jack turned to her. "In 1930 George murdered a stockbroker named Franklin Wilkes. Shot him point blank in the chest six times for no reason other than he'd lost money in the market."

For a moment Debra just stood there with an empty-eyed look. Then she turned to Jack.

"It was a long time ago. Georgie's not that way anymore. He's sick, he needs me to take care of him."

As Jack opened the iron gate and led George out onto the street, she followed along.

"Don't do this," she pleaded. "Georgie's ate up with cancer. You can see how sick he is. Would you have a dying man spend his last few months locked up in a prison cell?"

"Put him in the car," Jack said, passing Feldman to Schulte. He turned back to Debra. "Your nephew had twenty-five years of life that Franklin Wilkes didn't have. He was walking around free as a bird while Franklin was buried beneath the ground. George took a good man's life because he was angry over something that wasn't even Franklin's fault. So, yes, I am going to cart him off to jail, because that's where he belongs."

"But he's sick," she said through tears. "Can't you let him stay here under house arrest so he can die a merciful death?"

"Dying in prison is a far more merciful death than he gave Franklin," Jack replied. He climbed into the car and slammed the door.

As they pulled away, he glanced back and saw Debra Hettinger still standing in the middle of the street with her arms outstretched and tears rolling down her cheeks. In an odd way he felt sorry for her. She was yet another victim of George Feldman's vengeful crime.

IT WAS WELL AFTER MIDNIGHT when Jack returned home, and by then George Feldman had been fingerprinted and locked in a holding cell. There was no doubt his fingerprints would match those found at the murder scene.

The next morning Jack left early and stopped at Emory's apartment on his way into the stationhouse. He poured himself a cup of coffee and sat across from Emory at the breakfast table. For the first time he spoke to Emory of the search for George Feldman and explained how he had finally been found.

"Dear God," Emory murmured. "After all this time…"

"He'll be arraigned this afternoon," Jack said. "I thought maybe you'd want to be there."

Emory nodded. His eyes filled with water, and his voice was thick with emotion when he spoke.

"How can I ever thank you…"

Jack reached across the table and covered Emory's trembling hand with his own.

"Don't," he said. "I only did what I'm supposed to do. You're the one who should be thanked. Had you not held on to Franklin's story and believed that a day of retribution would come, the case would still be gathering dust in the Harbor Street warehouse."

They sat in silence for several minutes; then Emory wiped his eyes with the back of his hand and looked across at Jack.

"Franklin would have been real proud to have you as a son-in-law," he said. "Real proud."

"After all I've learned about Franklin, I would have been just as proud to have him as a father-in-law," Jack replied.

THAT AFTERNOON WHEN GEORGE FELDMAN was arraigned, Emory was sitting in the back of the courtroom. The man who stood beside a court-appointed defense attorney bore little resemblance to the newspaper photograph of so many years ago. He still had the same angry eyes, but his face had grown narrow and slack-skinned. His shoulders were narrow and rounded over; his arms hung at his sides and were thin as a child's.

The defense lawyer told of George Feldman's cancer and asked that he be released on bail to continue his treatments and convalesce at home, but even as he spoke his words were thin and without conviction.

The prosecutor argued that Feldman was a flight risk. He'd avoided arrest twenty-five years earlier by skipping town, and there was no reason to believe he would not do so again. The judge nodded.

"I agree. The accused is to be held without bail," he said and banged the gavel.

WHEN JACK LEFT THE COURTHOUSE, Emory followed him back to the station where they sat and talked.

"Have you told Christine yet?" Emory asked.

Jack shook his head. "I thought I'd wait until after the trial. After looking at how gruesome those crime scene photos are, I'd prefer she didn't see them."

Thinking back on how Laura had reacted to the single photograph published in the newspapers, Emory winced, rubbed a hand across his forehead and nodded.

"You're right," he said.

And so it was decided between them that nothing would be said to Christine until the trial was over and George Feldman shipped off to prison.

Although Feldman pleaded innocent, it was a cut-and-dried case. The defense attorney argued that the records were twenty-five years old and a number of witnesses no longer alive. The prosecutor claimed fingerprints were fingerprints and George Feldman's were not only all over the crime scene, they were also on the bullets taken from Franklin's body.

After less than two hours of deliberation, a jury declared George Feldman guilty. The judge set a sentencing date for the following month.

EMORY

Jack told Christine everything after the trial was over. She cried and said that she should have been there. I told her I agreed with Jack. Seeing that picture in the newspaper caused your mama to have nightmares for the rest of her life, *I said,* and Jack was trying to save you from the same thing.

The three of us went to the sentencing together and sat with her in between Jack and me. At that point they weren't showing evidential things like her daddy's bloody shirt and those terrible pictures of his body. It was just a feeble-looking man turned old before his time standing next to the young lawyer who'd represented him.

In a voice that was flat as a table, the judge looked down at George Feldman and said he'd committed a senseless and brutal crime, which he would now pay for by spending the next twenty-five years in the Brigham Correctional Center.

I could say that case was the making of Jack's career, but the truth is I always knew he'd make a fine detective. He's got a look that you don't see on many faces. When he listens to someone tell of an injustice, you can see the concern on his face. He cares about people, and he cares about justice.

More than once I've heard him say the law and justice don't always

278

see eye to eye. Although he doesn't come right out and say it, I know in his heart he's thinking that justice is the higher power.

I didn't choose Franklin for Laura and I didn't choose Jack for Christine, but given all I've seen I know my girls chose more wisely than I would have.

Rose, bless her sweet heart, always believed life was like a carousel. If you offer the world good and fair measure, it will in time come back to you. What goes around, comes around, she'd say. Although I didn't always see the wisdom of such a statement, I do now. This is the coming around.

FROM THE AUTHOR

*If you enjoyed reading this book, please post a review at your favorite
on-line retailer and share your thoughts with other readers.*

*I'd love to hear from you. If you visit my website and sign up to receive
my monthly newsletter, as a special thank you, you'll receive a copy of*

A HOME IN HOPEFUL

To sign up for the newsletter, visit:
http://betteleecrosby.com

*Beyond the Carousel is Book Five in the Wyattsville Series.
Other books in this series include:*

Spare Change
Book One

Jubilee's Journey
Book Two

Passing through Perfect
Book Three

The Regrets of Cyrus Dodd
Book Four

OTHER BOOKS BY THIS AUTHOR

Acknowledgments

Learn to do good; Seek justice, Reprove the ruthless,
Defend the orphan, Plead for the widow.
Isaiah 1:17

No successful novel is the work of a single person. Even the most skilled novelist is only as good as the people who support her. I am fortunate in working with a team that I consider the best in the business. Not a single day goes by when I don't thank God for providing me with the pathway that has brought these people into my life

This is especially true of Coral Russell, the Bent Pine Publicity Director. She is a friend, a partner, a publicist extraordinaire, a finder of new technology and perhaps most importantly a believer in all I do. To say thank you is woefully inadequate, for she is quite often the wind that carries my words to readers, friends and fans across the globe. From the bottom of my heart, I will forever be thankful for having met Coral.

I am equally blessed in knowing Ekta Garg, a super-talented editor who somehow manages to catch my mistakes without ever losing sight of my voice. Ekta's attention to detail constantly pushes me to go deeper into the story and I believe I am better because of this challenge.

Thank you also to Amy Atwell and the team at Author E.M.S. They are like the proverbial Fire Department, always there to help put out the fires. Thank you Amy for turning my manuscripts into beautifully formatted pages and for being so wonderfully organized and dependable.

I also owe a debt of gratitude to the loyal fans, friends and followers who buy my books, share them with friends and take time to write reviews. Without such fans my stories would grow dusty on the shelf.

Lastly, I am thankful beyond words for my husband Dick, who puts up with my crazy hours, irrational thinking, and late or non-existent dinners. Being an author is a life with as many ups and downs as a carousel, but no matter how many times I circle around I always return to the starting point and he is there for me. I would not be who I am without him for he is and will always be my greatest blessing.

ABOUT THE AUTHOR

AWARD-WINNING NOVELIST BETTE LEE CROSBY brings the wit and wisdom of her Southern Mama to works of fiction—the result is a delightful blend of humor, mystery and romance.

"Storytelling is in my blood," Crosby laughingly admits, "My mom was not a writer, but she was a captivating storyteller, so I find myself using bits and pieces of her voice in most everything I write."

Crosby's work was first recognized in 2006 when she received The National League of American Pen Women Award for a then unpublished manuscript. Since then, she has gone on to win numerous other awards, including The Reviewer's Choice Award, The Reader's Favorite Gold Medal, FPA President's Book Award Gold Medal and The Royal Palm Literary Award.

To learn more about Bette Lee Crosby, explore her other work, or read a sample from any of her books, visit her blog at:

http://betteleecrosby.com